PRAISE FOR THE
SAMUEL ROBERTS THRILLER SERIES

THE WICCAN WITCH OF THE MIDWEST

"I am impressed with how Scott was able to tell such a great story in such a short amount of time. [....] This would make my list of books to read during Halloween. It had quite an interesting twist. I was hooked from the very first page."
—*Fic Gal*

"If you enjoy mystery, humor, romance, and danger, you will find this book perfect for your library. Paranormal and magic thread throughout the telling and you will fall in love with the characters one more time. This would be a great book for the upcoming holidays. It is fun and enjoyable, one you will want to pass on to your friends."
—Leslie Wright for *Blogcritics*

5 Stars: "A great, entertaining story. I would definitely recommend it for those that like their mysteries with a little paranormal twist."
—J. *Bronder Book Reviews*

"A thrilling plot. [....] I especially like Sam and Bob. They play off each other humorously."
—*The One True Faith Blog*

"Scott has honestly done it again. He's given us another Samuel Roberts thriller full of intrigue, suspense, and so many unexpected twists and turns. [....] I couldn't put the book down. Looking forward to what Scott has in store next for Samuel."
—Lissette E. Manning, *Simplistik.org*

"A fun, quick and ha : I recommend it to all urban ιat

will hook you from the start, engaging characters, and a twist that will surprise the reader."
—*Reader Views*

"Equally suspenseful and humorous, *The Wiccan Witch of the Midwest* will delight the reader."
—*Celtic Lady's Reading Room*

THE FRATERNITY OF THE SOUL EATER

"An exceptionally entertaining read.... A master of the genre, Scott Lerner's latest novel continues to document his originality and skill as a storyteller."
—John Burroughs for the *Midwest Book Review*

"Not only is this an interesting plot full of twists and turns, but Lerner's characters, Sam and Bob, are witty and endearing. The book is not just plot-heavy, as many genre books can be. This supernatural thriller is full of characterization, which is perfect for fans of the series who already love Sam Roberts and also for new readers who will like him immediately and want to go back and read the first two installments."
—Margo L. Dill, The *News-Gazette*

"A quick and very amusing read. Even when they are getting whupped on Sam and his friend Bob, have a weird sense of humor, that just won't let them stop making smart remarks [....] This book isn't just funny, it has some mystery, and a bit of horror, and even some adventure."
—*Simple Wyrdings*

"Lerner gives us characters that are full of fun, bluster and charm, yet have that energy that you feel is trustworthy. His dynamics between his characters and protagonists are both strange and unlikely, but at the same time intriguing and interesting. You find yourself immersed in a story that takes you to the edge of darkness, twisting and realigning your own take on life [....] A fun and unique find."
—*Tic Toc Reviews*

"Another fun round with Sam and Bob [....] Bob always has a way of making light of whatever happens. Whether he shoots a cobra or sees a desiccated corpse, he finds humor in it. I like Bob. He reminds me of Shaggy from Scooby-Doo, right down to the van with purple shag carpet and the hash brownies."
—*Romancing the Book*

"The pace of the story is fast, so you're turning pages as fast as your eyes will allow…. My favorite character is Sam's friend Bob. Everyone has or needs a Bob in their life. He's there for his friend. He's handy with a computer and good to bounce ideas off. I don't want to give any spoilers but the story is a thriller mystery. It's fun, interesting, and good."
—*The One True Faith Blog*

"A suspenseful thriller that grabs you right from the start, it takes you into an ancient world of long held secrets and grotesque murders. A true page turner."
—*Tribute Books Mama*

RULER OF DEMONS

"*Ruler of Demons* doesn't feel like a horror story, but there's strong tension and entertaining banter throughout the book. It's the only novel about demons, mutilation, and the apocalypse that can potentially leave a smile on the reader's face."
—Brian Bandell for the *New York Journal of Books*

"A FUN book! The main character has a really cool sense of humor (even if he is a lawyer) and even when he is about to get killed he doesn't completely lose it. The book does have its dark side but on the whole it is the sort of book you should read when the weather is bad and you need cheering up ….The mystery part of the story was really well done too. You really don't know right up till the end exactly how it will go. Every time I thought I had it figured out…some other thing got thrown in to shake things up."
—*Simple Wyrdings Blog*

"*Ruler of Demons* is creepy and fast-paced, with a few thrilling

twists to keep the reader up at night. It's also sprinkled with the kind of humor one hears in a police procedural show, the wisecracks one imagines veteran cops make. They may not be the most realistic bits of dialogue, but the blurb on the back cover gives a good idea of the wild-ride tone of the novel: 'Only eleven shopping days till Christmas. And less than a week to save the world.'"
—Paige Fumo Fox for *Chicago Book Review*

"The novel is jam-packed with details from TV and movie references to mouth-watering descriptions of local cuisine. Lerner has a keen eye for the world his characters inhabit making it come alive for the reader in all three dimensions."
—Carol Robart, *The Plot Thickens Blog*

"*Ruler of Demons* is well written, with plenty of humor and plenty of adventure and Lerner's cast of characters are intriguing and intelligent. Readers who like a bit of weirdness and darkness in their reading (kind of like my oldest son!) will adore this."
—*Sharon's Garden of Book Reviews*

"One of the best techniques in this thriller is the pace. Your heart will race. But you won't have a heart attack, because the author is skilled in breaking up the pace with humor. Sam's and Bob's banter will make you laugh. Sometimes you have to stop and think, and then you'll guffaw…. They're clever, witty, and likeable. I think everyone will enjoy this story. You won't figure it out. You won't expect any of the twists the characters find themselves going through. You won't want the world to end."
—*The One True Faith Blog*

"Sam's belief in logic and living in the now directly opposes the nature of the crimes he's trying to solve, giving the book an added sense of tension as the reader is forced to look at things from the outside in…. *Ruler Of Demons* might not be bursting with peace on earth and yuletide cheer, but for the murder mystery fan who gravitates toward the macabre, it makes the perfect stocking stuffer."
—*Tribute Books*

"What pulled me in about this novel were the characters. Sam and Bob have a great friendship. I loved how Bob always talked about food, and how Sam managed to stay calm, no matter what. Their inside jokes made me feel connected to them. Sam was a bit of an average Joe, which made him all the more intriguing when he's thrown in the world of the supernatural. He's just a regular guy, and now he's dealing with all this stuff he knows next to nothing about, all because of that one time he fought evil and won. The way they manage to keep being lighthearted, even in the face of danger, made this book unique [....] All in all, a great, enjoyable read."
—Majanka, *I Heart Reading Blog*

COCAINE ZOMBIES

BRONZE winner in the Mystery/Cozy/Noir category of the 2013 Independent Publishers (IPPY) Book Awards

"A wonderfully written and fun—albeit somewhat scary—new novel.... The three best things about this novel are its fast pace with short chapters, Sam as the likable hero and the humor. 'I wanted to write a book I would also like to read,' Lerner said. 'The characters would talk and act like real people. It would be realistic, but at the same time, larger than life. I didn't want it to follow the same old tired formula.' He succeeded."
—Margo L. Dill, *The News-Gazette*

"A riveting thriller with plenty of twists and turns, very much recommended."
—*Midwest Book Review*

"Lerner's first-person, hard-boiled narrative—peppered with dark humor and historical and geographical facts pertaining to the Champaign-Urbana setting in which his story unfolds— slyly echoes the work of Jim Thompson, Dashiell Hammett and Raymond Chandler. Fellow Champaign Central High School alum Lerner has crafted a gripping tale, rife with colorful characters, to create a minor masterpiece of modern fiction."
—Don Gerard, Mayor of Champaign, Illinois

"Scott Lerner has created an everyman hero out of small-town lawyer Sam Roberts. Giving Sam a dry wit and gracing him with snappy dialog, Lerner sends him full tilt at the forces of evil that have invaded his humdrum life in Urbana, Illinois. Sam might see himself as a middle-aged schmo, but in Lerner's deft hands, that schmo and his sidekick Bob stumble toward saving the world as we know it. *Cocaine Zombies* is a blast!"
—Molly MacRae, author of *Last Wool and Testament*, *Lawn Order*, and *Wilder Rumors*

"Sam is a character who is easy to root for. He's smart (there are some great-accurate-legal scenes), funny without being sarcastic, brave without being reckless, and at the end of the day just wants to go back to his one-man law firm and resume his boring life. He's gonna have to go through a lot to get there, however, and it's a very entertaining journey."
—*Book Reviews by Elizabeth A. White*

"Ladies and Gents, allow me to introduce you to my new best friend: Scott A. Lerner. At a time when I, an avid reader and bookworm extraordinaire, found myself quickly approaching the point of being burnt out after reading book after book until the pages seemed to blend together – I stumbled upon this gem and have found myself putting my game face back on…. Sam is a down to earth lawyer with a sarcastic wit that had me laughing out loud several times while reading. His friend Bob was a man after my own heart – a modern day hippie of sorts. I couldn't help but picture actor Zach Galifianakis as Bob. Both of these men appealed to me because of how down-to-earth they were but also because they were so flippin smart!"
—*Not Now … Mommy's Reading*

"I couldn't put it down [….] It's full of suspense and murder [….] This book is by far one of my favorites [….] It will send chills up your spine and make you wonder about that little world of voodoo."
—*This and That Reviews*

Habitat for Human Remains

HABITAT FOR
HUMAN REMAINS

A Samuel Roberts
Thriller

~~~

SCOTT A. LERNER

Seattle, WA

CAMEL
PRESS

Camel Press
PO Box 70515
Seattle, WA 98127

For more information go to: www.camelpress.com
scottlerner.camelpress.com

This is a work of fiction. Names, characters, places, brands, media, and incidents are either the product of the author's imagination or are used fictitiously.

Cover design by Sabrina Sun

Habitat for Human Remains
Copyright © 2017 by Scott A. Lerner

ISBN: 978-1-60381-627-4 (Trade Paper)
ISBN: 978-1-60381-628-1 (eBook)

Library of Congress Control Number: 2017947571

Printed in the United States of America

I would like to dedicate this book to my wife, son, daughter, mother, father, sister and brother.

I would also like acknowledge the hard work and fine editing of Catherine Treadgold.

Also by the Author

Cocaine Zombies

Ruler of Demons

The Fraternity of the Soul Eater

The Wiccan Witch of the Midwest

Chapter 1

~~

A T A MINIMUM you would think the forces of darkness would bring cookies. Oh, who am I kidding? If they did, they would probably spit in the batter or replace the chocolate chips with newt eyes or grubs. They are called the forces of darkness for a reason.

It is hard to accept what life hands you when it is not what you wanted. Yet, life is not a cosmic burger joint. You can't send it back when the cosmic forces forgot to hold the pickles and lettuce. Destiny is in some ways worse than death. Death is the end. Even if death results in nothingness or a world with winged harp players, it is still the end. My destiny, however, seems never to end. It is relentless.

I have been through the five stages of grief. I have denied the fact that my destiny was to fight against the forces of darkness. Yet, there is no denying that evil continues to find me. I have cried and screamed, but it has done me no good. I have pleaded with whatever unknown force has cast the battle before me. And I have sat, dead-eyed, binge-watching *Breaking Bad*, eating too many Nutter Butters. At last I have achieved the final stage, acceptance. To paraphrase Ralph Ellison and Popeye the Sailor Man, "I am what I am." To take it a step further, the world is what it is.

Has this acceptance changed my life? In some ways, it has, and in others, it has not. I am still an attorney. I still try to help others in need of a divorce or in need of representation in criminal matters. I still show up at my tiny office in Urbana, Illinois, each morning and put in a day's work. Yet, I know that eventually I will get dragged back into the darkness and be forced into battle. I have never understood why I was chosen. I don't think I am particularly well prepared. I'm just an average guy, not very muscular, approaching middle age, pleasant looking. But no one would say, "Ah, that guy. Let's rely on him to save humanity!" I am needed nonetheless.

To make things worse, other than Bob, my best friend since high school, and Susan my ex-girlfriend who no longer speaks to me, no one knows of this terrible burden I carry. I can't go to a bar and brag about my adventures. Well, I guess I could, but I would rather not be locked up in a padded room.

It was Thursday, six o'clock at night, and I wasn't going to get anything else done today. For the middle of August, the weather was pleasant enough. I decided not to bring my briefcase home with me. I needed an evening with sushi, beer, and something decent to watch on television.

My desk was filled with piles of discovery that could wait until later. I needed to water the sad cactus that subsisted in a clay pot behind my desk. I needed to throw away the empty soda cans. My office was small—frankly, too small. It also didn't have any windows, thus explaining the depressed mental state of the cactus. I moved from my old house last year and have been looking for a new office space as well. It is just such a pain in the ass to move file cabinets and banker boxes filled with files. In Illinois, lawyers have to keep their files for at least seven years and the result is too damn much paper.

I had made it all the way to the door when the telephone rang. Out of habit, I ran to the phone and picked up the receiver. No doubt I would regret my decision.

"Sam Roberts," I said into the telephone.

"Mr. Roberts, It's Devin Avery," a baritone voice replied.

Devin Avery was a partner in the largest law firm in Champaign. I had run into Mr. Avery at various bar functions over the years. He was one of those smart lawyers who made a lot of money and never went to court. He focused primarily on estate law. Thus, it was odd for him to be calling. Particularly at six o'clock at night. Mind you, I work late all the time, but estate lawyers have the luxury of more normal hours.

"What's on your mind, Mr. Avery?"

"Have you read anything about the murder case involving Blake May?"

"Afraid not. Reading the paper tends to bring me down."

"Well, he is charged with murder. Supposedly he ripped his girlfriend into pieces."

"What a shame."

"His mother is Edna May."

"I don't know her."

"Well, I am the lawyer doing her estate work. I work for her son as well. He needs a lawyer and I don't do criminal work."

"Others in your office do."

"I would rather you do it. Our involvement with the mother's estate for so many years makes me a little nervous. I know the family too well."

"I would be glad to get involved, but it is a murder case. I would charge a retainer of twenty-five grand and another five if a jury is selected and we go to trial."

"I have no problem with that. I hold a financial power of attorney related to the family's finances. The mother is blind and her son, the one accused of the offense, has some mental issues, including severe agoraphobia. Come by and pick up the check. I will sign a fee agreement as well."

This was way too easy. Usually when I mention a retainer that large, people need time to consider. If nothing else they would come back with a counter offer. Then again, I was cheap when compared to Mr. Avery's firm.

"If this involves mental-health issues, she will also be charged for the costs associated with hiring an expert," I added.

"Of course. There is one other thing."

"There usually is."

"Will you go by and see her tonight on your way home? As a favor to me."

"The money's not a problem?"

"No."

"Then as a favor to you, and for the sake of the money, why not?"

"Spoken like a true lawyer. She lives at the old Frost Home."

"I know the place. I didn't know anyone lived there. I hear it's haunted."

"Are you afraid of ghosts?"

"Yes, but I have a greater fear of losing twenty-five thousand dollars. I will stop by, and thanks for thinking of me."

"No problem. You can pick up the check first thing in the morning. Oh, and one other thing ...."

"What?"

"Keep our firm's involvement out of any conversation with the press. I would rather the firm not know I sent away business."

"No problem."

When I hung up the phone, I thought, *That's odd. Why wouldn't the firm want to be involved?* Maybe it was just Mr. Avery who did not want the firm involved. Mr. Avery was a senior partner; he could do as he pleased. Then again I am not the type to look a gift horse in the mouth. This was a huge case, one I would actually get paid for.

Murder cases are as rare as hen's teeth. I guess I shouldn't say that. I have been appointed to represent clients in murder cases and I have represented clients in murder cases as an assistant public defender. Also, and sadly, violent crime seems to be on the upswing of late. Yet, in private practice, after I inform the accused of the retainer, they generally can't come up with the money. What can I say? Most people charged with murder aren't in the privileged set.

I checked online to see what I was getting into. I didn't have to look long. The alleged murder took place last Saturday. On the front page was written, BITING COLD MURDER AT THE FROST HOUSE. Blake May, the only suspect, had severe agoraphobia and had not left the house in twenty years. Mr. May was currently at the Marquee Mental Health Center. Even the state's attorney had acknowledged he was not fit to stand trial.

The police believed the victim to be Heather Kline, Mr. May's long-term girlfriend. She had not been seen since the incident and shreds of clothing at the crime scene had been identified as belonging to her. The remains were so crushed and torn apart as to make identification by fingerprints and dental records impossible. Her DNA was not on file. Detective Hood of the Champaign Police Department stated, "I have never seen anything like this. The body was in strips and chunks rather than pieces. I have seen a lot over the years, but this made me sick."

I know Detective Hood, and he is not prone to exaggeration. If anything, he is immune to the suffering of others. Articles like this were going to make it hard to get a fair trial. My guess was that there were a lot of other strange facts that the police had no intention of sharing with the press or the public.

I put my tie and jacket back on and grabbed a yellow legal pad and pen. It was time to speak with Mrs. May. A shiver ran down my spine as I was about to walk out the door. The telephone rang.

A familiar voice was on the other end.

"Dude, what up?" Bob sang into the phone.

"Heading to a haunted house."

"You want to bring me some food and we can check out a flick when you're done?"

"Sure, give me an hour and I will meet you at your place. I was expecting more of a reaction to haunted house."

"Oh, sorry. It is you, of course, so I can't say I'm shocked. What haunted house are you heading to?"

"The Frost Home."

"You're not kidding about haunted. That place definitely gives me the creeps."

"Now that I think about it, why don't you join me? I'm willing to pay for your time, and I suspect I'm going to need help on this case."

"Last time I helped out on one of your cases, I almost wound up dead."

"Suck it up, you Nancy. As Nietzsche said, 'That which does not kill us makes us stronger.' "

"Nietzsche can go to hell," Bob said. "He is already dead. I could use the bread, however. My motorcycle needs work."

"Cool. Meet me there?"

"Ten minutes, tops."

I hung up the telephone and headed out. Bob has helped me in the past and I was glad to have him on board at the beginning of this case. I had the feeling I'd need a guy with his particular talents. Bob does IT work from home, although I think he also has some kind of trust fund to help with expenses. His computer research skills and all-around detective work have proven invaluable over the years.

Chapter 2

~~~

I PULLED UP to the house. The Frost Home was on the National Registry of Historic Homes. It was built in the early to mid-1800s for Joseph A. Frost, a wealthy farmer and entrepreneur before and at the time of the Civil War. Legend has it that he had received news that his son, a Union soldier, was killed in the Battle of Lucas Bend. Mr. Frost was so distraught over his death that he killed his wife and two daughters before killing himself. As it turned out, his son was not killed but had been mistaken for another soldier. A mistake not uncommon in the days before dog tags and DNA testing.

The son, Morgan John Frost, was a member of the 133 Regiment of Illinois Volunteers and only signed up to serve for one hundred days. When he did return and found out what his father had done, he refused to spend a single night in the home. The Frost Home was sold soon after. Oddly, the architect, Antony Greer, killed himself the same year, although there was nothing to tie the deaths together.

The first floor of the three-story house was carved limestone and the next two stories were red brick. The woodwork was painted white, including the wrap-around porch. The roof was also white and curved downward around the edges. On top of the home was a widow's walk surrounding a cupola, a small metal structure resembling a square house. The house looked symmetrical at first glance. Upon closer inspection it was slightly off center. I found this to be slightly unsettling for reasons I couldn't explain.

The house's doors and windows were arched, and hand-carved brackets held up the roof and the roof of the porch. A large, round, stained-glass window on the third floor gave the home a Cyclops vibe. The window's design was a large yellow and gold daisy with a black center. Green vines wrapped around the edges of the glass.

The yard was oddly lacking in landscaping. There were no bushes in the front and only one tree—a gnarled oak that looked dead. The lawn was patchy and mostly dead. In the middle of the lawn were two small stone structures. The arrangement of rocks did not seem to be by design. They were piled haphazardly about three feet high.

I was familiar with the house, of course; everyone was. In middle school, I would cross the street to avoid walking past it. The house was haunted. Ask any seventh or eighth grader in town. You would expect such a mansion to be out in the country; yet, here it was, near downtown Champaign and surrounded by other homes and buildings. Not to mention very near to a school and library.

I parked near the house on the long dirt driveway. My hands shook as I walked up to the front door. In the back of my mind I heard Wendy Green's eighth-grade voice taunting, "Look! Little Sammy is afraid to go up to the door. What a chicken! Cluck, cluck." Well, as far as I was concerned, Wendy could cluck herself. I was no chicken.

In those days, we were always daring one another to knock on the door and run. To my knowledge, not a single middle schooler took the dare. Even not knowing the history and folklore surrounding the place, you could sense it had a creepy vibe.

My thoughts were interrupted by Bob's black van pulling up

behind me. Bob was wearing khaki pants and a plain black T-shirt. He looked mostly presentable other than his hair being uncombed and his goatee being a tad unruly.

"Man," Bob said with a shudder, "this place gives me the major heebies. Do you remember it from middle school?"

"Remember? It still gives me nightmares."

I have only known Bob since high school but we actually went to middle school together. We hung out with a different crowd in those days and I don't think we had any classes together. It would appear that everyone who attended our school had the same healthy fear of this place. "So, what are we doing here?"

"I am meeting the owner. Her son is accused of murdering his girlfriend. Apparently this is where it happened."

"Spooky."

We walked up to the porch. I looked for a doorbell and couldn't find one. Just as I was about to knock, the massive arched door opened. A large man in a black suit, white shirt, and bow tie held it open. He reminded me a little of Lurch from *The Addams Family*. He beckoned us to come in and pointed to a woman seated by an enormous fireplace. Closing the door behind us, he led the way toward the woman.

The house was grand on the outside but less impressive on the inside. The ceilings were high, maybe ten feet, but the carved molding and bric-a-brac I would have expected to see were missing. The main room was spacious but decorated much like an ordinary home. The furniture was antique and of good quality but not to the scale of such a mansion. The flooring was constructed of wide pine planks, giving it a less formal feel for its grand size. Even the fireplace—my height and large enough to easily accommodate a whole cow—did not have an impressive mantel.

I took a seat next to the old woman. Bob remained standing but walked behind me. There was an old oak table next to me with a single silver bell on it. I placed my legal pad and pen onto the table.

The woman had to be ninety years old. She wore a black dress with lace around the collar and cuffs, black earrings, and a matching black choker. Her straight silver hair was tied in a bun, pulling the skin back from her wrinkled face. She reminded me of Queen Victoria in the images created near the time of her death.

Hell, given this woman's age, she might have borrowed her dress from the queen herself. A black walking stick rested across the armrests of the chair. The handle was silver and carved into an animal's head—a bear or a wolf. With her left hand, she held onto the end, blocking part of the image.

What captured my attention most was her eyes. Her cataracts were so severe as to block out her irises completely. It appeared as though her eyes were white. She had to be completely blind.

"You must be Mr. Roberts." She held out a white-gloved hand, and I was unsure whether to shake it or kiss it. I went with the former.

"Yes, and you must be Edna May?"

"Who is your friend? I thought you were coming alone."

"This is Robert Sizemore. He has assisted me in many cases in the past. I believe he may be of help in your son's case as well."

She moved the chair closer to me, as though sharing a secret, "So you know why you are here?" she whispered.

"To represent your son."

"My son is everything to me."

"I understand."

"Will you save him?"

"I will do my best."

"Would you like something to eat? Toast with honey or jam?" She gestured as if to hold out an invisible plate.

"No."

"What about your friend?"

"No, thank you," Bob said politely.

"What can I do to help you help my son?" she asked.

Taking my legal pad from the table, I placed it on my lap and held my pen poised, ready to write. "First of all, I need the name and contact information for everyone at the house on the day this incident allegedly occurred."

"Why?"

"It will help me to determine what happened."

"Oh."

"I would also like to see where it allegedly took place."

The old woman leaned back in her chair and looked up at the ceiling, as if to gaze at unseen images there.

"You have met my assistant, Malcolm Conrad. He has been with me for twenty years and is incapable of murder. He also is incapable of speech. He is mute."

I wanted to reply, "You don't say," but held my tongue.

"I met him in Eastern Europe many years ago, and he has been with me ever since. He lives on the third floor with me. Laura James is our maid; she also runs errands, walks the dog ... that sort of thing. She lives on the second floor. She has worked for us for two years. Angel also lives in the home. He is the cook and does most of the shopping. He lives on the first floor and has only worked here for six months or so. That is everyone."

"Other than the people who live here, did anyone visit that day?"

We were interrupted by an attractive woman in her early thirties, wearing a black dress. Her long, curly brown hair was tied back in a ponytail. She was slender with mocha skin and intelligent eyes. In her arms was a silver tray with three bone-china cups and saucers. The tray also held two carafes, a sugar bowl, and cream pitcher. She placed it on the oak table.

"Sorry to interrupt, ma'am," she said. "I thought you and your guests could use some coffee or tea."

"Thank you, Ms. James. This is Mr. Roberts and his friend Robert. They will be looking into the ... unpleasantness."

I stood and extended my hand, "I was hoping to speak with you later about the incident."

She took my hand for a moment and let go.

Bob bowed his head slightly but did not extend his hand. The woman ignored him completely. She looked as though she wanted nothing to do with the situation.

"Whatever madam wishes," she said, bending slightly as she backed out of the room.

"Can I pour you a cup?" I offered.

"No, but help yourself. You had asked about visitors?"

"Yes."

"Devin Avery, my lawyer, came by to have me sign papers. That would have been in the morning. The mailman normally comes around noon. A carpenter stopped by sometime last week. I'm not sure what day. You could double-check with Laura. I normally stay on the third floor. Oh … my son's girlfriend, Heather Kline, must have stopped by, but I never spoke with her."

"When did the police come?"

"Maybe six or seven in the evening. It was last Saturday."

"Did they say how long the body was there before their arrival?"

"No."

"Did you speak with your son or Heather at all that day?"

"No, not that I can think of."

"All right, well, as long as I am here, I would like to talk to everyone in the home and see the room."

She raised her eyebrows. "Why?"

"I thought you wanted us to investigate this?"

"My son almost never leaves his room. He keeps his door locked most of the time. The police had to break the door down to get in. At least that is what I have been told."

"Maybe someone else came through a window?"

"His room is on the second floor. Besides, most of the windows in this house have long since been painted shut."

"He could have invited someone else into his room prior to locking it."

"It is possible."

"So, you think your son is responsible."

She waved her hand in an impatient gesture. "Of course not. He would have had to be out of his mind … insane."

"Did you see or hear anything that night?"

"I haven't seen anything for ten years. As for hearing, nothing unusual, but this house is well insulated for noise, and I spend most of my time on the third floor."

"How did you discover the body?"

"The dog was acting strange. He kept whining and scratching under the door. Laura called the police."

"If you don't mind, Bob and I will have a look around and speak with the other residents."

"Of course. Are you hungry? Do you want anything to eat?"

"No, but thank you."

Using her walking stick, Mrs. May rose slowly from her chair. She seemed unsteady for a moment but got her bearings before I could lend a hand. Feeling for the bell on the wooden table, she rang it twice. Laura rushed in.

"If you don't mind, Mr. Roberts and Mr. Sizemore, I will return to my room now. Please keep in touch. Laura, show Mr. Roberts and his assistant around the house and do what he asks of you. Malcolm, if you would help me to my room …."

I sniffed both carafes. Determining one to be tea, I poured myself a cup. I stood up and walked toward Laura, the cup still in my hand. Edna May was surprisingly sharp, given her age. She was probably right. If her son was in a locked room alone with Heather on the night of her death, that did limit our options. Given the condition of the body—assuming the newspaper article was right—it wasn't a suicide. People who choose to take their own lives generally opt for pills or a gun, not a potato peeler. I hoped the paper got it wrong. Many a great defense is ruined the minute a jury sees gruesome crime-scene photographs.

Chapter 3

~

LAURA TURNED TO me but waited to speak until Mrs. May had reached the staircase. When Mrs. May got to the first stair, a German shepherd came from another room to join her. The dog was large but looked surprisingly fluffy for his breed. He followed Mrs. May as she ascended the stairs.

Laura seemed uncomfortable, but I wasn't sure who was causing her discomfort—me or the lady of the house. She walked over to the table holding the serving tray and poured herself a cup of coffee. Her demeanor in front of Mrs. May was vastly different from the attitude she gave me. Once she finished taking a long sip of coffee, she confronted me, arms tightly crossed at her chest and lips pursed. She was defensive to the point of hostility.

"What do you need from me?" Ms. James said as she took the seat Mrs. May had vacated.

I returned to my seat. "I want to talk to you about what happened last Saturday. I also need to see the room where it happened."

"I don't want to go into that room," she spat out. "I already told Mrs. May that I wouldn't clean it either. If I didn't need the money, I would have quit last Saturday."

"Just point to the door."

She tossed her hair back and ground out, "Fine. What else do you want?"

"Why don't you start by telling me about Blake. What was he like?"

She narrowed her eyes. "Are you going to get me in trouble with Mrs. May? Are you going to tell her what I tell you?"

"I don't work for Mrs. May," I said. "I work for Blake May. My job is to help him. My job is not to get you in trouble."

"Fine," she said, "ask your questions."

"Blake, what is he like?"

"He is not bad-looking but kind of squirrelly. He rarely left his room. Until the police took him away, I'd never seen him leave the house. He wouldn't even let me clean his room. He was obsessive about his privacy."

"Anything else odd about him?"

She sneered. "Isn't that enough?"

"Just asking."

She rolled her eyes. "You will learn more when you see his room. He was a complete nerd. Obsessive compulsive as well. Didn't like to touch anyone. He wore gloves on those rare occasions when he left his room."

"What about his girlfriend?"

"Heather was stranger than he is. She was a lot younger. She worked as a page at the library, one of those people who shelve books. Yet, she acted like a queen or something. She had severe goth makeup, lots of tattoos, and a pierced nose. She was overweight and wore costumes from old television shows and geeky T-shirts. The only time she spoke to me was when she ordered food and alcohol. I don't mind running errands—it's part of my job description—but she treated me like a slave."

"So … you didn't like her."

She made a derisive sound. "I didn't like being ordered about by Blake's fat booty call. I didn't work for her." She hesitated for a moment, perhaps recognizing how it sounded. "I didn't want her dead, though."

"Of course not."

"You know how on television they interview a guy who lives next store to a serial killer and he says that the killer was a great neighbor and he would never have expected it."

"Yeah."

"This ain't that case. They were both weird as hell. Although, everything around here is weird as hell."

"What do you mean?"

"Mrs. May wanders the house all night. You should see her room. Its décor is *Night of the Living Dead* meets *Downton Abbey*. Not to mention the whole house is haunted. You should hear it at night. Strange noises … sometimes I think I see something and then it is gone. The place makes the Overlook Hotel in *The Shining* look like the Ritz Carlton."

With her bad attitude, Laura James had to be a whiz at hiding her feelings. "Then why do you work here?"

She threw out her arms in a *duh* gesture. "She pays me a lot of money and I get free room and board. In two years, six months, and ten days I am going to quit this job and move to California. I will never think of this house and these people again."

I shrugged. "Why wait?"

"I have to finish paying off my student loans and some other debts, but when I am gone, I will never say 'sir' or 'ma'am' again. I will never bring someone as much as a cup of water even if they are choking." She picked up her cup and finished off her coffee.

"Have you spoken with the police?"

"Saturday, I spoke to a guy for a few minutes. I can't remember his name. He asked if I saw anything and I said no."

"What time did Heather get here on Saturday?"

She shook her head. "I never saw her, but that's not unusual. She never knocks. She acted as if she owned the place. Although, she normally didn't come by during the day. My guess is she was here on Friday night and never left. She rarely left Blake's room when she was here. If not for ordering me to get her stuff, she could be here for a month without my knowing it."

Laura James was starting to get noticeably fidgety. I decided it would be best to walk and talk. I stood up and placed my empty tea cup on the small table.

"Why don't you show me the second floor?"

She held up a hand in warning. "Fine, but I won't enter the room. Yesterday we had a professional cleaning crew go through it for eight hours, but you can't fully clean the evil out of that place. The police made us wait for days before the crew was allowed in. I still have not gone in and neither has anyone else who lives here."

"I want to talk to whoever else was around last Saturday."

"There is Malcolm ... but he can't talk. Angel, but he won't be back until next week. He asked for some time off after the ... killing."

"What is Angel's last name?"

"Koch," she said.

"What about the carpenter?"

"Yes, Bill Sands. He does handyman work and maintenance. He is here fairly often. You can google him. I'm sure he wasn't here though. He doesn't work weekends."

"Do you think they will talk with me?"

"Sure, but they won't be of any help."

The staircase was not ornate and the steps were narrow and steep. I had no idea how Mrs. May managed it. I was tired by the time I made it to the second floor. Bob followed behind in silence. I didn't know if he was terrified or just being discreet. Bob is not a coward, but it was hard to ignore the creepy vibe of this place.

"I know this is none of my business," I said, "but what got you into this job to begin with? It has to be more than just the money."

"I agree."

"You agree?"

"It is none of your business."

"You were the one who discovered the body? The one who called the police?"

"I did … well, Mr. Fluffinator did."

"Mr. Fluffinator?"

"He's a German shepherd and don't give me no stupid look 'cause I didn't name him."

"That's a hell of a trick—a dog who can dial a telephone."

"Mr. Fluffinator must have smelled something. He was standing by the door, whining, so I started banging on it. No one answered and the door was locked. So I called the police. The dog didn't do none of the dialing."

The second floor was odd, in that the stairway ended in the middle of a room, almost like it does in some attics. The room had no windows. The floor was solid oak, and surrounding the hole where the steps led into it was a giant compass rose like you see on old maps. The letters N.S.E.W. as well as the star pointing to them was cut from exotic woods and embedded in the oak flooring.

There were no items of furniture, rugs, paintings or other decorations in the room. In the middle of each wall was a single door. The door on the southern wall was painted green, the door on the western wall, red. The northern wall was black and the eastern wall was white. I couldn't help but wonder if the decorator and architect had psychological issues.

"I know it looks kind of weird," Laura said, interrupting my thoughts.

"That's an understatement."

"Blake May lived in the western room, the one with the red door. I stay in the southern room with the green door. Come get me when you're done." She disappeared into her own room.

When the door closed behind her, Bob said, "She is cute, but about as friendly as a pit bull with a toothache."

"Agreed," I said.

I walked over and opened the door to the north. To my

surprise, the room was narrow and approximately twenty feet long. At the end was a staircase that obviously led to the third floor. Along the wood-paneled walls were paintings—old portraits in oil. Each depicted a different woman.

I closed the door. I was about to open the east door in an effort to further delay viewing the murder site but changed my mind. Instead I decided to bite the bullet and open the red door. It was hanging down from its cracked frame on a single hinge; the police had had to break it down. It swung open easily, and I was immediately accosted by the smell of bleach and disinfectant. The odor made me dizzy.

Chapter 4

~~~

BOB AND I entered a ten-foot-long hallway that led to a much larger room. I suspect it comprised much of the west side of the house. The space was in the shape of a giant capital T, except the long end of the letter was much smaller than it should have been and the top of the T much longer.

My bedroom at home is maybe ten by twelve. This room had to be ten times that size, although the dimensions were different. The main part was over a hundred feet long by twelve feet wide. It was actually silly to call it a room at all. It was more like a loft. To my right was a king-size bed with two end tables, a brass lamp on each one. Beside it was a picture in an aluminum art deco frame of a young woman with a pierced nose and severe makeup. I assumed that the photograph was of Heather. The size of the room made the bed seem much smaller than it truly was. It had a maroon velvet bedspread and decorative throw pillows.

The back wall to the west was red brick, and the remaining walls were white plaster. There were four arched windows against the back wall, at least ten feet of space between each one, with maroon velvet drapes that matched the bedspread. The drapes were all open.

In the space between the two windows closest to the middle

of the room was an enormous mirror. The antique mirror, close to eight feet tall, came to an arch at the top. The glass was wavy and some of the silver backing had disappeared over the years. The frame was wood but may have once have been gesso since bits of gold and plaster remained.

The thin oak planks on the floors reminded me of a basketball court. On my left on the east side of the room was a series of four doors. Each was modern and pine with contemporary hardware. The area with the modern doors was clearly a more recent renovation to the home. The walls were drywall rather than plaster, another indication that they were not a part of the original home. If not for this addition, the main portion of the room would have been even grander. Perhaps it had once been a ballroom.

Bob followed behind me, maybe a bit too close. "Nice place, a lot bigger than I would have expected."

"Yes, it is more like a condominium than a room," I said.

Bob headed over to the end of the room, as if something had caught his attention. I wanted to work at my own pace. I walked up to the first door closest to the entrance, which didn't have a lock. It opened outward to reveal a large bathroom with a white-tile floor and a Jacuzzi tub. The walls were painted light blue. I closed the door and moved on. Behind the second door was a small kitchen with a stainless steel oven, refrigerator, dishwasher, and microwave. There was a ceiling fan and a white tile floor similar to that in the bathroom.

Two stainless steel frames were built into the wall with a steel door and a handle at the bottom of each. Between the two frames was a steel panel like that of an elevator. After pulling up on the handle of the first panel, I realized it was a dumbwaiter. It was far too small for a person to fit into. I assume this was how Mr. May got his groceries and meals. The second panel opened to a garbage shoot. Perhaps it could accommodate a small person, but it would be a tight fit. I couldn't imagine anyone climbing up the shoot, which looked to be polished steel.

I closed the door and opened the next one. This room had a brass bar against the far wall that stretched the length of the space. Twenty or more suits and an equal number of button-down shirts hung in a row. All the suits were black and the shirts were white. Everything looked freshly pressed. Underneath the suits, more than twenty pairs of shoes were lined up, each facing outward next to its mate. The dude was definitely a neat freak. He needed to get dirty. Maybe that explained the messiness of the murder—his need to get his hands dirty. My guess was his bathtub had hot and cold running Mr. Bubble.

On the right side of the room were cubbies filled with pants, plain white T-shirts, shorts, and white Ralph Lauren underwear. A basket was filled with pre-mated socks. Against the left wall of the room was a burnt-orange washer and dryer set that couldn't have been more than six months old. The Haier Commercial Dryer was vented into the wall. Next to the dryer was an ironing board and a steam machine that looked like a large vacuum cleaner. As with the suits and shirts, it was clear from the organization of the room that Mr. May was indeed a bit obsessive-compulsive. I left the room and walked farther down to the last door.

This room was nothing like the others. It was longer, reminding me of a railroad apartment or the inside of an airplane. The walls and ceiling were constructed of sheets of riveted aluminum bent slightly at the top to give the space a curved appearance. Along the roof line was a single strip of green neon. That turned on as I walked in and gave the place a greenish hue. Adding to the futuristic ambiance, there were wall sconces every five feet or so designed to look like short light sabers. Bob must have heard me gasp because he was immediately at my side. His pupils expanded to the size of dinner plates and his breathing became audible.

"Holly shit, no wonder this dude never left the house. Why would he need to leave this room?"

"This is definitely impressive," I agreed.

At the far end of the room was a window looking into outer space. Upon further inspection, I realized it was not a window but an enormous curved television screen. In front of the screen was a metal chair with a sharp boxy design and dials and switches on the armrests. It was a replica of the captain's chair on the Starship *Enterprise*. Bob moved in to give it a closer inspection.

"Imagine the things Captain Kirk and Uhura did on this chair," Bob said.

"You need to get a life or at least get laid by someone who is not fictional character," I suggested.

"Like you're one to talk."

"Besides, Kirk and Uhura kissed once, but I think their relationship ended there."

"You are so naive. Kirk was a total ladies' man. Even the alien chicks found him irresistible."

"What about Picard? Did he and Counselor Troy have a thing?"

"No, although he and Dr. Crusher were totally doing it."

"You've definitely spent too much brain space thinking about this."

In the middle of the room was a steel table with a rubber mat. Electrical outlets and USB ports were built into the top. Circuit boards, small screwdrivers, files, and other hand tools were laid in neat rows on the rubber surface. There was a soldering iron as well as copper wire and a spool of silver metal in a clear bin at the center of the table.

Along the walls were clear Plexiglas cubbies. My client had an extensive collection of videogames and books. Most of the books were science fiction dating back to the late forties. In addition, he had textbooks and non-fiction books on the subjects of Quantum Physics, Theoretical Physics, and Astrophysics.

The other cubbies were filled with toys dating from the late forties and early fifties to modern times. They had to be worth something and might have filled a small museum. There were tin robots and ray guns and plastic models. I saw old film reels labeled "Buck Rogers" and "Flash Gordon."

I found hundreds of action figures, all in their original packaging. Tiny versions of characters from *Dr. Who*, *Star Trek*, and *Star Wars* stared down at me. I guessed that the characters I could not recognize were from less popular movies, anime, and comic books.

There were props as well, hundreds of them. Some had tags from Hollywood prop houses; others were made for mass consumption. This was a collection that any science fiction geek would truly envy. "Geek" was probably an understatement. To say that Mr. May was a bit of a nerd would be like saying Fonzie is a bit cool. Mr. May was a nerd's nerd. Perhaps the king of all nerds.

Bob interrupted my thoughts. "Do you have any idea what this shit is worth? There is not an action figure here that would sell for less than a hundred dollars. The movie props alone are worth twenty to fifty thousand. Not a one of them would go for less than a grand. Some of the toys from the fifties, the robots and ray guns—fucking priceless."

"I have never seen you so excited."

"Do you see that light saber and the cricket gun from *Men in Black*? The label says they were 'screen used.' How do you put a price on that? Dude, I am telling you, this is the holy grail of collectables."

"Should I step out? Give you and the room some time alone?"

He did a little twirl, arms spread, as if he were a model presenting the contents at a trade show. "I'm just telling you, this is the big leagues."

I was keeping an eye out for anything that might have been used as a murder weapon. Although, the police would have taken away anything obvious. There were loads of futuristic weapons: sonic screwdrivers, blasters, ray guns, phasers, and light sabers—none of which appeared to be functional.

There was a club from *The Planet of the Apes*, but it was made out of a harmless rubber. There was a Klingon bat'leth, but the blade was lightweight and unsharpened. There were also two curved knifes from one of the Riddick movies, but they were created for display rather than use.

When we left the room, I felt dizzy and disoriented. It was like going back in time. The transition from mid-nineteenth century home to science fiction room was jarring. This experience may not have helped me solve a murder mystery, but it told me quite a bit about my client.

Mr. May's shut-in status might have had less to do with his agoraphobia and more to do with simply having no reason to leave the house. Bob had already indicated he would be glad to stay here. What was the point of leaving? He had everything he needed. In this space alone, he had a kitchen, a bathroom, and a laundry room, and more square footage than most houses. He was certainly strange, but nothing I saw seemed to peg him as the homicidal type—whatever that means.

I had to practically drag Bob out of the room. When he finally stepped out, I quickly closed the door. I continued to look around the main area of Mr. May's space. Against the wall to the south was a mounted 60-inch television with a brown leather sofa and a treadmill facing it. A marble-topped coffee table stood in front of the sofa. Other than the large mirror, there were no paintings or other decorations on the walls.

The open space reminded me of a basketball court, except it lacked a team logo. The place could have used a giant "I" against the silhouette of the State of Illinois. When I reached the middle of the room, I realized I was mistaken. There was a design. Only it was mostly faded—an image of two crossed lines like a giant plus sign. At both ends of each line was a point like an arrowhead. It was another compass rose. A circle surrounded the plus sign and the negative space surrounding it was divided into four segments the same size but in different colors. Their colors were green, red, black, and white. The image was definitely old. In the middle, the paint had faded and was dark in some areas. In other areas the wood sealant had cracked or bubbled. It was so faded that if you weren't paying attention, you might miss it entirely.

We continued to walk around the room, on the lookout for some clue as to what had happened. I searched in vain for inspiration. I tried the windows, which did not open and perhaps were never intended to open. I didn't locate any secret panels. I took a bunch of pictures with my iPhone, but since I didn't know what I was looking for, it all seemed fairly pointless.

Bob returned to the collectable room while I was snapping pictures. When it was time to leave, I was worried he would insist on staying. The only time I had seen him so exited was at an all-you-can-eat buffet.

Back in the hallway with Bob, I tried to close the door. It wouldn't fit back into its proper space so I left it hanging by the single hinge. Laura was waiting for us. Her features were tense, and she was tapping her foot with impatience.

"Is there anything else I can do for you two?"

"Did you ever see the body?"

"Body? I saw what was left of it."

"What do you mean?"

"Picture six gallons of extra chunky pasta sauce." She grimaced. "You asked me how I came to take this job."

"Yeah."

"When I graduated from college, I owed a hundred thousand dollars in student loans. I already told you about the loans, although I didn't tell you the amount. I saw this job advertised in the paper. They didn't ask for references or require any special skills. Being an English major doesn't really prepare you to be a servant, except if you read a lot of Victorian literature. After working in this creepy place for two years, I now owe ten thousand dollars in student loans. I have a high tolerance for creepiness and the alternative seemed to be Burger Hut or Chuck E. Cheese's."

"Thank you for your help. I suspect we will be back around."

"Can you find your own way out?"

"Yes."

Ms. James was a bit rude and less than helpful. On the other hand, all this must have been shocking and unpleasant for her. I could definitely understand why she would not want to relive it. She did not strike me as a murderer, but no one ever did.

Chapter 5

~~~

I LOOKED DOWN at my watch. It was only eight thirty at night. That hardly seemed possible. I checked my phone to confirm that the LeCoultre—a prize from an earlier battle with evil—was correct. It was. Somehow the strange house had the ability to slow time.

The Frost Home definitely has a supernatural vibe. I have long since accepted that I am catnip to the forces of darkness. Given a choice, I would have been warm chocolate chip cookies to the forces of goodness.

"Are you ready to head to my place?" Bob asked.

"What's showing?"

"*Hellraiser* and *Batman*."

"Which *Batman*?"

"The one with George Clooney."

"Too scary for me."

"*Hellraiser* it is."

"I'll go get some food and be by in ten minutes."

"Cool. I will get the popcorn popping."

I HEADED TO the grocery store and selected two containers of pre-made sushi in plastic coffins, some fried chicken, two éclairs, and two pieces of chocolate raspberry cheesecake. I was afraid that at this time of night the éclairs would no longer be as light and flaky as I would have wanted. I also grabbed two six packs of Leinenkugel beer and a sugar-free Red Bull.

I arrived at Bob's house ten minutes later. Bob lived in a small, ranch-style home near Hessel Park. It was one of many similar houses built in the late forties/early fifties after World War II. The returning soldiers needed places to live, and affordable small homes were constructed in large numbers. I parked the car and walked up the path to his door, which opened before I knocked.

Since our visit to the mansion, Bob had changed his clothes. He was now wearing a tie-dyed T-shirt with "Cherry Garcia" printed across the front and a picture of a pint of ice cream below. I handed Bob the beer, sushi, chicken, and pastries. He placed them on the glass-topped coffee table in his living room next to a glass bong, which bore the fading image of a dragon. Although the room was never tidy, it seemed messier than usual. There were empty beer bottles and dirty clothes strewn on the floor.

I sat down on the brown-leather sofa facing the large flat-screen television and Bob sat beside me. Pulling out a beer, he handed it to me. I helped myself to a piece of cheese cake. Since Bob's was not the type of joint that provided forks, I began to nibble on the triangle of chocolate raspberry goodness as though it were a slice of pizza. The sushi and chicken could wait.

"So," Bob said, "tell me about this case. What do you want me to do? From the looks of that house and that creepy lady, I suspect there is a lot."

I gave Bob a rundown on what I had learned from the paper and Mr. Avery. The description of the body of the alleged victim caused Bob to put down his éclair. Despite having heard Laura refer to it as "six gallons of pasta sauce," I was pretty jaded at this point and didn't allow the conversation to affect my enjoyment of the cheese cake.

"I haven't met with the accused yet," I said, "so I have no theories as to what happened."

"What was the murder weapon—a food processor?" Bob gave no indication that he was trying to be funny.

"I have no idea," I replied.

Bob put both elbows on the coffee table and appeared lost in thought. Finally he said, "From what you told me, the dude was in a locked room, alone—or alone, other than the victim. He's a weird guy, but there's nothing to indicate that he's violent. Even his mother seems to think he did it. Given that he hasn't left the house in twenty years and he clearly wants to join Star Fleet Academy, an insanity defense sounds like an easy sell."

I leaned back into the couch. "It's not that easy. First of all, juries hate the insanity defense. Second, being insane isn't enough."

"What does that mean?"

"Our legal system is shockingly unsympathetic and backwards when it comes to mental illness. Most states still look at some form of the M'Naghten Rule."

"Sounds like legal mumbo-jumbo."

"In 1843 this guy, M'Naghten, killed a guy he thought was the British prime minister. When he was found to be insane, the public was outraged and a jury instruction was made that essentially said it is presumed a person is sane. To find otherwise, it must be proved that when he committed the crime, he didn't know what he was doing or if he did, he didn't know it was wrong. It seems crazy that we look to a case from the 1840s for direction when it comes to mental illness, a field we are finally beginning to understand today through modern science. It is barbaric, if you ask me."

"So what do you have to show in Illinois?" Bob asked.

"You have to show that the defendant suffers from a mental illness, and as a result of that illness, lacks the ability to appreciate that his conduct is criminal or he can't conform his conduct to the requirements of the law. All in all, pretty close to the M'Naghten Rule."

He grimaced. "Um, simple English?"

"Murder requires a state of mind. You have to knowingly act in such a manner as to kill someone. If you are so crazy you have no idea what you are doing, that might constitute an insanity defense. Yet, in Illinois, the jury can find a person guilty but mentally ill."

Bob gave me a sidelong glance. "What's that?"

"A jury can find that a person is crazy but understood the nature of their actions," I said.

Bob shrugged. "So they put them in the loony bin until they are no longer mental? That's a lot better than jail."

I waved a hand in denial. "That's not how it works. They normally *do* put them in the penitentiary. Although even if they didn't, a state mental hospital is just as bad. While locked up, they may or may not get treatment. If they are restored to good mental health—which would be unlikely, since you are putting crazy people in a prison—then they would still serve out their sentence."

"So, finding a person guilty but mentally ill is worthless."

"As tits on a bull."

"Didn't that one woman in Kankakee use that expression?"

"Yep, and so did my grandmother."

"You are messing with me now. Your grandmother never said that."

I took a sip of beer. "How about worthless as a top hat on a goldfish?"

He wagged his finger at me. "I believe your grandmother said that but it is never going to catch on."

I pointed at the TV. "Why don't you turn on the movie?"

"In *Hellraiser*, the dude was in a room alone with that strange cube and was shredded. Although I didn't see any wooden puzzle boxes in Blake's hangout."

"No, but he had a lot of movie props."

"No shit. If he goes away for a long time, do you think he would sell me some of them?"

"No, that would be a conflict of interest."

"The puzzle box thing would be the perfect defense. The killer is some kind of weird demon from another dimension."

"It wouldn't surprise me if that were true, but it might be a hard sell for a jury."

Bob scratched his head. "You think? Do you have any other ideas?"

"There was the dumbwaiter and garbage chute. Do you remember that Sherlock Holmes story where a snake crawled into a locked room to commit the murder?"

Bob snorted. "I see, so maybe they sent a snake up the garbage shoot or the dumb waiter?"

"Well, that's just stupid," I said. "A snake couldn't do that kind of damage. I was thinking a possessed Cuisinart."

Bob tapped his goateed chin, as if considering this possibility. "Of course, when you put it in terms of possessed kitchen appliances, that makes perfect sense. The real killer sent up an evil food processor, which hops up to the victim and attacks."

"I just realized there may be a hole in my theory."

"Just one. I thought that seemed workable."

Finishing off my beer, I said, "You could never find a food processor with a long enough cord."

"You want me to do some research on the length of cords on food processors?" Bob was opening another beer. "Or maybe cordless food processors?"

"Actually, I want you to do some research on the Frost Home. Could you look into the claims that it is haunted? I want to know about anyone who died there. I already know about the original owner, who killed his own family and himself after discovering that his son was missing in action in the Civil War."

Bob whistled.

I continued, "Was the house built on an Indian burial ground? That sort of thing. In addition, I will write down the names of everyone in the home around the time of the killing. See what you can find out about them."

Bob sat back and put his feet up on the coffee table. "You know Native Americans didn't have tombstones and marked cemeteries, right? This whole country is an 'Indian Burial Ground.' Given that we wiped out an entire society through war and disease." He wiped the custard from his éclair with the sleeve of his shirt.

I smiled. "You are filled with sunshine and rainbows."

He patted his belly. "I am also filled with chocolate and custard. You don't want this other éclair, do you?" He lifted the second éclair from its plastic sarcophagus.

"No, I'm good."

"Does anyone benefit from the girl's death?"

"Not that I can think of. She was a page at the library, so I doubt she was rich."

Bob pushed a button on the remote, and we watched the movie in relative silence. My mind was more on the case than what was on the screen. By the time the credits rolled, I was tired and ready to return home.

"I've got to get out of here," I said, standing to leave.

"What about the sushi and chicken?"

"You eat it. I'm stuffed."

"Cool. I'll call you when I find out anything useful."

"Try to avoid any evil appliances," I suggested.

I LEFT BOB's and got into my Honda. Soon into the drive home, I realized my need to urinate. Why I'd drunk a couple of beers and hadn't peed before I left was a mystery. I sped down the road with my legs pressed together, trying to think of dry things.

This case had the potential to throw me once again into the fray against the forces of darkness. The fact that I was not sure if I could make the seven-mile trip to my house without wetting my pants made me wonder if I was up to the task. I pulled into my driveway and got out of the car. While attempting to unlock the front door, I dropped my keys twice. By some miracle, I was able to empty my bladder into the toilet and not somewhere along the way.

After a quick shower, I headed to my bedroom. I tried to clear my mind of the case and get some sleep. It took a long time before sandman graced me with a visit. Thoughts of haunted houses and grisly murders kept creeping into my mind, disturbing the pleasant mental images of sheep jumping over fences.

Chapter 6

~~

WAKING AT SEVEN without an alarm, I got out of bed and helped myself to a large bowl of Cheerios with sliced banana. I printed out a fee agreement from my computer and put it in my beat-up leather briefcase. As I left the house, I grabbed a diet Red Bull.

My father wasn't exactly Kwai Chang Caine of *Kung Fu* fame or the wise old octopus in *The Rainbow Fish*. Yet, he did have his moments of clarity. Once he said to me, "Son, if someone has money for you, pick it up before they change their mind." This was advice I took to heart and decided to head over to see Devin Avery before going to my office.

My father had offered lots of good advice that I didn't always follow. He warned, "Don't whistle if you don't mean it, don't growl if you can't bite, don't spit in the wind, and don't pee on an electric fence." All of these lessons were profound and wise and helped guide my life in some way. When I strayed from his words of wisdom, it often resulted in a negative outcome. I should have never peed on an electric fence during my summer job as a corn detasseler in high school.

Donning a black suit with a red tie and my father's Tudor wristwatch, I headed to the office of Devin Avery. Located near the park, his firm was among the oldest in Champaign

County. The building itself was once a bank, and the façade was white marble with huge columns. It was one of the only Greek revival buildings in town. Carved into the façade above the columns were the words ENGLISH UNION BANK. At the very top sat a single black bird. The bird looked down at me with malevolent intent. In my life, black birds have often been harbingers of bad things to come.

I parked in front of the building and walked up the cement stairs past the large, two-inch-thick glass doors, past a wooden stairway to a receptionist behind a curved desk. The receptionist was polite, with long blonde hair and blue eyes. I helped myself to a few fun-size Snickers and waited for her to call Mr. Avery.

As Mr. Avery came down the stairs, I noted his black Armani suit, yellow silk tie, and pristine white shirt. He carried a large briefcase and looked extremely serious, although he always did, even at social functions.

He pointed to glass doors that led to a conference room. It was wood-paneled and had a fireplace with a green stoneware mantel at the far end. An enormous table took up much of the space. Chairs were lined up on both sides, with one larger leather chair at the head of the table, facing the door. Other than plants and framed photographs of Champaign-Urbana in the twenties and thirties, there were no decorations.

The houseplants were large and oddly waxy, considering the lack of natural lighting in the room. I wondered whose job it was to dust the leaves. I have actually bought leaf polish in the past but never used it.

Mr. Avery walked to the back of the room near the fireplace and took a seat at the far end of the conference table. I sat next to him, waiting for him to begin the conversation. There was a moment of awkward silence.

"I have spoken with Mrs. May."

"Yes, so have I."

"She likes you."

"She has impeccable taste."

"She has been a client of mine for more than forty years. I want you to do your best for her."

I wondered just how old Mr. Avery was. Assuming he was twenty-four or five when he finished law school, he would have to be at least sixty-five years old to have had a client for forty years. The likelihood was that he was much older.

I had always assumed Mr. Avery was in his late fifties or early sixties. He still had a full head of curly hair that was primarily brown, with very little gray. He had high cheekbones and a mustache and looked to be in good physical condition.

"I always do my best," I said. "Remember, my job is to work for her son. Ultimately, he will make the decision as to whether this case goes to trial or ends in a plea. I can't make that choice and neither can his mother."

He placed his briefcase on the conference table and removed two documents, each with the heading "Power of Attorney." He also removed a green check drawn from his firm's trust account and made out to my firm in the amount of thirty thousand dollars.

I stared at the check, a little wide-eyed. "The check is in an amount five thousand dollars more than we discussed. The amount I quoted was more than enough money."

"Never look a gift horse in the mouth Sam. Do you have a fee agreement?" Mr. Avery pulled a black Montblanc fountain pen from the inside pocket of his suit coat.

I removed two fee agreements from my briefcase. I changed the amount to reflect the new figure on the check and handed them both to him. He signed both copies without reading them. I countersigned them with my Zebra ballpoint and gave him one for his records. I also took the check and put it my briefcase.

I picked up the documents labeled "Power of Attorney." The first was for Mrs. May, and the second for her son. The language appeared to give Mr. Avery wide latitude and power to act on their behalf of his clients for any conceivable business or personal transaction.

Staring at the documents, I said, "I don't do probate work and I don't know much about powers of attorney, but … couldn't it be a conflict to have a power of attorney for a mother *and* her son? It seems the son would have incentive for the mother not to spend money. After all, he will presumably wind up with the money when she dies."

"No, I'm not worried about that. Mrs. May is blind and her son has mental issues. They certainly need someone to deal with their rather large estate. I am far more helpful than an estate planner, brokerage firm, or bank."

"That makes sense," I said, not knowing if it made sense or not. "Thank you for considering me for this case."

"No, thank *you*, Sam. I know you will do a good job. I assume you are going to speak with your client."

"Yes, do you know if he is still at the Marquee Mental Health Center?"

Mr. Avery tapped his fingers together in a restless gesture. "As far as I know, he hasn't been moved."

Rising to his feet, he offered me his hand, which I shook. We walked out of the room together toward the front of the building. There he took a left up the large stairwell, and I continued straight out the front door. The meeting had taken less than five minutes.

Across the street, the park was beginning to fill with white tents. I had forgotten that the Taste of Champaign began tonight. Vendors would be selling samples of local cuisine for tickets. Music was also part of the event, and they were setting up a couple of stands for bands and live entertainment.

I'd intended to see my client right away but decided to deposit the check first. It goes back to my father's advice: he always said it was best not to hold on to a check for too long. I wondered why the check was from the firm's trust account and not Mrs. May's private account. I decided it was best not to waste brain space on such things. The firm was less likely to give me a bad check.

Chapter 7

~~~

I STOPPED BY the drive-thru at the bank and deposited the check before heading to Marquee Mental Health Center. It was located not far from the bank and I arrived just a few minutes later.

The building that housed the mental health center was modern and composed of red brick. It was two stories high with a basement and spread out over an entire city block. I have had clients housed there but I have yet to be sent there for treatment myself. It may just be a matter of time.

A good number of their patients are teens and young adults being treated for substance abuse as well mental health problems. It is not uncommon in a divorce case to have a child who is placed at the Marquee Mental Health Center. It is sad how many divorce cases involve attempted suicides, drug abuse issues, and general mental health concerns. Based on anecdotal evidence alone, mental health issues seem to be more prevalent in family law cases than criminal ones.

I grabbed my briefcase and headed to the front door of the building, where they buzzed me in. I explained to the receptionist that I needed to see Mr. May. She pointed to a waiting area filled with people and handed me a red sticker with the word VISITOR printed in large black capital letters.

I had two magazines to choose from: one promoting craft ideas and another discussing the virtue of small organic farms. I decided to let Martha Stewart provide insight into the world of handmade greeting cards. Just as I was about to conclude that store-bought greeting cards were well worth the money, a tall bald man in khaki pants and a black polo shirt approached.

"You must be Mr. Rogers," he said.

"Although it is a wonderful day in the neighborhood, it is Roberts," I said.

"I apologize; the message must have gotten garbled. My name is Dr. Rudolph Hyde." He held out a hand and I shook it.

"I am here to see Mr. May."

"Yes, I got a call earlier from his mother saying you would be stopping by today. I also spoke to Mr. Avery this morning, who has Mr. May's medical power of attorney. Please follow me."

We walked down the narrow hallway and took a right to an area with two stainless-steel elevators. Dr. Hyde pushed the button and the door immediately opened. We got out on the second floor. The doctor used a key card to open a set of glass doors, and we passed the nurses' station and entered a room at the end of the hall.

It was an office with a small desk. The doctor closed the door behind us and had a seat in the large leather chair behind the desk. The walls were covered with the good doctor's certificates and qualifications.

"Please have a seat," he said, pointing to the chair in front of his desk.

"Thank you," I said.

He opened the single file on his desk. "What do you know about Mr. May's mental health condition?" he asked.

"Not a thing."

"He has a diagnosis of agoraphobia going back over twenty years. It is an anxiety disorder. He perceives the environment outside his house to be dangerous and uncomfortable. It is not particularly uncommon, but the severity of his case is most unusual."

"So," I said, indicating our surroundings, "he must not be loving it here."

"No, but he's coping. Yet, it is not exactly an illness that is going to get him out of his … predicament."

"I can't ask you to turn a banana into a buffalo. He is what he is," I said.

The doctor was tapping a pen against the table. I resisted the urge to grab it. "I want to do more work with him," he said. "He might suffer from schizophrenia."

"Does he have any prior indicators of schizophrenia?"

The pen stopped tapping. "Mr. May is forty-eight years old, and until now, he has been without a prior psychotic episode. At least one that was diagnosed. His speech and affect seem normal. His family does not have a history of schizophrenia, although there is some mental illness in their background. All pointing against a diagnosis of schizophrenia."

"I am no expert on the subject," I said, "but I have never heard of an initial diagnosis of schizophrenia in a person who is almost fifty years old."

The doctor inclined his head in agreement. "Men tend to have their first psychotic episode before their early twenties and woman before their late twenties. Yet a little less than five percent of women will have an initial onset after age forty. It is rarer in men for such a late onset. If Mr. May has been alone for so much of the last twenty years, who is to say he did not have a psychotic episode prior to this one?"

"So you believe he killed someone and did so during a psychotic episode?"

He shook his head. "I don't have enough information to make a professional assessment."

"What is your hunch?"

"Let's call it a hypothesis."

"All right."

"I believe he has had repeated and continuing psychotic episodes that began in his twenties. That in fact his agoraphobia was not agoraphobia at all but a symptom of schizophrenia. A dreadful misdiagnosis based on his affect being normal."

"So you think he's schizophrenic?"

"He clearly is delusional and has hallucinations. Yet, he is lacking other symptoms of schizophrenia. I should note the DSM-5 does not require me to find that a person has every possible symptom of the illness. I could make a diagnosis based on the hallucinations and delusions alone. I am not sure what to make of Mr. May just yet. I am consulting some other doctors. I *will* tell you that I am inclined to say he suffers from schizophrenia. Anyway, I will let you talk to your client."

"How do you know he's not faking it to try and create a defense?" I asked.

"I expected that question to come from the state's attorney. The truth is at first I thought he was. He reported auditory and visual hallucinations. Must people who see things have ingested LSD or other mind-altering drugs. Visual hallucinations, even among schizophrenics, are rare. Most lay people don't know that. So at first I thought he was just making stuff up to sound crazy. I will tell you this: I have spent a lot of time with Mr. May since he got here. I don't believe he is faking it. I would give that opinion in court. I am confident to a reasonable degree of medical certainty that he is not acting."

I stood up and gave Dr. Hyde my business card. "Call me when you make a diagnosis," I said.

I expected Dr. Hyde to take the card and lead me to my client. He remained seated. He was staring at his hands.

"Psychologists and psychiatrists pretend that the *Diagnostic and Statistical Manual of Mental Disorders* or the *DSM* is magic. Those of us in the field pretend that it is objective, reliable, and valid."

"You don't believe that?"

"As psychiatrists, we strive to be objective, but that is ultimately not possible. Did you know that homosexuality was listed as a mental illness in an earlier version of the DSM? It isn't today. Multiple personality disorder or what is now called dissociative identity disorder is in the DSM, but many in my field consider it to be made up."

"What's your point?"

"In the early seventies, when the book *Sybil* came out, the diagnosis of multiple personality disorder popped up everywhere. Politics, movies, and popular culture impact how we treat the mentally ill. Science should not be impacted by fads, religion, or politics."

He seemed to be looking to me for a reaction, so I said, "I am lost." I understood what he was saying; I just didn't get where he was going with it.

"Psychiatry is getting more sophisticated all the time, but we still can't begin to understand how the human brain works. In other words, I can't give an objective opinion as to what is going on in Mr. May's head. Yet, I believe he suffers from schizophrenia. Another doctor may disagree. It is not like diagnosing a broken leg."

"Is he undergoing any treatment?"

"We are providing him with low doses of some antipsychotic medications. That may make a difference. He is also in individual therapy, and I hope to introduce him to group therapy down the road. I am a bit cautious because he has not spent a lot of time with other people over the years."

"Thank you, doctor." I rose to my feet.

Dr. Hyde stood up as well. "I will let you know if I make any breakthroughs. Why don't you follow me? I will take you to see Mr. May."

Once again I handed the doctor my business card. This time he accepted it. I followed him out the door and down the hall. On both sides of the hall were rooms that looked like those typically found in a hospital. Each had a sliding glass door. Those that were occupied had a closed curtain to preserve the privacy of patient. The other curtains were open, revealing rooms that contained two electronic beds, two white dressers, a television, and two chairs.

At the end of the hall was a large, open meeting room with a number of couches and tables. It was well lit and looked surprisingly cheerful. I followed the doctor to the back of the room where a man in a black suit, white shirt, and red tie was sitting alone by a window. I assumed this was another doctor but was surprised to be introduced to Blake May. Mr. May had gray hair and matching gray eyes. He stood and offered me his hand. He was tall and looked like the captain in the movie *Airplane*. After Dr. Hyde made the introductions, he left so I could speak to my client.

I would have preferred to be in another room, but no one seemed to be paying any attention to us. There were only three other patients in the area; all were watching television. A single orderly stood at the other end of the room, looking bored.

I had to say I was shocked by Mr. May's appearance and his demeanor. It was unfair, but given the situation, I expected him to be wearing a tin foil hat and barking at furniture. I sat down and provided him with a Substitution of Counsel form I had taken from my briefcase.

"My name is Samuel Roberts. Your mother and attorney, Mr. Avery, paid me to get involved in your case. You still have a choice in the matter. If you want me to get involved, I need you to sign this form. It allows me to substitute in for the public defender as your attorney." I handed him a pen, then wondered if I was allowed to hand a patient a pen. I wasn't even sure his request to have me act as his attorney would be valid, given he was incarcerated in a mental health facility. He signed above his name and returned the pen and paper.

"So, tell me what is going on," I said.

"Oh, not much." He gave me a wan smile. "I have been yanked out of the only place I feel safe in the world and forced to stay in this hellhole, where the only thing I have to look forward to is the chocolate pudding on Wednesdays. Yet, it could be worse. I could be in jail, where I am sure the chocolate pudding is served less frequently. On top of that, the jail would provide buggery to kill the time."

"You want to tell me what happened?"

He smirked. "Yes, I am looking forward to that. I want to relive the hell that brought me here. That sounds about as much fun as the jail rape."

"If it means anything," I said, "I think the local jail is fairly safe. I won't vouch for all the penitentiaries."

He blew out a short breath of disgust. "You know, it *doesn't* mean anything. In fact it sucks."

"I read in the paper you are being held without bond. We could file a motion seeking a bond but it would probably be denied, until we have more information concerning your mental health. It looked like the judge had some concern about your fitness to stand trial and wanted you here or in jail pending a report from your doctor. I intend to stop by the public defender's office after this and get more information."

"I don't know how much longer I can take it here."

"I'm curious … how did you get appointed the PD when you clearly have money? The judge must have concluded you had mental problems before he sent you here. Did he bother to arraign you?"

"Arraign me?"

"Have you plead not guilty? Did the judge explain the charges?"

He threw up his hands at the futility of it all. "I don't remember much of anything. It happened so quickly and I was more than a little confused."

"Can you tell me what occurred at your house before you were arrested?"

"Meaning, did I murder anyone?"

I waved him off. "No, I don't want to get into that. At least not yet. I want to see the police reports first. I want to know if you saw anything or heard anything odd that night."

"Did the doctor tell you to ask that?"

"No."

"I guess this is one of the few times it's good to be crazy." Mr. May put a finger up to his head and rotated it clockwise in the universal sign for crazy.

"I am no expert but you don't seem crazy to me."

"That's because we just met."

"All right, tell me something crazy."

"Do you believe in time travel?" Mr. May asked.

"As in, we have been here talking for five minutes so we are traveling forward in time?" I said.

"I was thinking more in terms of physics and science fiction. You know, H.G. Wells type of time travel."

I looked around for an orderly. "You know … I'm going to see if we can talk in a more private setting."

"You don't want people to hear how crazy I am?"

I inclined my head. "No, I am good with that. I hope everyone thinks you are barking-at-trees nuts. I just don't want everyone to know how crazy I am. It's bad for business. Most people like to hire lawyers who are not completely out of their minds."

I walked over to the orderly and requested that we be allowed to speak in a private room. He signaled to another orderly, who informed the first that he would have to speak to Dr. Hyde.

Fifteen minutes later we were alone in Mr. May's room.

Chapter 8

I TOOK THE recliner and Mr. May sat on the edge of his bed. His hands were trembling. He looked afraid, but I didn't know of what or whom.

"Should I lie down? Isn't that how it is done with mental patients?" Mr. May asked.

"Do what you want. I'm not a doctor. Unless being a *Juris Doctor* counts? It does remind me of a joke."

He snorted. "You will forgive me if I don't laugh. Nothing in my life is at all funny."

"Then why don't you tell me what you were getting at earlier."

"Heather, my girlfriend, is … *was* a page at the library. Since I don't leave my house, I normally select books online and have someone pick them up." He cleared his throat and looked down at the floor. "I do have an interest in science fiction and Heather seemed to notice. I had Laura James, our maid, pick up a lot of books on the subject. Heather must have spoken with Laura, because she figured out that I lived in the Frost Home. She called me up one day and asked to have a tour."

"You guys ended up dating?"

"I haven't left my house in over twenty years. The idea of a woman who could be interested in a guy like me … I was instantly in love. It didn't hurt that she was kind of kinky. She liked to dress up as television characters from science fiction programs. I am not saying she was perfect, but I would never harm her. Besides, she was interested in the two subjects that I find the most intriguing."

I sat forward in my chair. "Let me guess, gardening and travel?"

He almost laughed. "Sex and the science fiction."

"How long had the two of you been together?"

"I don't know? Over a year. Actually, closer to two. I am not sure if 'dating' is the right word. We don't leave the house. I guess I should say *didn't*. I will never see her again, will I?" Mr. May was starting to cry. If this was an act, he deserved an Oscar.

"Tell me about what you would do at the house. You can skip the sex part."

"Heather was kind of strange."

"Yes, but it sounds like in a way you liked."

"She told me the Frost Home was designed as a hub for alien travel. That my room was at the end of a wormhole and creatures from outer space would come through to visit earth. Yet, according to her, someone had closed the door and they could no longer get through."

"Did you believe her?"

"No, not at first, but she had done all kinds of research and had lots of weird books and stuff. Not to mention, she was willing to have sex with me so I tended to give her the benefit of the doubt."

"What else did she say?"

Blake was getting increasingly fidgety the more we talked. Now he was drumming his hands on the bed. At least that didn't make a noise.

His eyes filled with tears as he said, "Heather claimed my room was the core of the house. She explained that we could open doors to other worlds. That without ever leaving my room, we could see things others could only dream of."

"That must be a pretty exciting notion for someone with agoraphobia."

"Yes." Blake wiped away the tears with the back of his hand.

"Tell me more about these doors to other worlds."

"There is a mirror against the back wall …" he paused.

"I have been to your room." I took out my iPhone and brought up images of the mirror.

"We would put candles around the circle with the arrows in the middle and chant spells from a small leather book she had. We would cut our hands and allow blood to drip into a silver bowl that we placed in the center of the circle. Then Heather used a brush to paint the mirror with the blood."

"That sounds like dark magic, not science or science fiction."

He grimaced. Now his leg was bouncing—another manifestation of nerves. "I thought it was stupid as well, but it worked."

"It worked? How?"

"Voices would emanate from the mirror … whispers."

"What did they say?"

"Nothing that made a whole lot of sense. Just whispers. Heather said that if we worked at it, the mirror would provide us the secrets of the universe."

I was trying not to stare at his bouncing leg. "Did you tell anyone about this?"

"No one, other than Heather."

"Why?"

"Two reasons: the first is that Heather told me not to."

"The second?"

"I didn't want to seem crazy. I can tell by looking at you that you think I am nuts." Now we both focused on his bouncing leg, and he somehow managed to make it stop.

"It seems odd you would cut yourself just to hear whispering."

He shook his head and waved his hands in adamant denial. "It didn't just whisper to me. It showed me things."

Now we were getting somewhere. "What sort of things?"

"I could look into the mirror and see images of a strange creature from another world."

"What did he look like?"

"Almost human, but he was bald with a big head and long teeth." He was gesturing as he described it, forming the shape in the air. All I could think of was Taz, the Tasmanian Devil from *Looney Tunes*. Although he wasn't bald, he did have long teeth.

"Was he green? Did he have antennas? Where was he from?"

"No, no, and I don't know. We're not talking about the Great Gazoo. It was real and amazing, like I had superpowers. Heather said if she continued her work, some day we could travel the universe and never leave my room. There was only one problem."

"What?"

He sighed and rubbed his hands against his thighs. "It wouldn't last. Once the candles had burned out, the image disappeared and the mirror returned to normal. Without Heather, I have nothing. She is the only one who can perform the ceremony. That is why I could never kill her."

"Not because you loved her?"

He fixed me with his intense gray stare. "I know this makes me sound like a jerk, but this was better than love."

I looked down at my phone. It was almost noon, and I suddenly felt the need to get the hell out of here. I was definitely starting to feel uncomfortable. I couldn't tell if I was dealing with science fiction or dark magic. If Mr. May was crazy or if there was some truth to his tale.

"Listen, I have another appointment," I lied. "Besides, I want to wait until I read the police reports prior to getting into more details."

He sat up straighter. "I understand, and I am starting to feel better. Thank you for getting involved. You said you had a joke, earlier. I would like to hear it before you go."

"It's not funny."

"Good, I don't feel like laughing, and if it's not funny, I won't feel obligated to do so."

"A guy goes into his psychologist's office and says, 'Doctor, all day and all night I fantasize about teepees and wigwams.' The doctor says, 'I see your problem. You are two tents.' "

He gave a brisk nod. "I agree, it's not funny. Please get me the hell out of here. I want to go home."

"I will do my best. One other thing. Do you have a picture of Heather?"

"I did—in my wallet—but the police took it."

"Why do you have a wallet if you never leave the house?"

"I don't know. That is what normal people do, I guess. I do have a picture of her on my bedside table. Why do you need it?"

"I want to find out more about her. Did you guys ever go anywhere together?"

"I didn't go anywhere with her or anyone else. Hell, if you can get me home confinement, I would take a life sentence."

"Yes, I forgot for a moment about your agoraphobia. Did she ever talk about where she hung out?"

"I know she worked at the library. She talked about a couple of bars she went to—The Cactus Pot and Snuggle and Meet. She also talked about going to bookstores, comic book conventions, and *Star Trek* conventions."

"That's a beginning. Thanks for talking with me. I'll get started."

I stood up and shook Mr. May's hand, promising to return after I received the police reports. I had a strong sense that Mr. May was not pretending to be crazy. I also sensed that he was not crazy.

If that was true, then I was dealing with some very strange shit.

Chapter 9

~~~

IT WAS CLOSE to noon, and I was about to get some lunch before heading to the courthouse. There was a place downtown called Seven Sins. Given that gluttony is one of the seven deadly sins, it seemed like an odd name for a restaurant. The place was dark, with a gothic vibe and known for serving sliders of all types. It was the perfect spot for a person in a contemplative mood to eat lunch. Just as I was about to slide into my car, the cell phone rang.

"Sam Roberts," I sang into the phone.

"Dude, what's up?" Bob said.

"I was just heading to Seven Sins for lunch."

"Cool, order me two buffalo sliders with cheese, waffle fries, and a Coke."

"I know you just got started, but did you find out anything concerning the house?"

"Actually, I have already found out quite a bit."

"Anything useful?"

"I don't know about useful, but certainly weird. That house definitely has a tortured history."

"I look forward to hearing the whole story. I will see you in a bit."

It took only a moment to get to the restaurant. I parked

across the street, got a table in the backroom, and gave the young blonde waitress our orders. Bob came in ten minutes later, just as our food arrived. He was wearing jeans and a black concert T-Shirt with the image of Neil Young holding an acoustic guitar. I had opted for the salmon slider and a salad as a healthier alternative to the buffalo sliders and fries.

As usual, I waited for Bob to inhale his food before engaging him in conversation. I've been friends with Bob long enough to know that it's pointless to discuss business before he's done eating. Besides, I was hungry myself and I suspected what I would learn might have a negative impact on my appetite.

"So, what did you find out about the house?" I asked.

"Dude, it wasn't easy. There was surprisingly little online. I eventually found a reference to a professor at the University of Illinois who wrote a book about it in the 1920s. I couldn't find the book anywhere. I checked Amazon, Barnes and Noble, and every antique book dealer on the web. Guess where I found it?"

"The library at the U of I."

He pounded his fist on the table, startling our waitress. "You suck! I mean it, you suck like a Dyson hopped up on steroids. How did you guess?"

"He was a professor at the University of Illinois and the university has the largest book collection of any public university in the country."

"It was in the rare book and manuscript library on the third floor of the main library—the one on Gregory. They wouldn't let me check it out, and I had to pretend to be a professor to look at it. I also only had a few hours with it so I will need to go back after lunch."

"I'm impressed you found it. I'm also impressed that they believed your cover story."

"It helps that I had an ID."

"How did you manage that?"

"Um, I had to borrow it. An older guy—emeritus maybe—

left it on top of a pile of books while he used the john. I'll leave it at the front desk at the end of the day. Fortunately they didn't give the ID a close look at the rare book room desk, because they probably know the guy." He grabbed the dessert menu, which was propped up next to the little bowl of artificial sweeteners. "Since you're paying for lunch, I assume you know I'm ordering dessert." Bob waved to the waitress, who immediately came to our table. "Can I get a cup of coffee and a slice of chocolate cake?"

"I'll have a cup of tea, Earl Gray, when you have a moment," I added.

"So, anyway, do you remember when you said something about an Indian burial ground and I said the whole country is an Indian burial ground?"

"Yes," I said.

"Well, you weren't completely off target. It wasn't an Indian burial ground, but it was sacred land to the Native American tribes in this area. At least for a while. Then something happened, and no tribesman would set foot on the spot."

"How did the author discover that?"

"Randolph Becker was a professor around the turn of the century. It was a time when spiritualism and séances were all the rage, and he took a scientific interest in the subjects. There was a group called the Obscure Thinkers—it must have been like some fraternal group back then. They met often to perform séances and other ceremonies."

"Did the group live there?"

"No, he didn't say who lived there. If it's important, I can find out easily enough from the recorder of deeds. He did say that the owner of the property was a spiritualist and believed the group was engaged in monumental work. The members had a policy to never write about or discuss their work. Despite that policy, the land was famous among a small group of people."

"It's odd that I've never heard of them until know."

"According to the author, Mary Todd Lincoln had been to

the home to try and communicate with her dead son, Willie."

"Hmm." It wasn't all that surprising that I'd never heard of the Obscure Thinkers, but it was odd that Bob was just learning about them, given his interest in all things weird.

"Mr. Becker claims that when Abraham Lincoln was a lawyer in Springfield, he was riding the circuit and had work to do for Mr. Frost. He was offered lodging free of charge. This was at a time when two lawyers might have to share a bed at a rooming house. Lincoln refused to stay at the Frost Home, claiming it was 'unsettling.' "

"Fascinating."

"Did you know that in 1875, a little more than ten years after Abraham Lincoln was assassinated, Mary Todd Lincoln was put on trial in Chicago to determine if she was insane?"

"I didn't know that."

"She was sent to a sanitarium in Batavia, Illinois, for around three months. Her own son Robert Todd Lincoln was the one who got the whole thing started. According to the author, who again does not provide his source, Robert Todd Lincoln was concerned in part about things his mother said about the Frost Home."

"What did she tell him?"

We were briefly interrupted by the waitress, who delivered a piece of chocolate cake the size of cinderblock, along with the coffee and tea. I expected an end to the conversation until the cake was gone but Bob answered the question. He must have thought this information was important.

"The book doesn't say. Yet, it must have been pretty freaky if he thought she was insane." Bob scooped a large forkful of cake into his mouth.

"He was a lawyer, wasn't he?"

"The author of the book?"

"No, Robert Todd Lincoln."

"Yeah, I think so."

"So who would trust a lawyer?"

He rolled his eyes. "Well, you know me, I would never trust an attorney, present company included, but he *was* a Lincoln."

"Were there any other famous visitors?"

Bob didn't answer the question immediately, and his delay heightened the suspense. He hadn't paused for effect, but rather to fork in an impressively large chunk of cake and wash it down with coffee.

"What do you know about Black Hawk?" Bob answered my question with a question.

"Does he have anything to do with the Hockey Team?"

I was kind of joking, but Bob took me seriously. "Yeah, I think so. At least I assume they named the team after him."

"Why don't people protest the Chicago Black Hawks like they did Chief Illini?"

He shrugged. "I don't know. This story has to do with the Native American chief, not hockey or any other sport." Bob said starting to sound impatient.

"Fine, just finish what you were saying."

"Black Hawk was born in Saukenuk, Illinois, and died in 1838."

"I'm not sure, but that may have been before the Frost Home was built."

"Well, Black Hawk had a son named Gamesett. Soon after the Frost Home was built, they held a séance there."

"So, Mr. Frost was into spiritualism as well?"

Bob nodded vigorously as he gulped down another hunk of cake. "The house was built for spiritualism." He had to stop a minute, having choked on that last bite, but he gulped down more coffee and soon recovered enough to continue. "The author of this book was studying spiritualism on his own. The University of Illinois didn't even exist until 1867. He was an undergraduate at Transylvania University, but his degree was in philosophy, not spiritualism. He went to a séance at the Frost and spoke to Gamesett."

"He went to Transylvania University? Was he into vampires?"

Bob slapped me on the arm a little too hard for playfulness. "Transylvania University is in Kentucky and happens to be one of the oldest schools in the country that is not on the East Coast. This story has nothing to do with vampires."

I rubbed my arm. "Fine, what did Gamesett say?"

"He said that on the land where the Frost Home was built, there was a stone arch so old that the Native American Tribes did not know who erected it. He also said that the land was once held sacred and was a doorway to other worlds. Then something happened and the land was cursed. The sacred became the reviled and profane. He said that his father would not set foot on the land. The ground no longer produced crops and sat empty until Mr. Frost built his home there."

"Go back to the 'doorway to other world' part. What other worlds? Could you choose your world like a spiritual bus station?"

"He didn't say anything more about it. At least so far. I've only had time to go through a small portion of the book."

"What happened at the séance the author went to?"

"I haven't gotten that far, but it must have been serious. After all, he wrote a book about the house."

"What about Mr. Frost and his role in the occult?"

"He was into spiritualism, and the house was intended to be a doorway to the occult. That's as far as I got."

"You said the book was written in the twenties?"

"*Published* in the twenties. It could have been written earlier."

"There has to be more than one copy of the book. After all, someone published it."

"Yes, but I have never heard of the publisher. I'm still doing more research."

I gave him a pat on the shoulder. "You've done a hell of a job in very little time. I appreciate that."

He blew out a breath and fanned himself. "Dude, it is some pretty freaky shit."

"Have you ever heard of the book, *The Doors of Perception*?"

"Yeah, it's by Huxley—about taking mescaline. Mescaline as in peyote. The Doors—the band, I mean—was named after the book. I never read it, though."

"Neither have I, but maybe this gateway to other worlds was just some shit made up by Black Hawk or perhaps he was under the influence of peyote or something."

"Dude, that's like hella racist. Not all Native Americans were into peyote, and those tribes are not in Illinois. You kind of need a desert for that."

I scratched my head. "Yeah, I vaguely remember a Supreme Court case on the subject of religious freedom. I guess I'm just grasping at straws."

He scraped the last bit of frosting off his plate with his fork. At least he stopped short of licking it. "This all might sound freakish, but it might also be true."

"Well, keep up the good work. Also, let me know when you find more information."

He waggled his eyebrows. "The house does have stories."

"Yes, it has three stories."

"Damn! You are as funny as a rubber crutch."

"Who could create such a portal to begin with?"

"Black Hawk told his son that the arch had always been there. He believed it had been there since the dawn of creation."

I smacked the table. "Damn, that is heavy."

"Heavier than a 1950s Cadillac Fleetwood."

I held up an index finger. "One other thing."

We talked about Mr. May's room, and I filled him in on my client's tales of the mirror and aliens. Bob seemed very interested but provided no additional insights. It was odd how Bob's history lesson and Mr. May's story about time portals and aliens could easily relate to the same case.

I paid the bill and Bob walked me back to my car, promising to continue his research. This house had a history featuring Abraham Lincoln and Black Hawk, so why wasn't it more famous … or infamous?

Black birds have always been harbingers of darkness for me. Black Hawk wasn't an actual bird, so I hoped the legendary chief's role in this saga did not bode ill. I had a bad feeling about that house.

Chapter 10

~~

Ｉ DECIDED TO head to the courthouse to get the public defender to sign off on my substitute of counsel. I also was curious to see if they had any further information about the case.

The Champaign County Public Defender's Office is on the first floor of the old courthouse. The courthouse looks like a large brick church, complete with bell tower, and takes up an entire city block in downtown Urbana. Its construction was completed in 1901. In 2002 an addition more than doubled the size of the building.

I went through security and took a right to get to Richard Goldstein's office. I've known the public defender for some time. He's about my age, balding, with a long face and beaky nose. He wouldn't stand out in a crowd. As luck would have it, he was the lawyer on the case and was in the office.

There was nothing unusual about his office other than the dying palm tree. It was a small space with a desk and three chairs, a number of file cabinets, framed degrees, and a photo of his wife and two children. He sat behind his desk, which was covered with paperwork, waiting for me to start the conversation.

"I am taking over Blake May's case," I said as I rummaged

through my briefcase for the substitution of counsel form. He signed the document and handed it back to me, a look of relief on his face.

"I can't say I'm disappointed to see him go. Everything about that case is strange," Richard said.

"What happened at the arraignment?"

"They did it over the video monitor. He was acting pretty crazy—screaming and jumping around. The judge read him the charges, and before I could ask, the state requested to have him evaluated for fitness to stand trial."

"What about the preliminary hearing?"

"I asked for one and the judge gave me a date of September fifth, but it's not going to take place. The assistant state's attorney told me they were going to have this brought before a grand jury instead. As you know, in Illinois, a preliminary hearing needs to be heard within thirty days of the arrest. The state told me that they don't want to bring him to court that soon because they don't believe his mental condition will be stable. Assuming he is indicted by the grand jury, you can avoid the extra court appearance for the preliminary hearing."

I tapped the papers in front of me. "If he is that crazy, how could Blake understand the charges against him and the possible penalties?"

Richard shook his head. "He couldn't, but I don't think that argument will get you anywhere. If he goes to trial and is convicted, the appellate court would find the argument that he was too crazy to understand the reading of the charges to be harmless error. Assuming it bothers them at all."

"I take it you don't have the discovery yet?"

"Not yet, but the assistant state's attorney is Amanda Babs. She told me she was just there for the arraignment and someone else is going to prosecute the case. She also said that the photographs of the murder scene are the most disgusting she has ever seen. I have the feeling she wouldn't be upset if he pled guilty but mentally ill. He is from a rich family and has no prior convictions."

I could see her point. "Jurors certainly love nauseating photographs," I said. "It makes it hard to get a fair trial."

"On the positive side, it's no longer my problem." His smile seemed to call me a sucker. "Good luck."

"Just out of curiosity, how did you get appointed? He obviously has money."

"The judge was anxious to get him out of there. The whole thing took two minutes. He just appointed our office because it was the fastest way to get it over with."

I leaned forward to shake his hand. "Thanks for your help."

"No problem."

Richard handed me the Manila folder, which I flipped through. It contained the information as well as some notes and an order to have a psychological evaluation. There was nothing of any interest.

After I had the clerk's office drop the substitution in the judge's mailbox to have it signed and approved, I headed to the second floor to see if Amanda Babs was in her office. Amanda was in court, so I left a message asking her to give me a call.

Afterward, I headed to the Frost Home to retrieve the photo of Heather from Blake's bedside table. I wasn't sure if it would prove helpful, but I wanted to learn as much as I could about the alleged victim.

Chapter 11

~~~

I ARRIVED AT the Frost Home a few minutes later. As I walked up to the door, I had a sense of foreboding. The house seemed ominous and alive. I thought of Bob's story of the barren land and the stone arch that was here before the house. If the arch in St. Louis is the gateway to the West, this house was a gateway to hell. AC/DC may have sung about the highway to hell, but I suspected you could avoid the traffic by taking a shortcut through the Frost Home.

I looked at the two piles of stones in the front lawn and wondered if they were cairns. Cairns are stone markers used to mark trails or reference important sites. If not, perhaps they represented graves. They also might just be piles of rocks. As Freud once said, "Sometimes a cigar is just a cigar."

Malcolm Conrad answered my knock. When I explained that I wanted to retrieve the picture from Mr. May's bed stand, he looked over at Edna May, who was seated by the fireplace where we had spoken earlier. By Mrs. May's feet was Mr. Fluffinator. His ears perked up as I entered, but he did not move or bark.

"Mr. Conrad, you will get the photograph for Mr. Roberts while he and I chat, won't you?" Mrs. May said.

She had to be over twenty feet away from us when I made

the request of Mr. Conrad. I had also spoken fairly softly. For Mrs. May, at her age, to have overheard what I'd said was miraculous. Perhaps losing your sight really does heighten your other senses. Mr. Conrad bowed and headed up the stairs.

"Mrs. May, what a pleasure," I said.

"I am an old lady. You needn't blow smoke up my ass. It is not the least bit of a pleasure for me to bother you with questions. I intend to ask them, anyway."

"Of course."

"Please sit down." I obeyed. "Have you spoken with my son?"

"Yes," I said.

"Is he all right?"

"Under the circumstances, he is holding up just fine."

"I'm glad. Even if he committed this horrible act, he was not in his right mind."

Mr. Fluffinator looked up at me as if curious to hear what I would say next. He seemed like a kind and intelligent dog.

"If it's not too much trouble, I do have a question of my own. I have heard a great deal about this house. I was wondering if you could share anything about its history."

She looked in my direction through her sightless eyes and quickly turned away. Whatever she saw, or didn't see, I assume she did not like it. Her demeanor instantly reflected a tense wariness.

"The history of this house is a little far afield from my son's case."

"You never know. I have found that minor, seemingly irrelevant facts can have a large impact on a case. It is better to throw a wide net."

Mrs. May held her hands tightly in her lap. "I have certainly heard rumors about the house being haunted," she said, "but I have never heard rattling chains or the moaning of apparitions."

We were interrupted by Mr. Conrad coming down the stairs. He was holding a 5x7 photograph of a person I assumed to be Heather. Mrs. May stood with some effort.

"I believe you have what you need. Good day, Mr. Roberts." She was curt and dismissive.

"Is Laura James here?"

"No. I'm afraid there was a family emergency. She will be on leave for the next few months."

"Few *months*? The police didn't ask her to remain in town?"

"Why would they? She is certainly not a suspect."

Mr. Conrad handed me the photograph and signaled that I should follow him to the door. I could tell Mrs. May was uncomfortable when asked about the house, but I couldn't figure out why. She clearly did not want to talk about it. She also didn't want to tell me what was going on with Ms. James. I hope Ms. James was not being punished for speaking with me.

I can't say I was treated warmly the first time I met Mrs. May but this time she was colder than an Alaskan Good Humor man in January. Perhaps she was simply upset about her son. I had no idea how she knew Mr. Conrad had the photograph in his hands. She was blind, after all. This woman definitely made me uncomfortable.

The library was just around the corner, and I took my time walking over. The building is of contemporary design and made of glass, steel, and concrete. The interior complements the exterior, with bamboo floors and modern furniture and lighting. At the information desk, I was directed to the third floor, site of the administrative offices. I had asked to speak with the director.

As I got off the elevator, I saw a middle-aged woman with short brown hair, heavy makeup, and cat's-eye glasses sitting behind a clear plastic desk. She was thin and wore a leather miniskirt, purple pantyhose, a pink sweater, and a Hello Kitty necklace. On her desk, a porcelain unicorn kept company with a glass elephant.

In a squeaky voice that made her sound fourteen years old, she asked me why I was there. After I told her, she politely informed me that the director was busy and I should have called ahead. But if I took a seat, she would see what could be done. I did as instructed and had a seat in one of four chairs surrounding a glass coffee table. Ten minutes later, a brown-haired woman in her fifties wearing a gray suit and white blouse came out to meet with me.

She brought me back to her office—a small, neat space with a large window looking out onto the parking lot—and closed the door.

"Wendy Faber," she said in a professional tone.

"Sam Roberts," I responded, handing her my business card. "I am investigating the alleged murder of Heather Kline."

"You know I can't discuss with you private information concerning our employees," she said, sitting behind an organized steel-and-Plexiglas desk.

"I understand. I guess I was just hoping to find out the last day Heather was at work and if there was anything unusual about her behavior."

"I read about her murder," Ms. Faber said in a cool voice just short of icy. "I know she has not worked here since at least a week before that. As for unusual behavior, I don't work with her directly. Most of her job was putting away books. Her schedule tended to change from week to week. I will tell you that she was an unusual woman but I've had no complaints about her job performance. I am very busy, however, so if you would like to make an appointment—"

"I have just two questions."

"That's fine, but I may not be able to answer them. Frankly, if you are working for the man who killed my employee, I don't feel compelled to help."

"I am just trying to get to the truth. Imagine if my client is innocent and a murderer is out on the street. I think it is best for someone to be looking into the case, don't you?"

"Fine, that is your first question. What's the next?" she said, smiling at her own joke. She had warmed to me somewhat.

"Do you do a background check, including the criminal history, of all your employees prior to their working here?"

"Of course, and I'm sure Heather Kline does not have a criminal record."

"Was she ever in the military?"

"No."

"Is there anything you can think of that might be helpful?"

Without hesitation, she replied, "I'm afraid not."

She stood up, clearly dismissing me. I asked if she would call me if anything further should come to mind. She did not respond. I left her office not too much the wiser, but more enlightened than when I came in. I had confirmed that Heather did not have a criminal background and was never in the military.

I returned to the office to work on my other cases, spending the next couple of hours returning telephone calls and doing research. At around six, I gave up. I found it hard to concentrate as thoughts of Blake's case crept into my mind.

Chapter 12

~~

O N THE WAY home, I stopped at the store to pick up sushi and orange juice. I wondered why the grocery store had only brown-rice sushi. Brown rice may be healthier, but it does not really work with sushi. It must be the texture. I like toast and I like ice cream but I don't like ice cream on my toast.

At home, I turned on the television, flipping through the channels until I alighted on *Phantasm*. I have seen the movie a number of times but it seemed oddly relevant tonight. The idea that there could be dimensions into other worlds made me think of the Frost Home. The scene with the mirror reminded me of the mirror in the old mansion.

Despite having no appetite, I ate the sushi, trying to clear my mind of the day's events. After dinner I turned off the television, leaving Reggie and Mike to face the Tall Man without my support. I brushed my teeth and got undressed, hanging my gray suit in the closet but leaving my shirt, tie, and socks in a pile on the floor. It was Friday, and I didn't bother to set an alarm. I got into bed feeling tired and a bit lonely. A dog or cat might have helped, but I wasn't sure if I could handle the added responsibility in my life. I thought about Mr. Fluffinator.

I closed my eyes, contemplating sheep jumping over a fence. A door opened on its own and I walked into a large room. It took me a moment to get my bearings. A round table and six chairs were set up in front of a huge mirror against the back wall. The table had no cloth, just two bowls, a plate, and some eating utensils. At first I didn't recognize the room, although the mirror was similar to the one in Blake May's room.

Similar but not identical. This mirror looked newer, the silver backing less worn, the frame's gilt fresh and shiny. I realized my failure to recognize the space stemmed from the room being much larger than the one I had visited at the Frost Home. The rooms that contained the kitchen, bathroom, laundry room, and the science fiction museum were all gone. From the ceiling hung an enormous brass chandelier. It looked like an octopus and held eight lamps. The wall sconces were the same ornate design, made of brass and sporting gas flames.

A thin woman with piercing black eyes stood next to the table. She wore a black dress with a tight corset. The skirt of the dress was bell-shaped with three tiers. The hem touched the wooden floor, hiding her feet completely. Her long black hair was tied back into a long ponytail.

Seated at the table was the sixteenth president of the United States, wearing a black suit and bow tie. His stovepipe hat was on his lap. He had a beard with no mustache and looked exactly like the image captured by Victor David Brenner on the penny. Next to him sat Mary Todd Lincoln in a black dress with flowers in her hair. She had a dower expression and seemed a tad heavier than Sally Fields in the movie.

At the table was a man with high cheekbones, wearing a black wool suit. Underneath the jacket he was bare chested other than a choker made of bones and beads. His face was heavily lined and his hair was shaven into a wide red Mohawk. Next to the man in the Mohawk was a man wearing a dark-blue jacket with gold buttons and lighter blue pants. His black boots were caked with mud. His eyes were open, but he was clearly dead. A good portion of the back of his head was gone, exposing old blood along with a portion of his maggot-filled brain.

Holding his hat against his chest, Lincoln rose to his feet and bowed low. Even by today's standards, he was a tall and imposing man.

"My name is Abraham Lincoln and this is my wife, Mary Todd Lincoln." His voice was not unpleasant but higher pitched than I would have expected.

"I am certainly aware of who you are, Mr. President," I said with a bow.

"This is my friend Black Hawk and the late Private Reginald Jones of the 133rd Regiment of Illinois. He died for his service to this great land." The corpse and the man with the Mohawk stood and bowed.

"I am your host this evening," said the woman in black. She remained seated. "Mr. Jones is the man who we were mistakenly told was our son when he died on the field of battle. I am Mrs. Frost. This is Mr. Jones. I do not describe him as the president did—'the late Private Reginald Jones'—since 'the late' is used to describe someone who is 'lately diseased.' Mr. Jones has been dead for over a century and a half." She glared at the president. Her demeanor seemed to indicate that she still blamed him for the false report of her own son's death. In any case, she was objecting to something other than his use of language.

"Mr. President, I was unaware that you knew Black Hawk or that you had spent time in this house during your lifetime," I said.

"I indirectly knew Black Hawk while I was alive. In 1832 there was a bit of a skirmish known as the Black Hawk War. I was a captain in that skirmish. My military service was not long or distinguished, but it was my honor and duty to serve. I don't believe I had met Mr. Blackhawk at that time. The United States was victorious. I did apologize to Black Hawk for the loss of lives."

Black Hawk broke in, "Of course I couldn't forgive Mr. Lincoln or the rest of white America for murdering my people, but I did appreciate his words of reconciliation." He did not rise from his seat.

"As for staying in this house," Lincoln went on, "I never did. Even shortly after the home was built, it had a reputation for being unsavory. I don't mean that it needed salt, but that it was spooky. Mary Todd came here after I died, but this dream of yours is the first time I ever set foot in the place."

"This is a dream?" I asked.

"Did you think, even if I was still alive, I would visit you in real life? I am the sixteenth president of the United States. At least I was."

I bowed my head. "Yes, of course."

"Not to mention every other person at the table is also long dead. Please have a seat and maybe we can figure out what your dream is all about."

I sat down and noticed that the eating utensils on the table were sterling-silver marrow scoops. One of the bowls contained what looked to be chunky marinara sauce. On the plate were long bones cut down the middle to allow access to the marrow. The last bowl contained silver jewelry, glasses, and human teeth.

"Hold hands and we shall begin," Mrs. Frost said.

"Is this a séance?" I asked.

"Why would we need a séance, Mr. Roberts?" Mrs. Frost said. "If you want to talk to the dead, we are all dead."

"There is no money or power to be gained from manipulating the dead," President Lincoln added. "I am on the penny and the five dollar bill, and I don't get anything."

"Elvis is dead and his estate still brings in over fifty million dollars a year," I said.

President Lincoln looked even more disgusted, if possible, although the set of his craggy features tended that way to begin with. "All I did was free the slaves. What did this Elvis do that was greater than that? Anyway, this house may be about money but has nothing to do with speaking to the dead."

I heard a hum like that of a fluorescent light and looked over at Mrs. Frost. Her irises had rolled up into her head until only the whites of her eyes were visible.

"She no longer needs her eyes to see," Black Hawk said while gazing at Mrs. Frost.

The mirror started changing and moving like liquid mercury. After a moment, it seemed to switch images and I looked for a remote control.

When I turned my head away, I saw myself lying on a white leather chaise-longue in a white painted room. Next to me was a balding man with a full mustache and beard. He was wearing a tweed three-piece suit and smoking a cigar.

"So you dreamt about Abraham Lincoln, Black Hawk, Mary Todd Lincoln, a dead Civil War soldier, and Mrs. Frost," Dr. Freud said in his thick Austrian accent.

"Yes," I said.

He continued, "On the table was a bowl of red sauce. The sauce matched the description you were given of a decimated human body. In addition you were given a utensil for the purpose of consuming the body."

"Nobody was eating," I said.

"Maybe the food had another meaning. The long bones and the marrow scoops must have something to do with the penis. They are both long and phallic. The cannibalism might represent some sadistic tendency on your part or that of another. The changing mirror … I want to think about that some more. You know men are more moral than they think and far more immoral than they can imagine."

"I think I have heard you say that before. Is it a famous quote?"

"The bit about the mirror?"

"No, the morality thing."

"Good to know people remember anything about me. May I continue?"

"Please."

"Black Hawk is an Indian?"

"Yes," I said.

"Indians, or as you modern people say 'Native Americans,' live in teepees and wigwams."

"I guess."

"Then I see your problem."

"What? I must know."

"You are two tents."

I awoke to the sound of my telephone. I looked over at the clock to see that it was ten thirty in the morning. I answered the telephone.

"Dude, you want to head to the taste today for lunch?" Bob said.

"Sure," I said, rising to a sitting position on the bed and stretching. "I will meet you by the big fountain. The one with the Native American man holding his arms up."

"Noon?"

"Works for me."

I showered and dressed, made a cup of tea and watched the news for a bit. I allowed the dream to replay in my mind. I knew there had to be some message there.

Chapter 13

~~

I GOT TO the fountain a few minutes prior to noon and located Bob right away. It was crowded, but his bright green and red tie-dyed shirt depicting a skeleton kissing a large mouthed bass was easy to spot. He had a small paper carton filled with chicken and rice on his lap and a half-filled bottle of Mountain Dew sitting next to him.

"Dude, got hungry and started without you."

He held up his dish to offer me a bite but I shook my head. In this crowd, it was too noisy to talk, so I suggested we move to a less congested area of the park. We found a seat in the back row where a lone folk singer was singing "City of New Orleans" on a beat-up acoustic guitar. He sounded more like Steve Goodman than Arlo Guthrie.

I got up to get some Taste Money and returned with half a gyro, some tofu Pad Thai, and an iced tea. When I returned, Bob was gone, only to return a few minutes later with a huge chocolate chip cookie and a snow cone. We ate in silence.

After we finished, I told him about my dream. I suspected it had no meaning other than to suggest my need to seek mental health treatment. Bob, however, seemed very interested in these night-time images.

"So, do you think I'm crazy?" I asked.

"After all these years, I know you're crazy, but the dream is no reflection of that."

"I am not sure how to respond."

The folk singer was singing "Blowin' in the Wind" in a credible Dylan imitation. I hoped the answers to our questions weren't going to be as elusive.

"You spoke with Abraham Lincoln," Bob said. "Did you ask if he was gay?"

He was humming along here and there, probably unawares, in a tuneless voice.

I gave him a long look, but he didn't crack a smile. "No, I did not ask the former President of the United States about his sexual preferences. Besides, he was married and had children."

Bob stopped tapping his foot and said, "So have a lot of gay people. There has been a debate among historians on the subject. That is why the gay republicans are called Log Cabin Republicans."

I blew a raspberry. "I don't believe it."

"It is just a rumor," Bob insisted. "No one knows."

"Not that," I said, trying to ignore the singer's annoyingly croony rendition of "Alice's Restaurant." "I just find it hard to believe that there are gay republicans. As for Lincoln being gay, who cares? It neither enhances nor diminishes his legacy. I will say he seemed very presidential."

Bob was gazing around as if plotting his next taste. It was hard to believe he could still be hungry after that dinner-plate-sized cookie, but with Bob, anything was possible. "I can't believe Freud didn't have more insight into your dream," he said.

"Yeah, I was a bit disappointed in that as well. Not to get off topic, but did you finish the book by the guy who was at the Frost Home?"

Bob's eyes widened. "I did, and I also found out more about the house from other sources as well. What I discovered makes your dream sound sane."

The guitarist on stage had started in on an uninspired version of that hammer song Peter Seeger made famous. Bob stared up at the stage for almost half a minute before turning back to me.

"Squirrel," I said.

"What is that supposed to mean?"

"You have the attention span of a poodle. You are like that dog in that Disney movie. Would you continue?"

Bob's brow furrowed, and he opened his mouth as if to protest, but then he went on with the story instead. "The book was published in the 1920s, so for anything that happened after that, I had to find other sources."

I rubbed my hands together. "Cool, give me the rundown."

"Sure, but let's get rid of our garbage first." When he returned from throwing away our cartons and plastic cutlery, Bob sat back down in his chair and continued his story. Fortunately the singer was taking a break. "Mr. Frost was a sailor. In the 1830s, he fell in love with a woman in Ireland who was said to be a witch. She married Mr. Frost and moved to America just before the great potato famine. This fortuity of that move supported her countrymen's belief she was a witch."

I frowned. "How could you know that?" I asked.

"Letters," he said, "from the book. After they married, he returned to New York and got a job working for a wealthy investor. Mr. Frost began investing in lumber and in the railroads and was doing very well. After a few years, his wife convinced him to leave New York. They planned to move to California. The Gold Rush was underway and she predicted if they moved they would become wealthy. On that Westward trip, they wound up in the area now known as Champaign. His wife was drawn to the land where the Frost Home is now located. They never left Champaign and built their home where it still stands. That was in the 1850s."

Bob looked up and I assumed he was putting his thoughts in order until I noticed a young woman in spandex yoga pants and a matching spandex crop top walk by. She had long brown hair and blue eyes and couldn't have been more than twenty-five years old. He did not look away until a four-year-old girl ran up to grab her hand.

"Don't you think she is a bit young for you?" I asked.

"Of course, you sick bastard! That child can't be more than four or five," Bob said.

I rolled my eyes. "I was referring to her mother."

"Oh, I didn't notice her. Besides, she wasn't necessarily that girl's mother. She could have been the nanny or babysitter."

"Does it matter?"

"No, I guess not. I just always thought that the future Mrs. Sizemore wouldn't have children from a prior relationship. Kids are cool. I can be flexible."

"Should I run out and buy a gift?"

"No not yet. I should wait until I meet her before I send out wedding invitations."

"She seems nice, but not your type."

"I can see that," Bob said. "Ordinarily I am not into physical perfection, long, flowing brown hair and eyes so blue you can see through to her glowing soul. I am willing to make an exception this once. What is your type, if I might ask? Susan was pretty cute."

"Let's not talk about Susan," I said, feeling my stomach drop. Susan had hung in there with me much longer than any reasonable person could have expected. I guess she finally concluded that my penchant for encountering world-threatening evil was too dangerous and that I would never shy away from it when it crossed my path. I added, "I prefer women who know I exist. Can we get back to the house now?"

"You're aware that Mr. Frost killed his family when he was told his son died in the Civil War. Yet, it turned out his son was still alive and the person who delivered the bad news mistook him for someone else."

"Yes, that fits with my dream," I said.

"Since the time it was built, the house was said to be haunted.

There were tales about visitors who were never seen again—not that unusual, given the war and the times in general. People tended to be more mobile and did not leave forwarding addresses. It didn't help that the Frost family was rich and his wife was known as a spiritualist and held séances and other odd ceremonies. Central Illinois in the mid-nineteenth century was not exactly enlightened."

Another singer was setting up on the stage. He was physically more or less a clone of the last one.

"What happened to the house after the family was killed?" I said, watching the man tune his guitar.

"The Frost's son in the military was the only remaining heir. He sold the home to a man named Robert May."

"Let me guess: it has remained with the May family to this day."

Bob put his index finger to his nose. "The home was sold to Mr. May in 1874. Mr. May was a farmer and not particularly wealthy. He was only able to afford the home because it sold at a good price due to its unsavory history. As soon as he moved in, however, everything changed. His farmland became very valuable thanks to its proximity to the railroad tracks and was sold to a highly motivated buyer. He became wealthy overnight."

"I assume a Midwestern farmer was not into the occult."

Bob wagged his index finger. "You assume incorrectly. He married a woman named Rebecca Corley. A known spiritualist."

"Let me guess: the séances, strange ceremonies, and missing persons continued."

Again, Bob placed his finger on his nose. "You got it. They had a single daughter around the turn of the century named Agnes May who was reportedly insane. For a short while she was committed to Bellevue Place—the same asylum in Batavia, Illinois, where Mary Todd Lincoln was held. She was moved, however, to a less prestigious state institution and spent a number of years there."

"Did she ever get married?"

"She never married but got pregnant and gave birth while still institutionalized in the late 1920s. Your good friend and benefactor, Edna May, was born in a mental institution."

I felt a chill go down my spine. "That's creepy."

"She ended up spending a number of years there herself as a baby. The lovely doctors assumed she must be crazy because her mother was. She was forced to undergo treatment as a toddler. When she was five years old, mother and daughter returned home. Agnes brought a woman from the institution with her to help raise Edna. Her name was Helen Wormwood. Ms. Wormwood had been institutionalized because she claimed to have magic powers."

I slowly shook my head. "That's crazy. What do you think it all means?"

He grabbed my arm and looked me straight in the eye. "Dude, that house is *evil*. People who spend time there seem to wind up dead, mentally ill, or they just disappear."

Bob fell silent, and I assumed he was deep in the contemplation of good versus evil, yet when I followed his gaze, I noted his spandex-clad prospective wife strolling by again. She did not have the child with her, so perhaps Bob was right and she was a babysitter.

"Would it be wrong to point out that you are shallow?" I asked.

He drew in a deep breath. "She even smells nice—sweet but with a hint of heat. What perfume do you think that is?" Bob asked.

"I believe it is eau de bulgogi taco. It is sold exclusively at that blue truck along with kimchi and some noodle dish. Assuming you don't have a date with that young lady, how would you like to go bar-hopping tonight? I want to visit a couple of the hang-outs of the late Heather Kline."

Bob sat back in his chair and gave me a speculative look. "I would be glad to. But why? What are you looking for in relation to the victim of the crime?"

"*Alleged* victim, and I'm not sure."

Bob raised his eyebrows. "Maybe you could meet someone. Have you gone out with anyone since Bridget?"

I hated it when Bob pursued this topic. "Sue me, but I am a little hesitant to jump back into the dating scene considering that my last girlfriend proved to be less than sincere."

"Sure, she was a bit of a witch. She was also cute."

I rolled my eyes. "So are lion fish, tigers, and blue-ringed octopuses."

"That's random. Besides, tigers are only cute when they are little. What time do you want to head out?"

"I was thinking ten. I will pick you up."

Chapter 14

~~

IDECIDED TO straighten up the house, but after an hour got bored and switched on the television. For the remainder of the day I wasted time. It took work to avoid thinking about work.

In preparation for our night out, I put on a pair of Levi's, a gray T-shirt, and tennis shoes. I wanted to blend in with the crowd as best as I could and so had chosen an outfit that was about as generic as I could get. Finally it was time to get Bob.

Bob was wearing the same colorful tie-dyed shirt he had on at the Taste of Champaign, along with jeans and brown slip-on canvas shoes. When I entered his house, he was watching a horror movie on his large screen television. Or rather I assumed it was a horror movie based on the images of a man chewing on a femur bone. It was one I had not seen. Bob turned off the television, grabbed a leather backpack, and we left.

"Dude, where are we headed?" he asked.

"The Cactus Pot and a place called Snuggle and Meet. I have never been to the latter."

We got into the car and Bob made a face. "I have lived in Champaign the majority of my life and have never heard of a bar called Snuggle and Meet."

"Same here," I said as I drove down the street. "I feel you

should meet someone before you snuggle. So at a minimum it should be called Meet and Snuggle."

"Not me," he said. "If the snuggle isn't so good, I wouldn't want to meet the person."

The Cactus Pot was a small downtown Urbana dive known for country music and cheap domestic beer. It has been at its present location for as long as I can remember. There is a small stage that I hoped would be empty tonight. The bands are mostly country, and in such a small bar, it's hard to have a meaningful conversation.

The place smelled of stale beer and cigarettes, despite the fact that you can no longer smoke indoors in restaurants and bars in the City of Urbana. "The Pot," as the locals refer to it, was dark, with fake wood paneling and neon signs advertising mostly beer. In addition to the signs, the décor included NASCAR memorabilia, a jukebox, and a few video poker machines.

I was pleased to see that there was no band or at least the band had yet to arrive. "I'm no angel" by Gregg Allman was playing in the background. I considered the song more rock than country. It had been popular in the late '80s at around the time Gregg was married to Cher.

Bob grabbed a table past the small dance floor near an electronic dart machine. I headed to the bar, and in an effort to blend in, I ordered a pitcher of Pabst Blue Ribbon. There were three or four patrons sitting at the bar, all ignoring one another.

The bartender was in his forties, skinny with long hair and a beard. He was wearing blue jeans, a flannel shirt, and cowboy boots. He didn't smile or acknowledge me other than to grab the pitcher.

"Can I buy you a drink?" I offered.

"If it is whiskey, I guess that would be okay," he said. "By whiskey I mean Jack." He had a slight country twang.

"Sure, whatever you like."

He turned around and removed a bottle of Jack Daniels from the highest shelf, separated by a shelf that contained two other bottles of Jack Daniels. I assumed from the reverence he had for this bottle that it must be a special edition. He poured two fingers into a dirty shot glass, returned the bottle to its shelf, and drank it down. He gave me the pitcher and I gave him a twenty. I did not expect change and so was not surprised when none came.

Removing the picture of Heather Kline from my jeans' pocket, I said, "By the way, have you ever seen this woman?" I held out the picture.

"What, are you a cop or a private investigator?" the bartender asked, opting not to look at the photograph.

"I am a lawyer."

"I had me one of those when I got divorced," he said.

"How'd it go?"

"I'm working here nights and I'm doing roofing work during the day. So take a guess. I ain't seen my daughter in two years. I also just spent five hundred dollars at the vet and my dog still might die."

"Well, you can't blame your lawyer for the dog's bad fortune."

"The hell I can't. That dog is the only thing I got to keep from the divorce. The wife let her go 'cause she knew she was sick. So what type of law do you do?"

"Mostly maritime law," I lied.

He gave the photo a quick glance. "Well, I ain't seen the woman in the picture."

I walked back to the table with the pitcher of beer and two glasses. Bob took one of the glasses and wiped the rim with his T-shirt before pouring a beer. I have seen Bob drink a beer out of a Frisbee after a dog caught it. Either Bob was becoming a lot fussier or this place did not meet even his standards.

A few minutes later, a woman got up from the bar and started walking in our direction. Her gait was a bit unsteady and I was not sure if that was due to her level of intoxication or the fact that she was large chested and wearing high-heeled boots. She was in her forties with bleached-blonde hair and makeup applied with a trowel. Her silk blouse had a cheetah pattern and was a few sizes too small, leaving nothing to the imagination. I wondered if she did her shopping on one of those television shopping channels or at a wildlife preserve. She sat down next to me and placed a hand on my thigh.

"My name is Jacqueline," she said. "I saw you talking with Keith, the bartender, and he's an asshole. Maybe I can help with that picture." She spoke with a slight slur.

She might have smelled of alcohol, but who could tell? I couldn't get past her perfume. It was the overpowering scent of a million flowers who killed themselves for smelling too sickly sweet. I handed her the photograph.

"I've seen her."

"Really? When?"

"A number of times. The last time must have been a month or so back. She tried to get me to go home with her. I said I prefer men." As she said this, her hand slipped from my lower thigh closer to the crotch.

I didn't react but was on the alert for the hand's further progress. "What did she say?"

"Something about meeting her boyfriend, and a threesome. I am not into that either." She looked over at Bob as if reconsidering this option.

"Did she say anything else?"

"Not that I can think of. She used to come here every so often. Never looked the part. I think she liked the music. Never saw her when there wasn't a band. She was kind of a slut."

"Thanks for talking with me. Can you think of anything else?"

"No not at the moment. How about buying me a drink? Maybe something will jar my memory"

I was already standing. "What can I get you?"

"Jack and Coke."

I headed to the bar and fetched a Jack and Coke for Jacqueline. When I got back to the table, her attention was completely fixed on Bob, who looked like a mouse in a snake cage. I handed Jacqueline her drink.

"You two are as sweet as a sugar cookie with a glass of lemonade," Jacqueline said.

"Well, I just wish we could stay longer, but we have to get going," I said, hopping to my feet.

"Afraid so," Bob agreed, pretending to look disappointed.

"Well, I will be here all night if you want to talk some more about that picture or anything else," Jacqueline said with a wink.

I could still smell her perfume even after we were a block past the drinking establishment. Maybe it had become embedded in my sinuses. If nothing else, we had confirmed that Heather frequented the Cactus Pot.

"Sorry to drag you out of there," I said as we got in the car. "I know we still had most of our pitcher of beer."

"That's okay," Bob said, "I wasn't thirsty anyway."

"I think Jacqueline liked you."

"In the same way a hyena likes a bunny rabbit."

"Yet, she was smart enough to avoid going home with Heather. There is something to that."

"What?"

"I don't know, but like Greg Allman on the jukebox, Heather wasn't exactly an angel. Or at least I am getting that impression."

Chapter 15

SNUGGLE AND MEET was located east of Urbana toward St. Joseph. I put the address into my phone's GPS and followed the directions. The map seemed to point to an area in the middle of nowhere. I was apprehensive; I don't know why, but this place gave me a bad feeling.

"I can't think of any bars in this direction. I know there is a cemetery and some houses," Bob said.

"Yeah," I replied. "There are also some farms and a seed research greenhouse."

Bob gave me a long, skeptical look. "Well, maybe I will find someone to snuggle and meet. Your luck with the ladies has not been fantastic either."

"Let's just say I am on a dating hiatus. If I want someone to rip out my heart and kick it around like a soccer ball, there are demons, witches, and voodoo spirits lining up for that privilege."

Bob, who appeared to be lost in thought, said, "You know, maybe the rest of the world is right. Football is a better name for soccer. In American football you never use your feet."

I made a disgusted noise. "You must have missed the Illini games. They use their feet all the time. They punt every four downs or so."

We drove past the Mount Olivet Cemetery, which was small and surrounded by cornfields on three sides. The ground was relatively flat, so the word 'mount' made no sense. I assumed the reference was to the Mount of Olives Cemetery in Jerusalem. Bob and I had had a chance to see the ancient burial grounds when we were in Jerusalem. The belief among some religious Jews and Christians is that when the Messiah comes, the resurrection of the dead will start there. It is based on a Bible verse, but I couldn't tell you which one. We were somewhere between Urbana and St. Joseph, Illinois. My guess is that the Bible did not describe this particular spot as prime for resurrection. That said, it still seemed like a nice enough final resting place.

The moon was almost full and brightened the night sky. The reflection was captured on the polished stones of the graveyard. There was a single mausoleum that looked older than the other graves surrounded by a cast-iron gate.

As we passed the cemetery, we noted a number of houses on one side of the two-lane highway. On the other side of the street was a drainage ditch, and behind that, rows of trees and brush. Behind the trees were acres of partially harvested corn and beans.

I thought about how the trees hid parts of the acres of land. Maybe there was also something hidden behind the ancient walls of the Frost Home.

Out of nowhere, I saw TIKI torches burning up ahead. This had to be the place. I pulled up onto a lawn filled with a strange variety of cars. Rusted pickup trucks were parked next to new Mercedes. There were sports cars, four-door sedans, and motorcycles. In addition, the license plates indicated that the vehicles were from all over the country.

The bar itself was an old church, complete with a steeple and enormous stained-glass windows depicting Jesus Christ performing various miracles. The outside of the building had little by way of lighting other than a neon sign that had

"S&M" written in purple glass. The stained glass was lit from inside the building and the images of miracles seemed to glow against the dark backdrop of the bar. The burning torches were not just for effect but for illuminating the parking area. We parked and got out of the car.

"Well, now I know why it is Snuggle and Meet and not the other way around," Bob said.

"Yes, I get it, S and M. It does make you wonder about the crowd," I agreed.

Bob and I walked up to the church. I felt as out of place as a juicy steak at a vegan café. As we got closer to the door, I could hear loud, heavy-metal music. As we got to the door, it opened on its own, emitting thick, sweet-smelling smoke. A large African American man in leather pants and vest pointed to a sign that indicated the cover charge was ten dollars apiece. I paid and Bob and I entered a world I was unprepared for. It was like H.R. Giger and the Marquis de Sade went into business together.

Against the far wall was a stage where a woman in a red shiny PVC cat suit was screaming something I didn't understand into a microphone. The drummer was wearing a black bodysuit that covered his face and head, making him near invisible. The other members of the band, one playing the guitar and the other a bass, were shirtless with black-leather pants. In front of the band, hanging from the ceiling on thick steel chains, was a teddy bear with a hook through its middle, dangling like a giant, fuzzy night crawler, and on a similar hook, what appeared to be a side of beef.

"I get it," Bob yelled to be heard above the band.

"What?" I said.

"It's Snuggle and *Meat* not Snuggle and Meet. Get it? M-E-A-T." He pointed to the cow carcass."

"Shouldn't this bar be in L.A. or New York?" I asked.

Bob nodded. "It is pretty fucked up," he said.

There was a large counter on the far right side of the open

area of the room and no tables or chairs anywhere. The lack of furniture was a good idea given the amount of people in the bar and the crowds who continued to stroll in. Most were dressed entirely in black with a few wearing bright neon colors.

I walked up to the counter, where a woman was handcuffed to a brass rail that ran along the top of the bar. The bartender was wearing a top hat and his face was painted half white and half black. His black shirt had a skeleton on it. UV lighting behind the back of the counter where the better bottles were shelved made the white of his face and the bones in the skeleton shirt glow. I ordered two beers. They were served in pint glasses with the image of a teddy bear eating raw steak with S&M written above it in script.

The woman handcuffed to the brass rail looked up at me, and I took a closer look at her. She was dressed in red spandex pants, with a diamond-patterned corset. Her hair was blonde pigtails dipped in pink, making her appear to be a mix of Harley Quinn and that girl from *Sucker Punch*. Her eyes were bright blue. As I was about to leave, she signaled for me to bend over closer, and when I did, she kissed me gently on the lips. When I looked up, she opened her hand to reveal two yellow pills, a smiley face on each.

Tilting her head slightly like a cat, she whispered, "Fifteen each, two for twenty."

I was about to walk away but remembered the photograph. I handed her a fifty and asked if she knew the girl. Wadding up the money, she put it in her cleavage and examined the photograph.

"She used to come here. Hung out upstairs, liked to take guys home—girls too, for that matter. Not so pretty but adventuresome from what I was told. Also, a bit of a bitch, but some guys like that."

"Thanks," I said, starting to walk past her.

"Wait, you forgot your Scooby Snacks," she said.

Bob walked up between us, holding out his hand. "I will take those. My friend is on a diet."

The woman placed five of the smiley-faced pills in Bob's hand. He pocketed the pills and we fought our way through the crowd to where I assumed the stairs would be. The music was too noisy to hear one's thoughts as we passed through the strange crowd. After a bit, we made it to the back of the room, where there was an old staircase blocked off with a velvet rope. An enormous bald, tattooed man who could have been a professional wrestler stood guard.

"What the fuck do you want?" the man asked.

I jutted my chin upward. "To go upstairs."

"Do you have an invitation?"

"Yeah," I said, pulling out a hundred-dollar bill. "Mr. Franklin asked me to meet him upstairs."

The man took the money and looked over at Bob. "Ben might have given *you* an invite, but what about your friend?"

I handed him a second hundred-dollar bill. He unhooked the velvet rope and Bob and I walked past. I turned around briefly to show him the photograph of Heather.

"I was wondering if you have ever seen this girl?"

"You think they hired me for my good looks?"

"Sure, why not."

"I know better. Do you want to know why I got this job?"

"Do tell," I said.

"I don't see shit … ever. I am so blind, a pocketful of Benjamins can't cure me." He covered his eyes with his hands. "I already forgot what you look like."

This guy was worse than the guard on *Hogan's Heroes*. It was clearly pointless to seek further information from him. Bob and I started to walk up the stairs. At the landing, he tried to hand me a yellow pill, but I refused. He popped the pill in his own mouth and swallowed.

"Are you crazy? You don't even know what that is," I said.

"We will find out," Bob said. "I sure the hell hope it ain't the type my mother gave me."

"You realize that it is a felony to possess any amount of Ecstasy, assuming that's what you just took."

"I need to take something," he protested. "I sure as hell don't want to deal with whatever is upstairs sober. My Spidey senses are tingling. Besides, Nancy Reagan is dead."

I was worried about Bob and shocked that he just took a pill from a stranger at the strangest bar I had ever been to. Yet, this was not the time and certainly not the place for an intervention. I continued up the stairs.

Like Bob, I was a little concerned about what we would find.

Chapter 16

∼∼

AT THE TOP of the stairs was a large, wooden-arched door with cast-iron hardware. I could see a pair of eyes looking through a small door within the door and then the larger door opened. A woman dressed in a nun's habit and nothing else let us in. When the door closed behind us, the pounding music from the bar disappeared, replaced by quiet elevator music.

The room itself looked like a doctor's waiting room—sterile and generic. The naked nun pointed to a glass coffee table with magazines surrounded by ten burnt-orange chairs. The only person in the room other than the nun and Bob and me was a skinny, balding man wearing dress pants and a corduroy jacket with leather patches. He reminded me of the newscaster on *WKRP in Cincinnati*. He was reading a magazine with a busty, naked woman on the cover and a single word: "Damn!" The magazine mostly covered his lap but it was still clear his hand was inside his pants. Bob and I had a seat at the other end of the room.

"Helga will be seeing you soon. Unless you want to wait for Ebony?" the nun said.

"Helga will be fine," I replied.

I picked up a copy of the *Sports Illustrated* swimsuit issue and sat down. The selection of magazines was eclectic, with a copy of *Martha Stewart's Living* on top of the latest issue of *Giant Jugs*. *O* magazine rested next to *The Big O* magazine. I found a seat next to Bob, who was already seated. As I looked at my magazine, Bob gazed uncomfortably around the room.

Ten minutes later, a woman with long red hair in braids and a Viking helmet came out. She wore brown leather pants with a matching leather halter and gladiator sandals. A hammer or battle ax would have gone better with her outfit, but instead she held a leather riding crop. It would have been a tough look to pull off for most women. Helga's large muscles and severe expression were more than enough to ensure no one would laugh at her attire.

"You two gentlemen are with me then," Helga demanded.

Bob pointed at the skinny, balding man. "That dude was here first," he said.

She narrowed her eyes at Bob. "He likes to stay in the waiting room. You two, on the other hand, look like you are in need of correction."

"Actually, we just need to speak with you for a moment," I said. "I feel very correct already."

"If you want to speak, come with me. We can talk about pain," Helga said, leading the way.

We entered a door against the far back wall and found ourselves in a medieval dungeon reeking of sweat. I saw no windows or doors other than the one we'd walked in. The floor was completely covered with what appeared to be a wrestling mat stained here and there with blood or hopefully fake blood for effect. Shackles were mounted in the gray-stone walls at various heights. One of the walls was lined with thick quilted padding like the type used in freight elevators. In the middle of the room was a medieval-looking wooden structure with holes for the head and wrists—the stocks, they called them. Against one wall was a wooden rifle cabinet with a glass door containing an array of whips and paddles hanging from hooks.

"Pain is candy. Welcome to my sweet shop, bitches. Now take off your clothes," Helga demanded.

"We really just want to talk," I insisted. "It will only take a moment."

In response, Helga grabbed me by the shoulders and pushed me to the far end of the room. After I was cornered, she bent over. I held up my hands to prevent having my ear bitten off.

"This is the only area of the room where a camera can't see us," Helga whispered. "What is so important that you are interfering with my job, Sam?"

"How do you know my name?"

"It's Beth," she said. "You represented me for a heroin case in Vermilion County a few years back and in Champaign County last year for prostitution."

"Wow, Beth, I would never have recognized you. You look fantastic."

"Thanks," she said. "I stopped using heroin and started working out. Put on twenty pounds of muscle. You know the old saying: users trade in the spoon for a fork. Well, the only weight I put on is muscle."

"You found a job here?" I scanned the room with wide eyes.

"This is a great gig," she insisted. "I'm not a whore anymore. Don't have to be. Most of the guys prefer the riding crop to my touch anyway."

"I am glad to see you have turned your life around," I said.

"Cut the bullshit small talk, Sam. You're not here for the whip, are you?" She held up her riding crop.

"No." I pulled out the picture of Heather. "Do you know this woman?"

"Yeah, a real bitch. Name is Lilith, although that is probably not her real name. She worked here maybe three weeks but got fired for taking home the customers. A major no-no. She was ugly, had a bad disposition, and acted like she owned the place. I was thrilled to see her go."

"Can you remember anything else about her?" I put the photo away.

"Nothing other than I wouldn't spit on her if she was on fire."

"Thanks, Beth. If you think of anything else, will you call me?" The cowering position was giving me a sore back, so I stood up.

"I've been meaning to call you anyway. I got a speeding ticket last week."

"We will deal with it," I said.

"I was thinking …. I am going to charge you anyway. Why not have some fun?" Beth gave me a coquettish grin and slapped the whip against her hand.

"Call me old-fashioned," I said, "but when it comes to romance, I prefer the inevitable emotional pain to the physical pain."

"Your loss," she said with a wink. "Once you go Viking, you never go back." Helga raised both arms and flexed her enormous biceps.

"How much is this conversation going to cost me?"

"What did you pay to get up the stairs?"

"Two hundred."

"What do you have left?"

I checked my wallet. "Looks like one hundred and fifty bucks."

"That will be one hundred and fifty bucks." Helga held out the hand not carrying the riding crop.

I handed her the money, thinking I should charge extra when she came in with her speeding ticket. She laughed and showed Bob and me to a door hidden behind the padding of the wall. It led to another staircase. We followed it down the stairs to the outside area behind the bar.

It took a while to find my car, since the bar had filled up noticeably since we'd arrived. Bob and I got in. The car was comfortable and familiar.

"That was definitely strange," I said.

"No shit, I thought that Ecstasy was no good but it's finally kicking in," Bob said.

"You're going to die if you get in the habit of taking unknown drugs from strangers in bars."

"Well, mom, if you haven't figured it out, our life spans are not going to be that long anyway." Bob's tone was even snarkier than usual.

"That's a bit harsh. I am just concerned."

"Sorry, dude. You know I didn't mean it. I just have a bad feeling about all this."

"Me too. I also have a feeling the alleged victim in this case was not exactly innocent. Why was she so hell-bent on bringing people home with her?"

"Maybe Heather just liked to snuggle with strangers."

"Maybe she was up to no good."

"Like?"

"Human sacrifice."

"Not too discreet, if that's what she was doing."

"I am probably just jumping to conclusions," I said with a shrug. "Given what we have been through over the years, I can be rash."

"Does it help your case," Bob said, "if you can prove the victim was up to no good?"

"No." I paused. "Well, *probably* no. There are affirmative defenses like self-defense. You can also act to protect someone else. If a terrorist held a gun to someone's head, you could shoot them to protect the hostage—that could be a defense to murder. Those defenses don't work if the threat is not immediate. I couldn't legally kill someone just because I knew they were picking up guys at Snuggle and Meat and taking them home or to a mirror to sacrifice them."

Bob's face fell. "So tonight didn't get us anywhere."

"For the case, probably not," I agreed. "For the battle against good and evil, it tells us that Heather may have been playing for the wrong side."

"I think Helga likes you." Bob waggled his brows.

"She was paid to like me."

Bob started to tap his fingers on the dashboard, moving his head up and down to the beat of an invisible drummer. "How about we head to another bar. I feel good. Maybe we could hang out downtown."

"How about heading to Elly May's and grabbing some grub instead?" I suggested.

"No, I'm not hungry. I am half tempted to return to Snuggle and Meat and see if the Ecstasy girl has a boyfriend."

I have known Bob for most of my adult life and have never known him not to be hungry. Not to mention that the bar at Snuggle and Meat was about as far from Bob's scene as I could imagine. I looked down at my phone. It was past midnight.

"I have got to get some sleep. Mind if I call it a night?"

"No problem, dude, but the night is young."

Bob seemed surprisingly talkative and cheerful when I drove him home. Was it the Ecstasy or something else? Whatever the cause, Bob was not himself. It worried me that he was taking strange drugs. At the same time, was it my place to tell him what to do?

I have handled a lot of drug cases in my life. If Bob didn't have a real problem, it was none of my business what he did. If he did have a real problem, he wouldn't listen to me anyway. Our state is broke, yet we spend more money housing a person for a drug conviction than it would cost to send them to college. When they get out of prison, they tend to go right back to drugs. Given the draconian sentences for drug convictions and the fact that illegal drugs continue to be consumed, it is clear people with drug problems need more than my nagging.

Hell, Bob's drug problem—if you could call it that—was probably my fault to begin with. If I didn't get him involved in all this crazy shit, he wouldn't need to get high.

Chapter 17

~~~

I DECIDED TO put aside the May case until after the preliminary hearing. It was silly to waste effort to prepare a case without having the police reports and other discovery, and I wouldn't get that information until after the preliminary hearing. In any case, the public defender had informed me he thought there would be an indictment anyway and thus no need for a preliminary hearing.

It was not as though I didn't have other cases to work on. Although my clients have never truly understood this, I actually have more than one client at a time. Thinking about that house did make it hard to concentrate on my other work.

IT WAS FINALLY September 12th, the day of the preliminary hearing. I had spoken to my client yesterday and explained that there might not be a preliminary hearing, and if there was, it would be short. I didn't intend to call any witnesses. I informed him that a police officer would be called as a witness for the state and that hearsay was admissible. If the court failed to find probable cause to believe a felony took place, the case would be dismissed. Yet, in a high-profile murder case, you had a better chance of sticking an entire jar of olives up one nostril, including the jar, than having the case dismissed so early in the process.

I appeared early and asked the bailiff if my client was at the courthouse already. I was informed that he was on his way up. There were two cameramen in the courtroom and the reporter from the local paper. A few minutes later, Amanda Babs showed up.

"Do you have a moment?" I asked Amanda, a tall, slender woman wearing a drab skirt suit. In her forties, she had pleasant features that were distorted by a perpetually sour expression.

"Sure, what's up?"

"Just wanted to know how long you think we will be here."

"The grand jury issued an indictment last week, so it won't last long."

"Why didn't you tell me?"

"Sorry, I just didn't get around to it," she said casually as she entered the courtroom.

I wasn't exactly thrilled with the lack of civility, but there was nothing I could do about it. When I entered the courtroom, the judge was already on the bench. I had a seat in the back. I had to wait as an eighteen-year-old with no prior record was admonished for, of all things, possession of half an Ecstasy pill crumbled at the bottom of a plastic baggie. She was informed that the penalties ranged from one to three years in the penitentiary for a class-four felony.

My case was called, and the bailiff brought in my client. He was wearing an orange jumpsuit and handcuffs. He looked extremely high. My guess was that the court and the mental health facility didn't want him causing trouble. It was ironic that he had probably been given a fistful of Schedule-I narcotics that would make Ecstasy seem like Skittles by comparison.

The judge called up our case, and I had a seat with my client at the counsel table. The judge read the indictment and I was provided a copy in open court. The court normally would ask if I wanted to waive the formal reading of the indictment, but in this case he wanted to be thorough and read it out loud. There was a single count of First Degree Murder. The state was not pulling its swing; it was aiming for the back fences. If I wanted a lesser offense to be presented to the jury, I would have to ask for that when the jury was given instructions during the trial. The judge turned to Mr. May, and even though he had already read the indictment, he proceeded to paraphrase it.

"Mr. May, the indictment alleges you have committed the offense of First Degree Murder in that between August fourteenth and August seventeenth, you killed Heather Kline without lawful justification when you knowingly performed acts that caused her death and you either intended to kill or do great bodily harm to her. Do you understand the charges?" the judge asked.

Mr. May nodded. I was not at all sure he understood.

"Mr. May, you must answer out loud, yes or no. No nodding, no 'yeah' or 'nah,' just yes or no."

"Yes," Mr. May said.

"Yes, what?" the judge said.

"Yes, I understand," Mr. May replied.

The judge looked over at the state. "Ms. Babs, is the state seeking a sentence beyond twenty to sixty? Is it your intent to seek natural life? Should the defendant be admonished as to any aggravating factors?"

"No," Ms. Babs said.

"Mr. May, if convicted, you will face a minimum term of twenty years in the penitentiary to a maximum term of sixty years. The offense, if you are convicted, is not probationable. In addition you also may have to serve a hundred percent of any sentence without credit for good behavior. Do you understand?"

"Yes," Mr. May said.

"Ms. Babs and Mr. Roberts, is there anything further we need to discuss today?"

"Yes, your honor," I said. "I have filed a motion to modify

bond. It appears that Mr. May is being held without bond pending the results of a psychiatric evaluation. I have not received the evaluation yet, but I would like to address the issue of bond."

The judge fixed me with a stern stare. "I have no intention of addressing that issue at this time," he said. "This is a murder case, Mr. Roberts, and until I have that evaluation, I have no intention of setting a cash bond amount. I will not unleash an alleged murderer into this community until I am fully informed of his mental state and any risk he might pose to the citizens of this area. Is there anything else, Mr. Roberts?" The judge kept looking toward a television camera as he spoke, reminding me of why I was not in favor of cameras in the courtroom.

"No."

"Ms. Babs?"

"No," she said.

The judge gave us a pretrial date and noted the due date when the discovery needed to be completed as well as the time limit for pre-trial motions. The judge left the courtroom, followed by the reporters and other observers. When it was empty, Ms. Babs handed me three Manila envelopes that together formed a pile over a foot tall. I assumed this was the discovery. Before I could discuss anything with her, she walked away.

I asked the bailiff if I could speak with Mr. May for a few minutes. He agreed and Mr. May, myself, and the bailiff remained in the courtroom after everyone left. It was pointless to ask the bailiff to allow us to talk alone after the judge made his comments about how dangerous Mr. May was. That was fine, because I had nothing confidential to discuss.

"I will go through this discovery and get back with you. Is there anything you don't understand?" I said.

Mr. May's dilated eyes reflected his desperation. "Can I go home? I don't like it at the institution."

"No, I'm sorry," I said. "I will ask to modify the bond when the psychiatric report is complete."

The bailiff led my client out the side door. He looked much worse than when I'd last seen him. I had a feeling he would completely crack if I couldn't get him out of the nut house soon.

As I walked out the door, I was approached by a short, blonde-haired woman in a tight blue skirt suit with a shiny purple blouse. There was a camera man behind her.

"Mr. Roberts, my name is Maria Charles from Channel Three News. May I ask you a few questions?"

I shook my head but knew better than to reveal my annoyance. "I really am in no position to answer questions at this time."

"How do you feel knowing your client was indicted for murder?" She had a high, chipper voice that would have been more appropriate for the fashion news.

I contemplated answering honestly. To tell her that indeed, I was not clam-like in my happiness. That it sucked that the grand jury indicted my client. I could have said that it was not surprising, since the state could get a grand jury to indict an orange if they wanted. I guess it could be worse; at least Illinois had gotten rid of the death penalty. Instead I responded, "I look forward to the trial."

"What evidence do you intend to present?"

"I do not feel it is appropriate for me to discuss an ongoing case," I said as I walked away.

Chapter 18

~~

I DECIDED TO return home rather than go back to my office. I needed time away from the telephone to read the mountain of discovery I'd just been handed.

At home I began opening envelopes and skimming through the paperwork. There was a lot of it, along with three computer discs. I inserted the first disc in my laptop, an audio file from METCAD 911. I assumed Laura James made the call, although her tone seemed a bit odd.

"METCAD 911, what is the nature of your emergency?"

"I can't get into a room of the house and the dog is sniffing by the door."

"I don't understand the nature of your emergency."

"I am afraid someone may be hurt or dead in the room."

"Is there anything else that would cause you to come to that conclusion other than the dog?"

"I started pounding at the door and no one answered." Almost as an afterthought the woman added, "It also smells like something may have died in there."

"How long has the person been in the room with the door locked?"

"I don't know."

"What is your location?"

The call went on for a few more minutes with little additional information provided. The caller was oddly calm. If it was Laura James, I didn't remember her saying that it smelled like someone had died in the room when I spoke with her originally. The 911 operator seemed calm but annoyed, as if she was contemplating if this call even warranted alerting the police. Yet she concluded by saying the authorities would be there in a few minutes.

The next disc was a series of photographs. Most of the pictures depicted the body. Although the top portion of a human skull was identifiable, the teeth and jaw bone were not. There were also no long bones. The body was not butchered or cut apart but pulverized.

The government removed separate bone fragments for the pictures. No individual fragment was more than four or five inches long. I wondered what the police would claim was the murder weapon—a sausage grinder? The bones were not cut but broken. In some of the pictures there were shards. It appeared as though the meat and bones had been chewed up and spit out by a large animal. There was shockingly little symmetry between the bone fragments. Some were longer and some were shorter. Some had a fairly clean break, while others were chewed apart.

It was clear that this was not a complete body. I could probably pour the remains into a large lobster pot. It was also odd that there was surprisingly little in the way of blood. The texture of the remains seemed chunky and thick. The color varied from almost black to deep crimson. No organs were readily identifiable. I have sadly seen dead bodies and human remains before—though not regularly, as luck would have it. Muscle tends to be fibrous, veins and arteries are stringy, and bones are hard. Human flesh tends to look more like pork than beef.

There was nothing normal about this crime scene. I found it hard to believe that any one person could do this kind of damage, not emotionally but physically. It would take far more than a few days for a single person to pulverize a human being so completely. Maybe if they had proper tools …. Yet a food processor, blender, or meat grinder would not produce a result like this. Unless the meat grinder was six feet tall. I also noted the lack of hair, skin, and clothing in the pile of remains. If I had to guess, I would say the person was killed somewhere else and brought in.

For dinner, I decided not to consider pasta sauce, soup, sausage, aspic, and most flavors of Jell-O. I was seriously considering becoming a vegetarian. Actually, I thought I might skip dinner entirely.

I figured I could find a doctor who would testify what it would take to decimate a body like that. If my guess was correct, it would take a long time. It might make sense to file a bill of particulars and try to force the state to narrow the scope of the date of the murder to a specific day rather than from August 14 through 17. I have had cases, particularly cases involving sex crimes, where the charging instrument would list a six-month period or more as to when the crime allegedly took place. Judges tend to give the state a lot of leeway in this regard.

The final disc was an interview with my client. In a room with no windows, Mr. May was seated at a steel table with a police officer sitting across from him. The officer read my client his Miranda rights and asked him to sign a form.

Mr. May was wearing black pants and a pressed white dress shirt. The shirt was impeccably clean with no blood or viscera on it. In response to each paragraph the officer read, he shook his head. When asked to sign the Miranda form, Mr. May crumpled it up and stuffed the entire page in his mouth. He began to choke as if he were attempting to swallow it whole. The officer, whom I didn't recognize, tried to pull the form out of his mouth but was bitten for his efforts. Three more officers entered the room—two men and one woman. The men forced his mouth open while the woman, who was wearing rubber gloves, removed the form.

"Why are you doing this to me?" Mr. May yelled.

"You murdered that woman!" the officer who had been bitten yelled in return.

"You will pay for what you are doing to me. Take me home now!" Mr. May yelled.

He stood up, looked toward the camera, and then back at the officers. He sat down, perfectly calm.

" 'If you continue in my word, then you are truly disciples of mine, and you will know the truth, and the truth will make you free,' " he said.

"I am already free, you dumb ass. You're the one locked up," the officer with the bitten hand said, unable to hide his disgust.

"It's a quote from the Bible, from Jesus," the female officer said. "Did Jesus tell you to kill that woman?"

"Who is dead?" he asked as if genuinely surprised.

"It's your girlfriend, Mr. May, isn't it? Heather …. You spent time with her after she was dead. You killed her and spent time cutting up the body."

"Heather is dead?" Mr. May said, again with complete sincerity.

"You killed her, you sick bastard," the officer with the bitten hand said.

"Heather is dead," Mr. May repeated. He was crying now, his hands covering his face.

The disc ended. It was brilliant. The police came across as overly aggressive, and Mr. May appeared genuinely shocked and horrified by the death of his girlfriend. Maybe his comments about Jesus would offend the conservative potential jurors registered to vote in this county, but maybe not. Maybe it made him seem religious.

He didn't strike me as the religious type, given there were no religious artifacts in his room. Also, since he never left his room, he certainly did not attend church. But if he was not religious, then why quote from the Bible?"

So far the discovery wasn't too bad. After looking at the photographs, I had a hard time believing Mr. May or any single individual with limited tools could do that to a body over the course of a weekend. I could actually see the beginning of reasonable doubt.

Chapter 19

~~~

I WAS GETTING through the discovery relatively quickly. Most of it was police reports. All the laboratory reports were missing. Their absence was not surprising. If they'd been sent to Springfield the day they found the body, we wouldn't have the results back yet. It looked like parts of the body had been sent away for DNA analysis. Other items were being tested to see if Mr. May's fingerprints were on them as well as his DNA.

If Mr. May's prints were on his cutlery, it wouldn't mean much, since he lived there. Perhaps if a knife had his fingerprints and his girlfriend's blood on it, it might be significant, but it wouldn't exactly be a smoking gun. He could have handled the "weapon" earlier. I noted that no clothing had been sent in for DNA testing. I assumed that meant they had not found any of Heather's clothing or that if they had, that clothing was clean. I should note the same as to Mr. May's clothes. For what should have been the world's messiest homicide, the crime scene was spotless. I have made brownies and created a bigger mess. My thoughts were interrupted by a telephone call.

"Dude, you're on the news," Bob said.

"No, kidding. How do I look?" I asked.

"Like a doofus."

"Why?"

"They interview a woman from the state's attorney's office who spends ten minutes talking about how guilty your client is. Then, when it's your turn, you don't say anything."

"It's not right to talk about a pending case."

"Your tie was kind of messed up too."

"When did you join the fashion police?"

"Why don't you come by tonight and we can watch a flick?"

"What time?"

"How about seven?"

"See you then."

After I ended the call, I continued to read the police reports. Two officers arrived at the home, and Laura James let them in and showed them to the second floor. When no one answered their knock, they broke the door down. They discovered the body or what was left of it in front of the bed, maybe ten feet into the room.

They did not have a warrant but claimed to have permission by Ms. James to enter the home and search the room. The officers also pointed out that exigent circumstances warranted breaking down the door. They claimed to be concerned that someone was injured. I used a highlighter and made a note to take a look at Fourth Amendment cases involving search and seizure.

After breaking in, the police immediately noticed the remains and found Mr. May naked and asleep on his bed. When confronted with the evidence, Mr. May seemed disoriented and denied any involvement in the murder. One of the officers noted he was sweating and acting suspiciously, which police always seem to note. Mr. May was allowed to get dressed but was then removed from the room. The minute he stepped over the threshold of his quarters, he became hysterical. The officers were unable to control him and it was not until other officers arrived that they were able to secure him in the police vehicle. I made a note to see if there was any recording of him while he was in the car. None was provided in the discovery.

There were four reports from different crime scene investigators. It appeared that the room was examined and all the windows were painted shut. Other than the door, there appeared to be no way in or out of the room. No blood spatter at all. In fact, one investigator said, "It was as though she were killed in a bucket and poured out." No female clothing was found in the room or clothing of any type with blood on it. No weapons were found in the main area near the body except for some knives, a cleaver, and a meat-tenderizing hammer taken from the kitchen. There was the Klingon weapon I'd seen in the attached room, as well as phasors, light sabers, and ray guns, but the reports didn't mention that room at all. The items taken were photographed and sent for analysis at the laboratory in Springfield. There was no visible blood on any of the kitchen cutlery. Photographs were also missing from the discovery. The bedsheets and other linens had been removed for DNA analysis, but again, that analysis did not appear in the discovery.

I made a note to look into the DNA of the alleged victim. So far there was no clothing, purse, or other evidence to support the claim that the alleged victim was Heather Kline. When I spoke to the library, they said she was not in the military, for they had done a criminal background check. If she was not a felon and had never been in the military, how did they have her DNA for comparison?

I did not see any indication in the reports that the officers had gone to Heather's house to search her hairbrush or toothbrush for a DNA sample. Even if the state were to get DNA from a toothbrush or hairbrush, it might not be useful. If you take a buccal swab of someone's mouth, you know it is their DNA alone. A toothbrush or hairbrush could contain DNA from others as well. One generally does not share a toothbrush, but given Heather's reputation for bringing people home, she might well have shared her oral-hygiene utensils. At this point I was unsure how the state could prove the identity of the alleged victim.

The police had been extremely thorough in their crime scene investigation. The investigators had used luminol, which is usually only reserved for CSI on television. Luminol is a powdery solid that can be dissolved it into a liquid that contains hydrogen peroxide and other chemicals. Placed in a spray bottle, it can be used to locate bloodstains invisible to the naked eye. The liquid causes a blue glow when sprayed onto bloodstains. This type of testing works even if the blood has been cleaned up or after a substantial period of time. The testing with luminal had revealed a glowing blue river all the way from the remains to the mirror. The officer made a point of saying that the frame of the mirror appeared to be painted in blue.

For fans of CSI, the scope of this investigation wouldn't be surprising. I personally have never seen the show. For Champaign, Illinois, the scope of this investigation far exceeded the norm.

Although the laboratory analysis was yet incomplete, one of the crime scene investigators put in his report that the condition of the body was strange and that he couldn't guess at the murder weapon. He stated, "The color and uniformity of the remains suggest that the body had somehow been mashed together." Other than the upper part of the skull, he couldn't identify a single complete body part.

He concluded that the organs must have been pulverized and the skin was likely gone. He made a point of mentioning that the laboratory would weigh the remains, but he was sure that the body would weigh less than a full-size human being and thus part of the remains were missing.

The general consensus was that there was no way in or out of the room other than through the entrance door. The police made a point of checking the garbage disposal and any garbage and laundry chutes to see if part or all of the body had been disposed of in that way.

There was additional speculation that Mr. May had consumed part of the body, and they toyed with the idea of forcing him to vomit. That idea was rejected by the head of the investigation. Although aware of drug cases where an individual, after a warrant was issued, was given medication to force vomiting to retrieve balloons of heroin, the crime scene investigator felt it was not worth the effort to get a warrant in this case. Instead, he had an officer search Mr. May's mouth and throat with a flashlight. This revealed no evidence.

He also suggested that once Mr. May went to the restroom, they should save his feces to search for Heather's blood in his stool. That had apparently not been done. He made it a point to inform everyone involved in the investigation that should Mr. May vomit on his own, said vomit should be collected and saved.

My job may not be dignified, but at least it does not involve searching feces and vomit for blood.

A few of the officers remarked that the room smelled a bit like incense. One said that it was kind of a ginger scent while another described it as cedar. The officers agreed that it did not resemble the overpowering odor of patchouli commonly used in dorms to hide the scent of marijuana. I made it a point to highlight this section, but I was not sure why. It seemed important.

The investigators used UV light and blue light to further search for invisible organic materials such as semen, urine, and bone fragments. This turned out to be of little value to their investigation. Given that the alleged victim and Mr. May spent substantial time in the room, nothing they found could be relevant. Perhaps it would give the government more credibility with the jury to go over all the steps they went through to gather evidence.

At this point, I concluded, the state could not prove their

case. They could not identify the alleged victim. They could not identify the time of the offense. They didn't have a murder weapon. They didn't have a confession. They had no witnesses.

They had interviewed all the people in the house at the time. Edna May had told the police that her son was acting strangely around the time of the offense. She did not give more details. Her son never left his room and she respected his privacy. She did say that she thought she'd heard Heather's voice. Since she was blind and never entered her son's room, I was unsure how she would know he was acting strangely. Apparently the police had not questioned her about this seeming inconsistency.

Her assistant Malcolm Conrad, being mute, had been asked to respond to police questions in writing. He did not know if Heather Kline had been at the home at the time of the alleged murder. He did assert that she spent a great deal of time there. He would often hear odd sounds coming from the room, especially during the time when the police alleged the murder took place. He described the sounds as banging and whispering. When asked if he could distinguish the voice of Heather, Blake, or some third party, he shook his head.

Mr. Conrad did have two prior felony convictions, one for aggravated battery and the other for stealing a car, but neither was within the last ten years. Laura James was also interviewed. She claimed that during that weekend, she'd seen Heather Kline enter the home and never leave. She further said that she heard screams at one point and pounding. The officer who interviewed her reported that her room was next to the room where the murder took place, so she might have been able to hear what happened. She informed the officer that Mr. May had a temper and was easily upset. She had seen and heard him lose his temper on numerous occasions.

The oddest part of the discovery, and the most lengthy, was over a hundred pages of notes and documents allegedly written and gathered by Mr. May. I made a note next to these that the state had not yet requested a sample of my client's handwriting or consulted an expert on handwriting. I did not know if this was because they felt the identity of the author was irrelevant or if they simply had not gotten that far in their investigation.

Included in these articles was one by Albert Einstein concerning his general theory of relativity, as well as various articles on relativity and time travel. Also Stephen Hawking's discussion of the Fermi Paradox and Enrico Fermi's explanation of why Earth has not been visited by aliens given how many planets in the universe could support intelligent life. A few articles by other lesser-known scientists published in the 1970s and 1980s addressed similar issues.

There are also notes related to Hindu mythology and the *Mahabharata* as well as ancient Buddhist texts translated to English. The mythology was centered on the idea of time travel or at least the concept that time could move forward at an accelerated rate on earth when one is visiting deities.

Mr. May seemed obsessed with the idea of aliens and time travel. He concluded that if traveling away from earth at a fast enough rate, a person would not age as quickly as those on earth and might in essence move forward in time. He was also obsessed with the idea that aliens had visited the earth before the written word. He had downloaded or clipped various articles concerning ancient Egypt and how aliens helped build the pyramids.

The juxtaposition of ancient texts and recent articles related to relativity and quantum physics seemed bizarre. Yet, given the books in Blake's other room, this was not shocking. I also noted transliterations of what I assumed to be ancient spells. There were other documents in a language I couldn't identify. It looked a bit like they were in the Tai-Kadai or Hindustani.

I was clearly out of my depth. I hoped Bob could sort out all this craziness. I should note that the pages said nothing about killing anyone. That was certainly a plus. They also never mentioned Heather or anyone else. The sole focus of the writing was science and magic. No wonder the state didn't care about a writing sample. This was of no use to their case and might help mine. It did support the theory that he was crazy.

I copied the relevant pages of the journal to bounce ideas off Bob this evening.

Chapter 20

~~

I LOOKED AT the clock and was shocked to see it was after six. I called the Bubble and Cluck and ordered the Bucket o' Wings and the sushi special with a side of coleslaw and baked beans to go. On the way, I stopped at the liquor store to pick up a six pack of beer. I decided on a beer I had never tried before called Blood of the Unicorn, mostly based on the image of a unicorn covered in blood going into battle. I have nothing against our unicorn brothers and sisters. It just made my life seem less disturbing by contrast.

On the way from the liquor store to Bob's, I was confronted by the corpse of an opossum in the middle of the road. The dead beast was bloated with a foot raised firmly in the air like a twisted salute. Perhaps more disturbing was the large black grackle picking at the body. For me, black birds had never been omens of good things to come.

I arrived at Bob's ten minutes before seven. It took a few minutes for him to answer the door. His hair looked unkempt and his goatee was a bit scragglier than normal. He was wearing black sweatpants and a pink tie-dyed T-shirt that had "Fuck the Man" written in black across the front. The coffee table had a bong on it, which was not unusual, but it also had far more empty beer cans and fast food wrappers than was the norm.

"Cool! The Bubble and Cluck," Bob said as he took the bag of food and the beer from my hand.

"You look tired," I said.

"Hell of a night, dude."

"Do you want to talk about it? Maybe I could live vicariously through your actual social life."

"It would be too much for you."

I took the rolled-up pages of Mr. May's journal from the back pocket of my jeans and handed them over to Bob. He unrolled them like a sacred scroll, sat down on the sofa, and began to read.

"Where did you get this?"

"From Mr. May's journal. It came in the discovery. All about time travel, I think. Do you have any theories about whether or not time travel is possible?"

"It is on the silver screen. It is a big part of *Star Trek* movies and the television show. There is the book *The Time Machine* by H.G. Wells as well as two movies with the same name. One of the *Superman* movies had Superman go back in time to save Lois Lane."

"What about in reality?"

"Einstein hypothesized that if a person going close to the speed of light traveled away from Earth, the traveler would age slower than the people left on earth."

"So, the traveler would be able to go back to Earth and predict the future."

Bob wrinkled his nose at me. "No, because he wouldn't have seen the future. If he returned, he would just see a bunch of old people. A number of scientists believe that since we essentially move forward in time just living our lives, it may be possible to *travel* forward in time."

"What about going back in time?"

"Some scientists think it's possible. Most don't. Stephen Hawking believed if people could go back in time, it would create a paradox that made it unlikely. By way of example, if you could kill your grandfather, you could cease to exist. Others believe there might be a wormhole that would allow people to go back and forth as a shortcut through space-time. I got to tell you, dude, I don't think time travel makes sense. At the same time, I am no Einstein."

"Closest person to Einstein I know."

He laughed. "I believe that; however, your friends aren't too smart. I just wonder why Mr. May was so interested in it."

"Me too." I paused. "So, what's on the schedule?"

"Double feature, *Phantasm* and *Oculus*."

I had seen *Phantasm* recently but never *Oculus*. Bob turned off the lights and divided the food. He handed me a beer and took one for himself and went to the kitchen to put the rest in his refrigerator.

After the credits of *Phantasm* rolled, we sat in silence for a while before he loaded the second movie, *Oculus*. When it ended, I was anxious to discuss the flicks but knew Bob well enough that I didn't want to rush things.

When Bob seemed ready to speak, I said, "You picked those movies because of Mr. May. Both had people coming through mirrors. *Phantasm* had a gateway to another world."

Bob was sitting on the edge of the couch, looking uncharacteristically solemn. "Yeah, the mirror in the Frost Home is like that; no one could get in or out."

"The journal might support that theory. That and the police reports that claim there was blood all around the mirror. Also, the body may have been incomplete and there was no obvious murder weapon."

Bob stroked his scraggly beard, deep in thought. "Where else could the rest of the body have gone? No way did it go out of the room."

"He could have flushed it or put it down the garbage disposal …."

"If so, that's a hell of a good plumbing system for a house that old."

We sat in silence until I heard a woman's voice call out Bob's name. I looked over at Bob, who was smiling sheepishly. A few minutes later, a woman in blonde pigtails wearing a black Twisted Sister T-shirt and nothing else walked into the room.

It took me a moment to recognize her: the woman handcuffed to the bar at Snuggle and Meat—the one selling Ecstasy. The lights were dimmed so I couldn't see clearly, but I suspected Bob was blushing.

"Sam, this is Candy," Bob said. "Candy, Sam. Actually you two already met at the S&M."

"How could I forget? I didn't recognize you without your handcuffs."

In response, Candy raised her right hand. A set of handcuffs dangled from her wrist. "Nice to see you again," she said in a girlish voice while dipping in a curtsy and holding out the hem of her long T-shirt. Even in the dim light, I could tell she was far older than she pretended to be.

"Now I understand the 'hell of a night' comment," I said.

"I don't think you have that good of an imagination," Bob said.

"Well …" I hemmed and hawed, "I'd better get going. I am really tired. Besides, three's a crowd." I was surprised she'd managed to stay so quiet during the movies. Maybe she'd been sleeping off the effects of last night.

"Not necessarily," Candy said. She walked up to Bob, kissed him gently on the cheek, and sat between us on the couch.

Candy smelled of alcohol and Jolly Rancher watermelon candy. Up close I could confirm that she was older than she'd appeared at the bar by about ten years. I had to admit she did have a certain charm. I hoped she made Bob happy. On the other hand, she was also a drug dealer. Not a great prospect for a long-term relationship. Maybe I was just jealous. Given my last girlfriend, I wasn't qualified to give relationship advice.

I got up and excused myself, explaining that I had a long day tomorrow. Candy looked up with a slight pout and Bob walked me out. When we got to the door, he whispered, "So, what do you think?"

"She seems nice."

"Trust me, she is anything but nice. One other thing ...."

"I am all ears."

"I think you need to have a serious talk with Mr. May."

I nodded my agreement and headed out the door. Although Bob's date was interesting, I was more interested in the idea of a mirror being used as a portal. Could the mirror in Mr. May's room take him to other worlds or different times?

I returned home and was about to go to sleep but decided to do a quick google search on the topic of mirrors. It turns out mirrors have been around for thousands of years. From polished obsidian around eight thousand years ago to the use of polished copper in Mesopotamia and ancient Egypt around 4,000 BCE.

The modern mirror with glass painted with a silver backing was invented in 1835 by German chemist Justus von Liebig. Thus, if the mirror at the Frost home was purchased soon after the house was built, it would be pre-Civil War. That would make it a very early mirror.

Folklore and superstitions about mirrors arose soon after the mirror was invented. There is a superstition that breaking a mirror results in seven years of bad luck. A mirror breaking on its own is said to foreshadow death.

Yet, that was not what interested me. I found various tales about mirrors used in magical rituals for viewing another person or place. These tales were not simply limited to viewing but communication as well. Mirrors could also be used for fortune telling, a tradition that went back to Ancient Greece.

I decided I needed sleep. In the morning I would return to the mental health facility and have a talk with Mr. May. I got undressed and slipped into bed. Not surprisingly, sleep eluded me. I thought about the game Bloody Mary and how teens would dare each other to recite the words "Bloody Mary" into a mirror three times until the ghost arrived. The "Candy Man" was also supposed to appear if his name was said three times. What had Helga said at Snuggle and Meat? "Pain is Candy."

While in high school, I attended wrestling camp at the University of Illinois. We had to do squats with another wrestler on our shoulders. One of the college wrestlers who was also an instructor yelled that my squats needed to be deeper. I told him that his mother had made a similar demand of me the night before. In response, I was assigned as his wrestling partner for the rest of the day. He punished and pummeled me nonstop. As he crushed my body and spirit, he would say, "Pain is candy and I am the Candy Man." I wondered if Helga had picked up the expression, "pain is candy" from that wrestler. I am not sure she couldn't have taken him in a fight to the death.

I learned from that man that a high school wrestler is no match for a college wrestler. I was completely out of my league. I had the same feeling about this case. I was not prepared for what was ahead. I lay in bed waiting for sleep.

Chapter 21

~~

ILOOKED UP to find myself at a table in Mr. May's room at the Frost Home. There were only two other people at the table this time.

Albert Einstein was sitting across from me. His long white hair was wild and uncombed, his mustache slightly darker than the hair on his head. He was wearing a tweed jacket and a white button-down shirt without a tie. In the other seat, with her back to the mirror, was Bridget, a witch I once dated. Her long black hair was combed straight behind her. She wore a silver pentagram around her neck that glowed against the ample cleavage exposed by her black dress.

"You are interested in time travel and my theory of general relativity," Einstein said in his slight German accent.

"I am interested, but I might not understand even if you explained it," I admitted.

"I once said that 'God does not play dice with the universe.' Do you know what I meant by that?"

"That the rules of physics don't change here, in space or in other worlds," Bridget interrupted him.

"That is how I predicted that gravity could bend light," he said. "I was able to predict that gravity from the sun could bend space and light. I improved upon Newton's law. I predicted that if you move through space at near the speed of light, time would go slower for the traveler than the people who remain on earth."

"So you could come back to Earth and know the future."

"No, you might come back and see that Earth has changed, but you would not see the world changing. You would be somewhere else at the time."

"I don't understand."

Einstein leaned toward me and gestured with his forefinger. "You can go forward in time but not backward."

"Magic can change the laws of physics," Bridget said. Her body language was relaxed, her elbows resting on the table.

"What are you talking about?" Einstein said, full of scorn.

She laughed. She seemed to be enjoying herself. "I can fly. I can defy gravity. I can create fire out of nothing. I can cross the line that separates the living from the dead," she bragged.

Einstein was still excoriating her with his eyes. "Can you travel back in time?"

"No, but I can use the tarot to see into the future," the witch insisted.

"That is impossible. God does not play dice," Einstein huffed.

She gave a magnificent shrug, which made the pentagram in her cleavage shift around. "God has nothing to do with it. Magic has its own rules that trump the laws of physics."

"What is the point of this?" I asked, forcing myself to look away from Bridget's assets.

She was speaking in that sensual, persuasive voice I'd found so difficult to resist. "The *point* is that magic is about demons, spirits, and forgotten deities. It is powered by spells, blood, ceremonies, and worship. A bit of eye of newt can't hurt either. It is about Earth, Wind, Fire, and Air. I honor the rules of nature but I can also bend them to my will."

"Why are you here?" I asked, directly my question at Bridget.

"It's your dream," she said, raising one eyebrow. "I assumed I was here as some sort of erotic fantasy. I haven't figured out the whole Einstein part. I can only assume you have some very twisted desires."

I was interrupted by a strange ringing. I stopped to search my pockets for my cell phone and awoke to the ringing of my alarm.

I got up, showered, and dressed. As I went through my morning ritual, I swore off watching scary movies, drinking beer, and eating wings right before bed. That had indeed been one twisted dream.

I got to my office by nine. After I watered the plant, I called the mental health facility and was transferred twice before getting Dr. Hyde directly. He informed me that if I hadn't called, he would have. He said that he would like to speak in person and could make himself available anytime. He also arranged for me to speak with my client alone that morning at ten thirty.

I placed Mr. May's file in a large briefcase. It was still early, so I decided to grab breakfast at Elly May's Diner. The diner bore no relation to Mr. May or his family other than having the word "May" in the name. It was also not named after Elly May Clampett of *Beverly Hillbillies* fame. Either it was named for the owner's daughter or simply chosen because it sounded homey. I've heard it both ways.

After all, Betty Crocker was a fictional character created by Marjorie Husted. For a woman to create such an iconic advertising character would have been quite an accomplishment at the time. That was in the 1920s, and the Nineteenth Amendment, allowing women the right to vote, had just been ratified.

The diner had a number of locations, and I chose the one in downtown Champaign. I found a seat at a booth and the waitress approached. I obviously eat here more often than I thought since the waitress knew me by name. She bore a vague resemblance to the TV Hillbilly Ellie May as you might imagine her in late middle age—pretty but soft around the edges, with platinum blonde hair tied back in a messy bun.

"Sam, you want hot tea, two eggs basted soft, and corned beef hash?" she asked.

"Yeah, dry rye toast as well, if you don't mind."

"Bob's not coming in today?"

"No, he's too busy."

"Shame," she said, "I do enjoy watching him eat. It is rare to see such enthusiasm for our cooking."

"I will do my best to clean my plate with more gusto."

"You do that," she said, her tone vaguely condescending.

I ate my breakfast without the promised gusto, my thoughts still on the dream. Only a fool would dismiss Einstein's words. Bridget also seemed to be conveying something important.

I only ate half my breakfast and left the money on the table. When I got up to leave, the waitress gave me a disapproving look. I wasn't particularly worried about her opinion of me, especially at this moment. I needed answers, and the place to get them was at the Marquee Mental Health Center.

Though I arrived early for my appointment, I was immediately ushered into Dr. Hyde's office. His outfit struck me as eccentric: not so much the olive-green suit and black shirt as the mustard-yellow tie. He motioned for me to take a seat. I kept the briefcase on my lap.

"I am willing to testify that Mr. May suffers from agoraphobia and schizophrenia," the doctor said. "He is in need of treatment, not jail. I will testify in court that he should be found guilty but mentally ill."

"All right," I said.

The doctor raised his eyebrows. "You don't seem as pleased as I thought you would be."

"I believe he may be mentally ill," I said. "I don't believe he is guilty."

"Well, I spoke with the state's attorney this morning. She seems to have a different opinion."

I drummed my fingers on the briefcase. "She would, wouldn't she? I assume the office wouldn't have charged him if they didn't think he was guilty. I think they are wrong."

"I see."

"Have you written a report? Do you believe he is fit to stand trial?"

"Yes, I have written a report." He pushed a sealed Manila envelope across his desk. "He should be fit to stand trial once I get him stabilized with medication. Maybe two weeks."

"Can I see him?"

"He is in his room, alone, waiting to speak with you."

"Can we go for a walk outside?" I said. "Do you have a courtyard?"

"He is not ready for that."

The doctor picked up the phone and asked a nurse to show me to Mr. May's room. It had a sliding glass door and contained two hospital beds. Mr. May was dressed in his usual uniform of black suit pants and a white button-down shirt. His silver hair was combed back neatly. I looked around and noticed a video camera in one corner of the room.

Pointing to the camera, I asked, "Is there somewhere more private we could talk?"

"The bathroom doesn't have a camera."

"All right, the bathroom it is."

Mr. May sat on the toilet and I sat on a white bath stool in the shower. My client seemed alert but he was also a little off. Perhaps it was the medication. I handed him the journal.

"Did you write this?"

"Yes," Mr. May replied.

"Why time travel?"

"Just curious."

"That is bullshit," I said. I didn't disguise my annoyance. "If you want me to help you, quit feeding me bullshit."

He slowly shook his head. "I can't."

"The mirror … it's a wormhole, a portal through space-time?"

"I don't know."

"Tell me what the mirror does."

"I don't know," he insisted. "Ask the man in the mirror."

"Who is the man in the mirror?" I pressed. "Is it you? Michael Jackson? Who is the man in the mirror?"

"I don't know," he said. "I was trying to find out. Maybe he comes from the future. Heather claimed he would tell her things. He never told me anything. I just heard whispers."

"What type of things did he tell Heather?"

"She claimed that if we gave him enough blood, he would tell us ways to make money. She said he knows the future."

"So he could give you winning lottery numbers or tell you whom to bet on in horse races."

"No, not like that."

"Does he come out of the mirror?"

"No. I give him blood, *my* blood. I wipe it on the mirror. I don't kill anyone. It is my blood."

"What about Heather?"

"Heather gave it blood too, but voluntarily. I didn't kill her. We didn't give it enough blood to kill anyone."

"The man in the mirror wanted more, didn't he?"

Another mournful shake of the head. "I don't know."

"What about Heather? She would be willing to give it more blood, wouldn't she?"

"Heather would have sacrificed anyone or anything to the mirror. She also understood it was my house and my room. She never provided more blood than we could safely give."

He became agitated then and grabbed a bar of soap, throwing it hard against the mirror above the sink. Made of polished steel, it didn't break. However, his sudden movement caused me to fall off the stool and land on the shower's hard, tiled floor. The residual water was soaked up by my pants.

I held off speaking for a long moment out of concern that my client was dangerous. Yet, his outburst seemed to calm him.

"Sorry," Mr. May said.

I perched once again on the stool, placing a towel on it first, and went over the discovery with Mr. May. At first he seemed oddly uninterested but became agitated and red-faced upon hearing the comments by his mother and Laura James. "Ungrateful bitches!" he muttered.

After I was done going through the discovery, I opened the envelope from Dr. Hyde. His report stated that Mr. May suffered from agoraphobia and schizophrenia, adding that these illnesses could never be cured but could be controlled. He further concluded that Mr. May must have had multiple psychotic episodes that were never reported because his agoraphobia kept him from seeking medical help. He felt that over time, with the help of medication, Mr. May would be able to function in society. That, however, would not be possible in the foreseeable future. Though mentally ill, the patient understood the nature of his criminal conduct and acted knowingly. At least that was Dr. Hyde's opinion to a reasonable degree of psychiatric certainty.

After a moment of silence, Mr. May asked, "What does that mean?"

"It means the doctor would not say you are not guilty but would go along with a finding of guilty but mentally ill."

"Where does that get me?"

"No prison, but perhaps, given your age, a lifetime of places like this."

He slashed the air with his hand. "Fuck that! I want a trial. I am not guilty." After that brief outburst, his anger again appeared to subside.

"It is up to you," I said. "I can't make that decision for you. I will keep working on your case with the assumption we are going to trial."

"Thanks," he said in a deflated voice. "Sorry about the soap."

"That's okay."

He looked around at the tiny but immaculately clean bathroom. "You know what I hate the most about this place?"

"No."

"The smell."

I sniffed the air. It smelled clean and certainly did not reek of anything unpleasant. "It smells like nothing."

"Life *should* smell," he said. "Perfume, flowers, shit and vomit. This is not life; it is purgatory. This is the waiting room of Hell."

Chapter 22

~~~

A s I LEFT the mental health facility, my mood was grim.
Sliding into the driver's seat of my Honda, I thought
about what my client had said: "Life should smell." These
words haunted me, kept running through my mind like a
jingle for Diet Coke. My cell phone went off and I picked up on
the second ring. It was Amanda Babs from the state's attorney's
office.

"Have you spoken to Dr. Hyde yet?" she asked.

"Yeah, just now."

"He told me your client, Mr. May, was mentally ill at the
time he committed the murder. I have a onetime offer. He can
plead guilty but mentally ill. He can spend his life in a plush
institution rather than prison. Let's get this done."

"I spoke to him about that. I can ask him again, but I am
pretty sure you are looking at a trial. I also went through the
discovery. Unless you have information I don't have, I find it
hard to believe you could prove this case."

There was a sneer in her voice as she said, "I guess we will
find out. I will tell you this: I would rather lose than dismiss
this case and let a murderer go free."

"Assuming a murder took place," I said, "and I would not

concede it did. If Mr. May does go away to prison, you may be guaranteeing that the real murderer goes free."

"What are you talking about? We have the body."

"No, you have a mess of blood. You have no DNA. At the moment we don't even know for sure if the blood is human. If it is, we don't know who it belonged to. It may be scraps from a hospital. Besides, I thought you were getting off this case. Letting someone else take the reins."

"Not so far. I am hoping they let me keep it."

"Yes, a finding of 'not guilty' might be good for your humility."

She was spitting mad now. "Fuck you, Sam! As far as I'm concerned, Dr. Hyde needs to evaluate you. You are crazier than your client."

"Sticks and stones," I said in a singsong voice. She hung up on me.

I knew it was a rude and juvenile thing to say. I was also aware it is not a good idea to taunt people with power. Yet, at the same time, she was not telling me the whole story. She was well aware that her case had problems.

It was odd with such a high-profile case that the state's attorney herself was not handling it personally. If not the state's attorney, then at least her first assistant. Amanda Babs is a good attorney but not their best. This was not a case I would expect the state to entrust to anyone but the best litigator in the office. It was going to result in a lot of press coverage and a lot of scrutiny. Maybe they'd bring in the big guns as it progressed.

I kept thinking about my client's comment, "Life should smell." As my mind struggled to give this sentence meaning, the telephone rang once again.

"Mr. Roberts?" The voice sounded as if it belonged to a young woman.

"This is he," I responded.

"I am the secretary for Mr. Avery. He was wondering if we could set up an appointment."

"What for?"

"He wanted to speak with you about Blake May."

"Sure, let me get to my office and check my calendar."

"He suggested six this evening at our office."

"I know I don't have anything after five. I will see him at six."

"Thank you, Mr. Roberts. I will let him know."

I wondered what that was about. I returned to my office and worked until five. There was a Thai place nearby called Thai One On where Susan and I used to eat quite often. I didn't feel like eating there alone so I ordered curried chicken to go.

I walked into the store-front restaurant, taking in its familiar yellowish-orange walls and temple rubbings on rice paper. Told my meal would take a few more minutes, I was offered water and a seat. I could smell sandalwood and absentmindedly wandered to the back of the restaurant, where there was a spirit house of carved teak with an arched gold top like a Thai temple. In front of the spirit house was a pile of brown rice with three sticks of incense burning.

A spirit house is meant to give the spirits shelter so they will not cause trouble in the restaurant. This was clearly a well-made house, since I had yet to run into a spirit while eating there. This small wooden structure did far more than appease the spirits. It guided my mind to an epiphany.

Mr. May said, "Life should smell." By the same token, death should stink. In the discovery, Ms. James called the police because the dog could smell something by the door. She also informed the police that it smelled bad. The officers contradicted her claim, stating that the room smelled of incense.

There were no exigent circumstances to break into the room if it didn't smell like death. Thus, the warrantless search may have been illegal. The state would argue that there was no need for a warrant because they were invited in, but there were two problems with that argument. One was that Ms. James probably lacked the authority to consent to the search. She didn't own the house. The second was that even if she could invite the police into the house, Mr. May's room was in a separate area. I had some research to do, but if the search was illegal, then the court might have to throw out the illegally obtained evidence. The whole case would fall as flat as my mother's chocolate soufflé.

A short Asian woman approached with a paper bag, which I assumed contained my dinner. She bowed slightly and handed it to me. I returned to my office and scarfed down the contents as I contemplated the police reports related to Mr. May's case.

As I drove toward Mr. Avery's office, I continued to consider the possibility that this case might be winnable. I might be able to avoid going to trial at all. It might be resolved by a pre-trial motion to suppress evidence based on the Fourth Amendment. If that motion was granted, the case would likely be dismissed. Even if it went to trial, it might never go to a jury. If they couldn't identify a body, it could be dismissed on a directed verdict.

I have won cases on a directed verdict before. The court ruled that the state's evidence, even taken in the best light, could not prove each element of the offense. Yet, who wins a murder case on a directed verdict?

Things could change, of course. The state could further identify the remains through DNA testing. They could find more information in ways I had yet to contemplate. Yet, even if I went to trial, the jury might still find my client guilty but mentally ill. The doctor would support that finding, testifying that Mr. May was mentally ill. I couldn't help but think that there was very little risk in rejecting the plea offer.

It bothered me that the state had called me right away. Why had Dr. Hyde called the state first? Was he siding with the government over Mr. May? Did the state prefer this result to an outright finding of guilt?

I had no problem finding a parking space on the street. Across the street was a park. Usually people wandered around there, but at this time of night it was empty. The entire area was surprisingly devoid of people. The marble façade of the law office basked in artificial light from floodlights mounted on the building and along the path to the door, even though the sunset was just beginning. The building seemed ominous, like a giant mausoleum. I thought about the movie, *Phantasm*, when the hero is chased through an ancient funeral home. I thought about Lincoln's tomb in Springfield and the white marble halls. I shivered involuntarily. Why should a law office bring images of death to mind? Maybe because Mr. Avery handled probate cases.

As the sun continued its path downward, the sky grew hazy. Shades of pink and purple were reflected upon the polished marble. The glass doors were unlocked and I pushed into the lobby, where I was greeted by a young woman in her twenties.

She had long black hair tied back in a ponytail. Her outfit—a simple black dress with a white collar—made her look more like a young girl on her way to church than a lawyer or a secretary. I found this unsettling but couldn't explain why.

"Mr. Avery is expecting you," she said by way of greeting.

"My name is Sam Roberts," I said, extending a hand.

Ignoring my gesture of introduction, she turned and led me up the enormous wooden staircase to the second floor. I had been to the second floor of this office before, but never to Mr. Avery's office. In the main area were small offices, glass cubicles, and desks not protected by walls. Normally the cubicles and desks were filled by paralegals and secretaries and the offices by associate attorneys. It was after six, but lawyers tend to work late. This entire area was empty, giving me a strong case of the heebie-jeebies.

I was led toward the back of the building to a set of large mahogany double doors. I had never noticed this area in the past. The door handles were bronze and substantial. My guide opened the door and left. I walked in feeling nervous but unsure why.

Mr. Avery stood at the back of the room, in front of an old tapestry. The image was of a shield with three lions sewed into it and flowers around the edges. In front of the hanging was an antique partner's desk in carved oak. The walls were paneled mahogany. Three large Persian rugs covered most of the wide planked red-oak flooring. Framed images of knights and battles decorated the walls. I recognized a copperplate engraving by a sixteenth-century German artist whose name escaped me. Above the fireplace were two medieval polearms—matching halberds that consisted of a long wooden staff topped with an axe blade and a spike. The metal portion was dark gray with gold inlays. The staffs were crossed like a crossbones on a pirate flag.

Although the office building was built around the turn of the century—that is, the nineteenth to the twentieth century—it had been remodeled more than once. I would describe most of the offices as modern, most of the furniture as unadorned. Mr. Avery's office, however, seemed to harken back to another place and time entirely.

"Good of you to come, Mr. Roberts," Mr. Avery said, turning around. He was wearing black pants and a white shirt. Rather than a suit jacket, he wore a satin smoking jacket in dark maroon with black lapels.

"Why did you call for me?"

"Please have a seat." He pointed to two brown leather captain's chairs near his desk.

"I really do have to get going. Is this something important?" I asked while sitting down.

"It's about Mr. May."

"What about Mr. May."

"I have heard that the doctor said he was mentally ill and the state is willing to allow you to have him plead to being guilty but mentally ill."

"I won't ask how you could have heard that."

"Is it true?"

"I am not comfortable talking to you about the specifics of an ongoing case."

"I paid you a lot of money, damn it," Mr. Avery said, anger creeping into his voice.

"*You* have not paid me any money. Mrs. May paid me money on behalf of her son. I don't work for you or Mrs. May. I work for Mr. May."

"I assume you will not let your client wind up in prison for the rest of his life. I have spoken with Mrs. May. We both want him to take the deal. We will make sure Mr. May lives a safe and well-cared-for life."

"Thank you, I appreciate your advice," I responded.

"What do you intend to do?"

"It is not my decision to make. Whether to go to trial or take a plea is up to the defendant alone."

"I know that. I am a lawyer, in case you forgot."

"A lawyer who does not handle criminal cases and asked me to get involved. Yes, I am well aware."

"What advice do you intend to give him?"

"It's getting late," I said, turning toward the door.

"Don't turn your back on me. You have not been dismissed." Mr. Avery spoke loudly, his voice beginning to tremble.

I turned around to see Mr. Avery staring at me, his fists clenched at his sides, his face red and eyes wide. "I do not work for you," I said. "I am not your servant or slave. I will do whatever the hell I want to with my case." I spoke calmly but I could tell from the look on his face that he understood I was on the edge of anger. "What I want to do is help Mr. May. If that means a plea, I will recommend a plea. If it means a trial, I will recommend a trial. No matter what, it means waiting to decide until I have all the facts. I don't have the laboratory reports yet. I don't even know if the remains were human. My malpractice provider frowns on lawyers who decide to enter into pleas without being informed."

"I am trying to help Mr. May," Mr. Avery said, still firm but in better control of his anger.

"Then let me do my fucking job," I said.

"You have a chance to make sure he does not go to prison."

I blew out a frustrated breath and wiped my brow with the back of my hand. The room was stifling. "We have been through this already. Even if I wanted to, I can't decide if Mr. May will go to trial or not. I can decide on strategy. I can file motions on behalf of my client. I can make decisions on how to prepare a case for trial. I can't decide if Mr. May will take a plea. He and he alone must make that decision."

"Well, he is crazy."

"He may have a mental disease or defect, but he is fit to stand trial. He is also fit to decide if he wants a trial. If he wants a trial and I want him to plead guilty then I will do my very best to be prepared for trial. So let me do my job and let Mr. May do his."

"I have his power of attorney."

"Then you can file any motion with the court. Argue that you should decide what he should do as far as a plea. I have never heard of anyone making such an argument, but be my guest. I might learn something."

"I may be able to get you more money."

"Thanks," I said, "I do enjoy money. Feel free to give me as much as you like. You should know, however, that money will have no impact on how I handle this case. Is there anything else? May I be excused?"

"No, there's nothing else," he said, his tone glacial. "Now get the hell out of here. If Blake does go to prison, I hope you can live with yourself."

I walked at a brisk pace out of his office, down the stairs, and out the door. When I got to my car, I looked back at the building and noticed a crow on a ledge of the façade. The artificial lighting cast a long shadow across the building. The bird was clearly not a harbinger of fluffy bunnies and kittens to come.

I was starting to sense a conspiracy. I am not a conspiracy nut. I believe Lee Harvey Oswald acted alone. I believe Osama bin Laden orchestrated the September 11 attack on the World Trade Center. Even as a child, I never bought into rumors that Hubba Bubba had spider eggs in it. No, I consider myself to be a realist.

Yet, this case was different. From day one, Mrs. May talked about making sure her son was found guilty but mentally ill rather than not guilty. The people in the house all seemed to have a negative view of my client. Ms. James seemed almost antagonistic. This, along with Mr. Avery's attitude and the fact that he knew the doctor's and the state's position at the same time I did, was starting to make me believe in conspiracies.

What incentive did everyone have for wanting Mr. May to plead guilty? Yes, it would avoid the risk of a finding of guilty. However, I had a feeling it was something else. It was about the house. Maybe they wanted the mirror all to themselves …. That might explain the behavior of those living in the home. Yet, what about Mr. Avery and Dr. Hyde?

It is not good politics or good Karma to piss off everyone in town. Mr. Avery had engaged my services to begin with. I would have to deal with Ms. Babs in the future. I didn't know why this case was bothering me so much.

I looked at my telephone. It was ten to seven and I hadn't eaten dinner yet. I decided to call Bob and see if he could do some computer research for me. I was curious if he could find a connection between the good doctor, Mr. Avery, and Mrs. May.

Bob didn't answer until the sixth ring. "What's up, dude?" he croaked into the phone.

"Have you eaten?"

There was a long pause before he answered, "No."

"How about meeting for dinner?"

"Cool, food is good."

"Half hour. You pick the place."

"The Blue Crayfish?"

"I will be there."

The phone clicked off. I was concerned that Bob was asleep at seven at night. I was also concerned about his choice of the Blue Crayfish. Bob rarely preferred a chain restaurant and we had never eaten at this one.

Chapter 23

~~

W HEN I GOT to the restaurant, I understood why Bob had chosen it. A large banner advertised that it was the tenth annual Crayfish Feast. Although there were no balloons or streamers, a sign indicated that one could purchase all-you-can-eat crayfish, hush puppies, and Asiago Cove Rolls for the low, low price of $14.99.

The Blue Crayfish had corrugated metal walls and a worn wooden floor reminiscent of a boat dock. Mounted on the walls were boat oars, water-skis, and fish of all types. Bob had yet to arrive so I took a seat in a booth in the back near the bathrooms.

I ordered a vodka and cranberry juice. After my meeting with Mr. Avery, I needed a drink. When I finished my adult beverage, Bob had still not arrived. The Stoli provided no comfort for my restless spirit.

I was about to order another drink when Bob came in. He seemed less together than normal. His hair was uncombed and he had apparently not shaved in days. His tie-dyed T-shirt looked like it had gone through a trash compactor. I waved and he headed in my direction.

"What's up, dude?"

"You look terrible."

"Gee, thanks, way to greet a guy. Did you order already?"

"No, waiting for you."

He slid into the booth. "You didn't have to wait. It is the crayfish celebration, of course, so I want the all-you-can-eat crayfish."

"It is the Crayfish 'Feast.' If you call it a celebration or festival, they may not feed you."

The waitress came to the table. She had red hair out of a bottle, eye shadow in hues of blue, and neon-pink lipstick. Her T-shirt read, "I HAVE CRABS" in capital letters with "lobster, crayfish, and fish as well" in smaller print below. Underneath was a picture of a bright-blue crustacean. We both ordered the all-you-can-eat crayfish. I ordered another vodka and cranberry while Bob opted for a tequila sunrise.

After the waitress left, I gave Bob the short version of the day's events and told him I wanted to research if Mr. Avery and Dr. Hyde had any prior connection. I also wanted to know if Mr. Avery had any involvement with anyone who lives or lived in the Frost House. Finally, I wanted to see if Mr. Avery or his firm had made any donations to the state's attorney during the last election. Bob agreed to look into these matters.

I couldn't recall if I had told Bob my dream involving Einstein and Bridget. I wanted to see if he had any insights. Bob appeared contemplative as he stroked his goatee. The waitress interrupted us momentarily when she brought rolls to the table.

"You had an earlier dream with Freud in it?"

"Yes," I confirmed.

"You should have dreamed the second dream first and then asked Freud to interpret it."

"Why? I don't think the dream with Einstein and Bridget had anything to do with my penis, my ego, or my mother."

"You did have a thing for Bridget."

"Fine, I will ask the good doctor, should he visit my dreams again," I said.

He gave me an ironic little bow. "Calm yourself, my impatient grass hopper," he said, channeling Kwai Chang Caine.

"I *am* calm," I said, knowing I sounded anything but.

He tapped his scruffy chin. "You know, I actually do have a theory about your dream. It takes me back to Mr. May's journal and his desire to understand time travel."

"I am all ears."

"Einstein was making the point that the laws of physics do not change, our understanding does. Einstein's theories took us ahead of Newton's law of universal gravitation. The laws of physics follow the same rules here or on the moon, now or into the future, God does not play dice with the universe."

"All right," I said. I leaned my elbows on the table, convinced that I was hearing nothing new.

But Bob was not done. "Magic, however, has different rules. Witches respect nature and the elements but manipulate them. In the musical *Wicked,* the witch defied gravity—one of the fundamental rules of nature. By definition, magic is supernatural and does not follow the rules of nature or physics."

I slapped the table. "Why is that important?"

Despite my impatience, Bob stayed on point. "If the mirror were a portal to another world or another time, it might explain how someone other than Mr. May could commit a murder in a locked room. From his journal, it was clear he was looking to science to explain the mirror. Yet, it is also clear Heather and he were not ruling out magic. Perhaps the two don't mix."

The waitress arrived with our drinks, leaving them on the table without looking up. Bob held up the tequila sunrise.

"Tequila, orange juice, and grenadine. All in separate layers. Like magic and science not mixing. I think Mr. May was looking for a rational explanation for a magical phenomenon. Other than in *Star Trek*, there are no known worm holes that allow travel through time and space."

"I think I understand. The mirror needed blood. If it was a wormhole, why did they need blood?"

"Exactly."

"So this is about opening doors to other worlds. It is not about other times. It is a doorway to Hell or some other dimension. Perhaps a passage from the world of the living to the world of the dead."

Bob nodded sagely. "That's my theory."

"Hell of a jump, based on limited information."

"Get me more information and I will revise my theory."

"Are you still seeing that woman from the bar?"

Bob held up his hand, palm out. "Slow down. If you change directions that fast, I am going to get whiplash."

"Sorry, I needed a break from the strange and mysterious."

"Then you never looked at that woman. Strange and mysterious is a hell of an accurate description."

"So, are you still seeing her?"

He examined his fingernails while avoiding my eyes. "No, it didn't work out."

"Why not?"

Bob looked up. His nails were surprisingly clean despite his general disarray.

"Her husband seemed disproportionally large. I was worried he might be the jealous type."

I nodded. "I can see how that might adversely affect your relationship. You have to kiss a lot of frogs, handcuffed to bar rails, to find your one true love."

"I guess, but she is awfully cute."

"So are bunnies, until they poop on the carpet."

"I would rather spend time with her than any bunny. Other than the bunnies who hang out with Hugh Hefner. Did you know he went to college at the University of Illinois?"

"Yeah, I heard that. If it were up to me, I would skip the woman one meets handcuffed to a bar or naked on the covers of magazines."

He snorted. "Says the man who has not had a date in over a year."

"Remember what Helga said that night at Snuggle and Meat?"

"Something about a whip and calling us 'bitches.' "

I gave him a little slap on the arm. "She said, 'pain is candy.' Well, I don't have much of a sweet tooth."

"Maybe you're right. Why not just join a monastery?"

"I'm not religious."

"Do they discriminate?"

"I'm not sure, but I think so."

After an hour or so, we finished eating. I could tell the waitress was impressed that Bob managed to shovel down three plates of crayfish before I could clean my first plate. I was more of a marathon guy and Bob was a sprinter. We left the restaurant, and Bob promised to call in the next couple of days with the information I'd requested.

I was tired and just wanted to go to sleep. Bob was right, of course. I was in no position to comment on his love life. He was also right that magic and science don't mix. When it comes to dark magic, blood is always the key. The spilling of blood, especially innocent blood, can open doors. The question is doors to what?

I thought of the sign above the gateway to Hell in Dante's Inferno, "Abandon all hope, ye who enter here." I suspected that this house did not guard an entrance to Hell, but it did have a major creepy vibe. Perhaps it was a gateway to "heck" or "purgatory." I've been told that if you are bad but not awful you will be forced to spend eternity watching the movies that score less than ten percent on *Rotten Tomatoes* over and over again.

I think Bob told me that, or perhaps it was a television evangelist. Either way that would suck. In comparison, fire and brimstone might not be so bad.

Chapter 24

～～

FOR THE NEXT few weeks I tried to concentrate on other matters until the rest of the reports came in related to Mr. May's case. It was early October and I came home early from work and put on a sweatshirt. With the cooler temperatures, I should have been wearing a coat. It had been a few days since I'd bothered to check my office mail, so I brought it home. I had quite a stack, mostly bills. There was, however, one letter that caught my attention—a large envelope that was either a holiday card or an invitation.

The card inside inexplicably filled me with sadness. It was an invitation to Susan's wedding. She was marrying a man named Zachery Young. The name made him sound like a fraternity boy. The ceremony was at a church downtown, and the reception was at the country club. The wedding was set for early January.

I was jealous, of course. Yet at the same time I wanted Susan to be happy. Although there was a good possibility I would never be happy again. I grabbed a Diet Coke from the refrigerator and added two fingers of Maker's Mark.

I sat on the couch and played music through my Bluetooth speakers using iTunes on the random setting. I let my mind wander, trying to forget about monsters, demons, and Susan.

Tomorrow I might go shopping for a wedding gift. I might even call Susan and congratulate her. I would acknowledge to myself that this was best for both of us. Tonight, however, I would think of nothing and let the music and the whiskey numb my brain.

Helga was wrong. Pain is not candy, or if it is candy, it is not good candy. It is a Milky Way filled with maggots or a Mars Bar filled with mucus. The news hurt down to my soul.

I got off the sofa and returned to the kitchen. Digging a Twix bar out of the freezer, I returned to my seat. I began gnawing at the frozen caramel like a desperate hamster while downing my bourbon and Coke. The candy and my cocktail mixed in my mouth like bile.

The telephone rang, but I didn't answer, allowing voicemail to pick up. I just sat there, unmoving, waiting for sleep to overcome me. I hoped for a dreamless night.

I AWOKE THE next morning at eight, showered, and dressed. I decided to head to the office to do some research on Mr. May's case. I still believed the search of his room to be illegal. In addition, the work might keep my mind off the invitation. Of course this was bullshit, but I couldn't just sit here, drowning in self-pity.

The Fourth Amendment to the United States Constitution guarantees:

> The right of the people to be secure in their persons, houses, papers, and effects, against unreasonable searches and seizures, shall not be violated, and no Warrants shall issue, but upon probable cause, supported by Oath or affirmation, and particularly describing the place to be searched, and the persons or things to be seized.

In Mr. May's case, there was clearly no warrant issued. As time goes on, the courts have allowed more and more exceptions to the warrant requirement. These exceptions include but are not limited to if the officer is in hot pursuit, or if there is fire in the house, or even if the officer needs to stop the destruction of evidence. Another exception to this rule is if the officer is invited in.

In this case, the police would clearly claim that they were invited in. In addition, they would claim it was an emergency and they were concerned about the occupant of the room or his girlfriend being seriously injured or in need of immediate medical care. To be successful, the police must be acting in an objectively reasonable manner. In the case of Katz v. the United States, the Supreme Court specifically pointed out that a search must be reasonable and a warrantless search is "presumptively unreasonable." In a 2009 case, the United States Supreme Court in Michigan v. Fisher held that it was reasonable for the police to enter and search a home without a warrant to provide emergency aid. That case, however, was clearly distinguishable from Mr. May's. In Mr. Fisher's case, the officer saw Mr. Fisher through the window, acting crazy. They had found blood outside the home on a damaged vehicle as well as broken windows and other damaged property.

Even if the police believed Mr. May had killed someone, the only support for that theory was Ms. James' concerns. There was no objective evidence to support this claim. They had heard no screams nor seen any blood or signs of a struggle. The claim that the room smelled bad was contrary to the police reports.

If the evidence was obtained in violation of the Fourth Amendment, then the court should bar the use of the evidence based on the exclusionary rule. Thus, the illegally obtained evidence should be suppressed. Not only should the evidence be barred but any evidence obtained based on the illegally obtained evidence should also be inadmissible in court. The courts have found what they refer to as, "the fruit of the poisonous tree" is equally inadmissible. Thus, if you obtained a confession by beating a prisoner until he admitted where he hid the drugs, not only is the confession inadmissible but so are the drugs themselves. All the evidence in this case relied on the illegal search of the home. If that was thrown out, the entire case would topple like a row of dominoes.

I didn't need to do a lot of research to determine that the search was illegal. There was no objective exigent circumstances that would allow the warrantless entry into Mr. May's room. The real question was whether Ms. James could grant permission to the authorities to enter the house and furthermore allow them to enter Mr. May's room by breaking down a locked door.

Did Ms. James have the authority to consent to the search of the house? The general rule is that in order to give consent to search property, the person giving consent must have that authority. Ms. James clearly did not. There is, however, a United States Supreme Court case, Illinois v. Rodriguez, which holds such searches may be valid if at the time of the search the police believed she had authority over the premises. I had little doubt the police would claim they believed she had the authority to allow such a search. The trial court could go either way.

Yet, there was another issue here. Mr. May's quarters were separate from the rest of the house. They had their own lock and key. They included a bathroom, kitchen, and laundry room. He never left. It was clear to me that his expectation of privacy would be the same as if he were inhabiting a separate dwelling.

There are a number of cases involving hotel rooms. Courts have found that the consent of the owner or manager of a hotel is not sufficient to allow the search of an individual tenant's room. If you rent a room at a hotel, you have an expectation of privacy. There are similar arguments related to dorm rooms at colleges. This was the crux of my argument.

I spent the next two hours writing a motion to suppress evidence. My argument was that there was a warrantless search and no exigent circumstances to justify it. If the police had to get a warrant, the delay would not have led to the destruction of evidence or anyone being further injured or hurt. Even if Ms. Kline was dead, there was no indication she was in the process of dying when the police were present. They heard no screams, squeals, or heavy breathing. The police did not witness any signs of foul play. They did not smell or see anything unusual.

In addition, Ms. James did not have the authority to consent to a search of the home. She did not own or rent the property. Should the court find she had real or apparent authority to allow the search, she had no such authority over Mr. May's room.

The motion would need to be set before the court prior to trial. That meant an evidentiary hearing. As a general rule, courts don't like motions to suppress. The idea that a guilty person might go free because the police failed to follow rules can be bothersome. Yet in this case, I felt confident that the motion would be granted. If the motion was granted, the state would have no case against Mr. May.

They didn't have a body or murder weapon. Yet, that was an issue for trial. A motion to suppress would be heard and decided prior to trial. I could prevent this whole case from going forward.

I spent the next hour writing up my motion to suppress and memorandum of law to go along with it. I mailed a copy to opposing counsel and the circuit clerk as well as a courtesy copy to the judge. I felt good about this case; it made no sense to enter into the plea recommended by the state. If the pre-trial motion was denied, maybe then I'd consider a plea. Yet, even if I lost the motion, the state needed to prove that Ms. Kline was killed to begin with. The decision was ultimately my client's, but he seemed to have no inclination to jump into a plea, despite the desires of the people around him.

Chapter 25

~~~

IT HAD BEEN a couple of weeks since I'd filed my motion to suppress evidence on the May case, and the court had already given me the date of October 31—Halloween. I was not sure if this was a good sign. It did seem oddly appropriate. There was not a whole lot to be done related to the case until the motion was heard, and I was pleased to have heard nothing from either Mr. Avery or Mrs. May.

I got to my office at around nine. With no court appearances and no appointments scheduled, I was wearing jeans, a T-shirt, and a black leather jacket. Finally, a chance to get my paperwork done! I dove into the pile of files waiting for my attention.

At eleven, I went down to get the mail. When I returned to my desk, the telephone was ringing. I picked up on the third ring.

"Sam Roberts," I sang into the receiver.

"Dude, what up?" It was Bob.

"Just working."

"I did that research, looking for connections between Dr. Hyde, Mrs. May, the state's attorney's office, and Mr. Avery."

"Find anything?"

"Not much. Mr. Avery's law firm contributed to the campaign

for the state's attorney's election but did so for the current state's attorney and her competitor in equal amounts. He was on the board of the hospital that owns the funny farm where Mr. May is staying, but that was some years back. I couldn't find anything about Dr. Hyde and his involvement with Mrs. May or Mr. Avery."

"If he saw Mrs. May professionally, you wouldn't find anything, HIPAA and all."

"They do all have one thing in common."

"What's that?"

"They are all members of the country club."

"It's a small town. That probably doesn't mean much."

"No, but speaking of the country club, I heard a friend of yours is getting married there."

I sighed. "You want to talk about Susan getting married? I am fine with it. Okay, maybe not 'fine,' but you don't have to talk me in from the ledge. I don't need you to dull my steak knives and hide my rat poison."

"Dude, I just wanted to make sure you are cool with it. I got the invite and thought I would tiptoe around the subject until you told me how you were dealing. Offer you a shoulder to cry on maybe a cup of bourbon."

"Fuck that," I said. "I am cooler than Fonzie." I was, however, starting to get upset.

"I can see that you are even more the iceman than Drake."

"The hotel?"

"The rapper."

"Never heard of him. I will stick with the Fonz or maybe Bruce Springsteen, if you don't mind. I prefer old-school cool."

"Can I get you some prune juice and Geritol?"

"Sure, as long as you put ice in them. That's how I roll."

He paused. "Seriously, how are you holding up?"

"It's for the best. I want her to be happy."

"So you feel all right."

I took a few deep breaths. "No I feel like I got hit in the

testacies with brass knuckles. That doesn't mean I am not okay. It just means I need time."

"I dig it. Like that Viking girl said, 'pain is candy.' "

"Words to live by."

"Thanks for looking into that stuff for me."

"No problem," Bob said.

Afterward, I looked through the mail and noticed a thick Manila envelope from the state's attorney's office. I put aside the rest of my mail. I had a number of criminal cases pending, but I had a feeling this was about the May case. When I opened it up, I was not disappointed.

The envelope included various lab reports. It appeared that the remains did contain human DNA. The laboratory did not rule out that the DNA could be from more than one person. Did they think this case involved a serial killer?

The analysis also confirmed that the remains appeared partially cooked and ground into a human stew. There was nothing to even hint at what had happened to the body, or more precisely, bodies. The heating of the remains made it difficult to determine how long they had been there.

No blood or bodily fluids had been found on any of the knives in the room. There was no blood on Mr. May's clothing or on his person. Maybe someone, or some group of people, had been murdered. Yet, they couldn't prove Ms. Kline or any specific person was killed on any particular date. They had no murder weapon or explanation as to how or by what means a murder took place. I was actually looking forward to this trial.

But first, I looked forward to speaking to my client. Also Mrs. May and Mr. Avery. Without more evidence, I couldn't imagine how the state could win this case.

The telephone rang.

Chapter 26

~~~

"**S**AM ROBERTS," I said into the telephone.

"It's Amanda Babs. I am calling on Mr. May's case."

"Yeah, I just got the lab tests. Good stuff. I would be looking forward to the trial but I don't think you will get past my motion to suppress."

"Look," she said with an audible huff of air, "I am willing to reduce the charge to aggravated battery for probation, if he wants to plea."

"I will have to talk with my client before I say no, but I will recommend he go to trial."

"Why take the chance?"

"Because it is unwinnable. It is built on a foundation of illegally obtained evidence. Yet, even if all that evidence gets before the jury, it is still a horrible case."

"You never know."

"That's true, but I am confident that even if you could find a jury who would ignore the evidence, the verdict would never survive an appeal."

This is where Amanda lost her cool. "Fuck you, Sam. Your client is not just a murderer, he is a serial killer. He cooks his victims and eats them. He is worse than Jeffrey Dahmer." Her voice was shaking.

"I guess I will leave that up to the judge and jury."

"I will *nolle prosequi* in the morning," she said in a firmer voice. "I intend to refile if I find more evidence. And I *will* find more evidence. I hope you can live with yourself when he kills again."

"The job of a prosecutor is to do justice, not to obtain convictions."

"Don't tell me how to do my job, Sam. If being an ass was against the law, I would prosecute you in a heartbeat."

The telephone went dead. I was going to call Blake but decided that this was more face-to-face news. He would be going home tomorrow. He would be happier than a clam on cocaine. I wanted see him in person so I could share a little in his joy.

I was at the hospital in less than fifteen minutes. At the front desk, a neatly dressed older woman informed me that I was not allowed in until they could contact Dr. Hyde. Five minutes later, a nurse escorted me to Dr. Hyde's office.

The doctor was sitting behind his desk. He looked up but did not stand to greet me. His attention was on a piece of paper on his desk.

"Mr. Roberts, what brings you for a visit?"

"I am pleased to say that I believe the state will be dismissing the case against Mr. May. I wanted to give him the good news in person."

The doctor did not seemed surprised or pleased. He also did not seem displeased. He spoke with a flat affect devoid of emotion. "He is in the group area with the television and game tables, where you met him last time. The nurse will take you there."

He got up and opened his office door. The same nurse who'd brought me to see the doctor was speaking to an orderly a few feet away. She looked up as the door opened.

"Nurse Fletcher, would you mind taking Mr. Roberts to see Mr. May in the group area?"

I followed the nurse down the hallway. On the way, we passed one of those old self-cooling water fountains from the 1940s or 1950s. I stopped to get a drink. The porcelain-coated steel was cold to the touch. The image of a Native American brave was stamped into the steel front. The nurse seemed annoyed that I stopped for a drink and tapped her foot until I was done.

I looked at her more carefully. She had cold gray eyes. Her uniform was a traditional white nurse's dress that seemed from another time. The lines on her face showed a life filled with more sorrow than joy.

"Mr. Roberts, can we go on?"

"Yes, of course. I just needed a drink."

"I often need a drink, but my job does not permit me time to dilly-dally."

If there was ever a person in need of both a drink and time to dilly-dally, it was Nurse Fletcher. I suspected that she has not been dillied or dallied in years. I wondered why such a woman had become a nurse. Had she started out warm and caring and traded her warm fuzziness in for cold prickliness as the years progressed, or was she always this way?

When I got to the group area, I saw Mr. May sitting at a card table looking up at a television set. I walked over to his table and sat across from him. The movie *The Lone Ranger* was playing loudly and Mr. May was enthralled.

This was the modern version of the tale starring Johnny Depp. I had seen the movie at the theater. I liked Johnny Depp in the film, but it definitely did not require or deserve the rapt attention Mr. May was giving it.

Mr. May did not look like himself at all. His hair was wild and unkempt. He was wearing scrub bottoms and a T-shirt with slippers. His eyes were the worst part. When I was in law school, a professor said to a student during a test, "Looking at you is like staring into a flat EEG." Well, in this case it was exactly like that. There was no life in his eyes.

"I have good news, Mr. May."

"Do you know the Lone Cabbage's sidekick's name?" Mr. May said, his voice calm and flat with no humor evident in his tone.

"No."

"Kimo-coleslawbe."

"That is funny," I said without laughing, "but I am going to get you out of here. You may go home as early as tomorrow. They know they can't prove the case against you."

"They have pudding tomorrow."

"Do you understand me? You are going home."

"Yes, I look forward to going home."

He didn't seem drunk or drugged, just not present. His eyes, once clear and full of life, were now unfocused, staring off into the distance. I hoped he was drugged—that when he got home, he would return to his former self. That was my hope, but I had an odd feeling that his essence was gone. That he would never be the same.

I returned to Dr. Hyde's Office. At the door, Nurse Fletcher blocked my path. I pushed her aside. Nurse Fletcher entered the office at the same time, her face red and angry.

"Sorry, Doctor, he just barged in," Ms. Fletcher said, her anger barely in check.

"That is fine, Nurse, you can leave us," Dr. Hyde said authoritatively. "Now, Mr. Roberts, what is so important that you need to barge in and upset my staff?"

"What the hell did you do to Mr. May?"

"I shouldn't discuss this with you—HIPAA and all."

"I'm his fucking lawyer." I wasn't yelling, but I was close to it. "His mental health is an issue before the court. I would be glad to subpoena you and have you testify as to his mental condition and treatment before the court."

The doctor remained calm. "I thought the case was being dismissed."

"Fine," I said, still bristling with anger, "if you don't want to talk with me, then you can make whatever argument you and your attorney come up with."

He leaned back and shrugged. "Look, I am not avoiding a conversation. In fact I would enjoy discussing the case with you. I was just thinking out loud. Please sit down. Mr. May is a severe schizophrenic. Much of the time he has been in the grips of a major psychotic episode haunted by nightmares and audio hallucinations. He even claims to have had visual hallucinations. His heart rate was dangerously high, he couldn't sleep or eat, and he was violent. He threatened to kill himself and harm others, including myself, on any number of occasions. If I'd done nothing, he would probably be dead."

"So what did you do?" I demanded.

"I started with various mixes of anti-psychotic medications and sedatives. They were having little impact unless I kept him completely unconscious. That is not very healthy, so I looked into other treatment alternatives. At one point I even considered psychosurgery but decided against it."

"Psychosurgery? Like a *lobotomy*?"

"I know it seems severe and desperate but Mr. May's condition was severe and desperate. I also decided against it. I did try Electroconvulsive Therapy."

"Electroshock therapy? That's barbaric." My hands were curled into fists.

"It may have been at one time, but now we use anesthesia and use a lower voltage of electricity. I am not sure exactly why it works, but it does. I should say it *did* work. Mr. May is no longer fighting the demons in his head."

"He doesn't look like he could do fighting of any kind. What authority did you have to do this? Certainly not from the court."

"His lawyer—"

"I'm his lawyer."

"Mr. Avery and his mother and I have been in touch daily. We have worked together on this treatment plan every step of the way. They have his medical power of attorney and I believe his best interests at heart. I understand Doctor ... *Mr*. Roberts that you may not approve of my methods, but I assure you they have been effective in this case. This is not *American Horror Story*. I am doing my best and my best has possibly saved your client's life."

I despised this man but had no evidence to base my feelings on. Maybe he was right. Maybe he'd only done what was necessary. Perhaps until now I'd only seen Mr. May at lucid moments. For all I knew he was ordinarily a maniac. Maybe his present condition was a bad reaction to the drugs and when it wore off, he would be fine. After all, I'm not a doctor. Although I do have a *Juris Doctor* degree, it's not the same thing.

"My question is why a man who was perfectly lucid when I spoke to him last is a fucking carrot today?"

"Last time you were here, an hour after you left, Mr. May struck Nurse Fletcher with the board from the game *Clue* and nearly broke her nose. Since his last treatment, he has not hurt anyone. Better a 'carrot' than a man who will cause harm to himself and others. Yet, he is far from a 'carrot,' as you so artfully say. He has a slightly flat affect because he is a schizophrenic who is not having a psychotic episode. That is the norm for a person with his diagnosis. Now, I have patients to see and people to help. It is always a pleasure, Mr. Roberts."

I got up to leave. I did not tell him that hitting Nurse Fletcher is not an indication of madness but of good sense. I did not tell him he could stick a carrot up his ass. I wanted to tell him to go to hell but the truth was I didn't know if he was evil or doing his best. In a flash, I visualized striking Ms. Fletcher with a full-size candlestick from the game *Clue*. If anyone could read my mind, they would keep me here. Who knows? Maybe I *was* crazy.

I left the hospital and got into my car. This case was like the month of March. It came in like a lion and went out like a lamb. Perhaps it would be more appropriate to say it came in with a roar and left with a whimper. It was over. I had saved Mr. May from an unjust conviction. I still had no answers as to what was going on with that mirror or with that house, but I was done. I had no direction, no case, and no peace of mind.

I felt angry and confused. I turned on the radio in my car. I could hear Katy Perry roar as the telephone interrupted the song.

"Dude, what up?" Bob sang into the phone.

"It's a long story, but Mr. May's case will be dismissed tomorrow."

"Wow, you are one rad lawyer."

"No shit, Sherlock. You should be in the FBI."

"That's my line. You don't sound too happy about it …. Anyway, I did find out a little more information on the house, but I guess it doesn't matter."

"Do tell. I feel cat-like in my curiosity."

"On a lark, I checked the recorder of deeds. Every person who has owned the house had a mortgage that was released within the first year of ownership."

"That is interesting, but it only shows that the owners paid off the mortgage. And that they all had money or made money."

"Also, I have found a large number of people who have been missing after visiting the home or in the area in the neighborhood surrounding the home. They were never found again. No bodies, no sign of them. They just … disappeared. It does not end in the past, either. Last year two people were reported missing within two blocks of the house."

"You think the house ate them?"

"I report 'Just the facts ma'am.' You can interpret them any way you want." Bob was doing his best impression of Joe Friday from *Dragnet*. Pretty convincing.

"Thanks for your help and don't call me ma'am."

Chapter 27

THE NEXT MORNING, the state dismissed the case against Mr. May. I was surprised to see no press in the courtroom. The judge did not react to the state's motion to *nolle prosequi* a murder case. In truth it was all a bit of a letdown. My client was accused of murder, and the state dismissed the case.

If the government sticks you in a mental institution pending a trial and then later dismisses the case, then the government should be required to provide compensation. If nothing else, they could give the falsely accused a cookie a day. If I ran for the governorship of the great State of Illinois, I'd run on a free-cookie platform. Considering that most of our governors go to prison, I could hardly be the worst governor the state has ever had.

When I got to work, I couldn't concentrate. I didn't have anything that had to get out that day, so I headed home early. When I arrived home, there was a black envelope with silver calligraphy on the front in the mail. The last formal letter I'd received had foretold Susan's coming nuptials. This one was equally menacing.

There was no return address and no stamp, so it must have been hand-delivered. The card inside invited me to a party at the Frost Home to celebrate Mr. May's release from the institution and the dismissal of his case. I was to be the guest of honor. It did allow for a "plus one." The party was of course on the same date the motions in the May case were to be heard, All Hallows Eve—Halloween.

I couldn't help wonder how they got this invitation to me so quickly. The case had only been dismissed today. The printing on the invitation was embossed and looked professionally done. I wasn't an expert on invitations, but this seemed impossible to me. If the mirror or the Frost House as a whole were truly evil, then the forces of darkness had to run their own printing operation.

I felt some very bad mojo. I decided to give Bob a call. I was tired of putting his life on the line. This time I did not need him to be my "plus one," but I did need to borrow a "plus nine" millimeter.

"What's up?" Bob sang into the telephone.

"Not much, other than I've been invited to a party at the Frost Home on Halloween. Apparently in my honor."

"Spooky. That house is scary enough on the average Tuesday, let alone Halloween. Let me guess: you need a date and no woman in her right mind would go out with you so you are asking me?"

"No, I don't need a date. If I did, I would just ask your mother."

"You bastard. You know my mother died in a horrible accident while out on a date," Bob said, anger creeping into his voice.

I was taken aback. "That's not true. Is it?"

He laughed. "No, just fucking with you. My mom is fine."

"It occurs to me that your earlier statement implies that women are more selective than men."

"Well, I assume, based on the number of times I have been rejected by men versus women that women are more selective. I get turned down by women all the time and have never been rejected by a man."

"How many men have you asked out?"

"None."

"I don't know how well your theory holds up."

"Fine." He paused. "What did you want, anyway?"

"I was hoping you had a Beretta I could borrow."

"If you need a gun, I am not letting you go to that party without me."

"I don't need a gun. I mean I might, just in case, but I don't think so."

"I'm the paranoid one. If you think you need a gun, you need one. If you think you're in danger, you're right. I am not letting you walk into this party and get sliced and diced and served up like a crab cake. Certainly not without my help."

"You want to help slice and dice me?"

"You know what I mean."

"I'm probably just being paranoid."

"We are talking in circles. Why don't you come over and watch a flick tonight?"

"What's showing?"

"The Picture of Dorian Gray."

"From the 1990s or the black and white one from the 1940s?"

"Black and white."

"What time?"

"Seven."

"Cool. I will be there."

I did some work around the house that involved laundry and dishwashing and I watched a few episodes of *Gotham* on Netflix. By the time I was done, it was a quarter to seven. I picked up some food from the Bubble and Cluck and a six pack of a beer.

Bob was wearing flannel pajama pants and a black T-shirt with a picture of Neil Young and the words, "I felt like getting high" written in a gothic font below the image. He looked frazzled, as if he had not slept recently. Normally he has a bit of a paunch, but I saw no evidence of it this evening. He'd clearly lost weight. I took a seat on the sofa after first removing an empty can of beer resting on the couch cushion.

On the coffee table were fast food wrappers and a book titled *Bunny Blood Feud*. The cover depicted a ridiculously fluffy rabbit that looked red with pink eyes. Upon closer inspection, the rabbit was white but so covered in blood and gore as to create the illusion of being red. The tagline was, "So fluffy you are going to die." I couldn't decide if this book was intended to be funny like the rabbit in *Monty Python and the Holy Grail* or nightmarish. The image on the cover supported the latter.

"Do you want to borrow it?" Bob asked, pointing to the book.

"No, I am good," I said.

"It's supposed to be based on a true story. A genetics lab that goes out of control. I have only read the first two chapters. So far, so scary."

We watched the movie in relative silence. Bob seemed less than his exuberant self. Given his love for sushi and fried chicken, I was concerned for his health when he did not finish his meal. I have known Bob for many years and have never known him not to finish his dinner from anywhere, let alone the Cluck You Special from the Bubble and Cluck. The meal included a chicken leg and thigh with a biscuit as well as a California Roll, cut into four pieces, and six pieces of tuna nigiri. These are among Bob's favorite foods.

When the movie was over, I asked, "Are you going to eat the tuna? I think it's bluefin."

"No, go ahead," Bob replied.

I grasped the sushi firmly with my chopsticks and popped it into my mouth as Bob looked on indifferently. Prior to tonight, Bob would have stuck a fork in my eye if I so much as thought about eating a piece of his sushi.

"What's wrong? You would sooner part with a kidney than your favorite dinner."

He shrugged. "I'm just not hungry."

"Is that like a shark not feeling like swimming? Hunger is part of your essential nature. As Descartes once said, 'I eat, therefore I am.'"

He smirked. "I think you are putting Descartes in front of the horse."

"You are hilarious."

He was staring straight ahead as if lost in thought. "I was just thinking of Oscar Wilde and Jews."

"That's random. I was just thinking of Oscar the Grouch and Methodists."

He was still staring into space. Ignoring my smartass reply, he said, "Oscar Wilde wrote the novel the movie we just saw was based on in 1890. People believe he was anti-Semitic because Dorian calls someone a 'horrible Jew' in the book."

I snorted. "I thought he was gay. You'd think he would be more sensitive to other religions and lifestyles."

He gave me a sidelong look. "You are getting me off topic. What is the central idea conveyed in the movie we just watched?"

I frowned. "I don't know. I guess the portrait in the attic had, locked within it, Dorian's true self. All his ugliness. What has that to do with Jews or religion at all?"

"Did you know that Jews cover mirrors when people die?"

I nodded. "Sure, when people sit *Shiva* after a death, they cover the mirrors in the home—I assume so they don't have to worry about how they look during mourning. They can concentrate on something other than themselves."

"That was what I thought as well. Remember that Rabbi we met in Jerusalem a long time ago when those nuns were being sacrificed?"

I made a face. "How can I forget?"

"I called him today."

"Why?"

"To ask him the same question."

"What did he say?"

"He gave the same answer you did. He also added another reason."

"What?"

"He said there was a small sect who believed that after the death of a family member the soul might wander the house before going off to the afterlife. This sect believed the soul outside of a human body could get trapped in a mirror and lose its way. I checked, and this is an Appalachian superstition as well. Native Americans also have customs related to the dead. The Navajo put a hole in the roof of their hogans after someone dies to make sure the soul has a place to escape. In Denmark, they open a window when someone dies to allow the soul to be released."

I scratched my head. "I think you're reading way too much into this movie."

"Dude, I wasn't thinking of the movie." Bob was leaning forward, gesturing emphatically. "I was thinking about the Frost Home. What if the land was possessed by an evil spirit or an evil soul? What if that spirit or soul was captured within the mirror in Mr. May's room after the house was built?"

I gave this some thought. "Couldn't they just break the mirror?"

His eyes grew wide. "Maybe they don't *want* to break the mirror. Maybe they are afraid of the spirit that would be released or maybe the mirror is giving them something. Besides, who can say what would happen if the mirror was broken, other than bring bad luck."

"It does appear the owners of that house tend to get rich. Yet how can a mirror give you anything?"

He sat back on the couch. After a moment, he said, "I have no idea. Although, the mirror in *Snow White* gave advice."

I held up a hand. "That must be it. Although, I am not sure how one profits by knowing 'who is the fairest in the land.' "

"You are hilarious."

"Your theory is interesting, but I have got to tell you, it seems a bit of a stretch. On the other hand, I would love another look at that mirror."

He wagged his forefinger at me. "Don't get too close."

"Why?"

"Remember what happened to Alice."

"She chased a rabbit?"

"She also fell through a looking glass. They made a movie."

Just then my telephone rang. As I clicked the "on" button, I continued to ponder what Bob had said. It was impossible, of course, but Bob and I have dealt with the impossible many times.

"Sam Roberts."

"Sam, it's Beth."

"All right …."

"Beth from Snuggle and Meat—your former client. I also go by Helga. The one with the whips and riding crops."

"Sure, how could I forget? What can I do for you?"

"Guess who is at Snuggle and Meat tonight?"

"Can you give me a hint? Celebrity? Politician? Narrow it down."

"That girl in your picture, Heather."

My heart started to beat faster. "Is she the same one you knew as Lilith? Are you sure? She's alive?"

"No doubt to all three questions."

"Thanks. I will head out there. I definitely owe you one."

"I will take you up on that."

I pushed the off button, noting the curiosity in Bob's eyes. I wasn't sure how much of the conversation he'd overheard.

"Do people say they 'hung up' a telephone anymore?" I asked.

"Huh?"

"You 'end' a call on a cell phone. Do people say 'I hung up the phone' when you are not hanging a handset on a cradle?"

"What was that call about?" Bob said, ignoring my stupid question.

"It was Helga at Snuggle and Meat. She claims to have seen Heather Kline."

"The dead woman? Did she have a vision?"

"Apparently Heather is alive and well and at the S&M."

"I think I need a drink."

"Snuggle and Meat has drinks."

"Give me a minute to get out of my lounge wear."

Bob returned a few minutes later, wearing black jeans and a black turtleneck with a matching black windbreaker. He looked like an agent from some kind of military special operations.

"You don't have a gun, do you?" I asked.

"I'm no Boy Scout, but when I go for a meeting with a corpse, my rule is 'always be prepared.' "

"Leave the gun," I said. "We'll be in a busy club and the odds are far better that we will get pulled over for driving dirty than attacked in public."

"I hope you're right," Bob said, removing the windbreaker, the shoulder holster, and the gun beneath it.

"Have I ever been wrong?"

I was glad Bob had put down his beer or I would have been drenched in a spit take. His guffaw was involuntary and caused him to bend over with the effort. I was amused and insulted all at the same time.

Chapter 28

SNUGGLE AND MEAT was far less crowded than the last time we'd been here. Yet, given it was a weeknight, the fact that anyone was here at all was surprising. My gold Jaeger-LeCoultre indicated it was eleven in the evening.

As we entered through the doorway of the former church, my ears were assaulted by the pounding beat of the band. The band members each wore red makeup and black horns, giving them an oddly demonic appearance. Their name, Blood and Pus, was written in neon above their heads.

The place had a different feel without the hordes of people. We walked over to where Bob and I had met the woman handcuffed to the bar the last time. The bartender looked over at us.

"What are you drinking?"

"Stoli and grapefruit for me," I said.

"I'll take a Jack and Coke," Bob added.

"We're looking for Helga," I said.

"Yeah, a lot of guys are. She's upstairs, but you need an appointment."

"We're old friends. She asked us to come over."

"Upstairs."

The band took up a strange version of "Lookin' for Love," a

song Johnny Lee made famous in the 1980s. The synthesizer mimicked a harpsichord and the drummer and standup bass joined in. The lead singer played rhythm guitar on a red Gibson. He was shirtless, with his entire body painted a deep red. His black leather pants and matching black horns were a sharp contrast to the red.

As we headed over to the stairs, I noticed the band had changed the lyrics to better match their image. They were no longer looking for "love" but for "blood." When we arrived at the stairs, the large bald man we had met the last time we were here greeted us.

"Helga said you were coming. Must have had a good time before."

"Good times," Bob said in a flat voice.

"Head on up," the man said, reminding me of a beefed-up version of Monty Hall on *Let's Make a Deal*. He unhooked the velvet rope to allow us passage. When we had made it up a few stairs, I heard a cough. I looked back to see the man's hand out. I pulled out my wallet and passed him a twenty.

"A little light?" the man said.

"We're guests, not customers," I said, turning around and continuing up the steps.

This time we were alone in the sterile waiting room. Bob sat down and picked up the *Sports Illustrated* swimsuit issue. I walked around, looking for Helga or Beth or whatever she was calling herself. She entered the waiting room from a hidden door.

She was no longer dressed as a sadistic Viking but instead wore tight red-leather pants, high heels, and a corset. Her makeup was cartoonish and her previously red hair was now black and in pigtails.

"Sam, you made it. I see you brought your friend."

"How do you know he's not a customer?"

"You both could be. I am flexible if the price is right."

"Flexible in terms of the money or in terms of what you will do?"

"Both. Follow me. I told Heather you were coming and she agreed to speak with you."

"You do good work," I said. "I thought the two of you didn't get along. I'm surprised she agreed to meet."

I gestured to Bob, who got up to join us. We entered the same room as before. Heather was standing in the center. The first thing that caught my attention was the large pistol in her hand. She wore a red velvet robe. Other than the change in outfit and the gun, she was clearly the woman in the photograph I had taken from Blake's room.

"Beth, please shut the door," she said.

"You don't need a gun," I assured her as I turned to Beth for help.

In response, Beth removed a small handgun from her corset. It was a 9mm with pink grips. She adjusted it in her hand and pointed it at me.

"So, is there a reason you are pointing guns at us?" I asked.

Bob didn't look surprised. "My guess is for the same reason anyone points a gun at anyone," he said. "They want to fucking kill us."

"Don't be silly," I told Bob. "We just have a few questions and have no intention of bothering them after that. Why would they want to kill us?"

"I do enjoy killing in general," Heather said. "Yet, I have also heard a lot about you Mr. Roberts. I feel I will enjoy killing you in particular."

"What if I scream like hell until somebody comes to help?" I said.

She made a sweeping gesture with her arm. "This room is soundproof, of course. It is designed for screaming. That said, please go ahead. It gets me so excited to hear a grown man scream. You will have plenty of time to scream later, so you need not raise your voice now. Let's start with your friend. Can I call you Bob?"

"I prefer to be called 'the guy who is going to rip the head from your neck and piss on the stump,' " Bob said.

In response, Heather's gun exploded in her hand. A bullet struck the door we had just entered with a thud and a hole appeared in the leather apron attached to the hook. Judging by the trajectory of the shot, the bullet had missed the top of Bob's head by inches. The report was ringing in my ears. The room must indeed be soundproof.

"Bob is fine, or Robert, whatever you prefer," Bob said, more agreeable.

"Take off your T-shirt and get into the stocks or I will call you meat puppet with holes in it," Heather said.

I turned to Beth. "Beth, don't listen to her. We can help. Is it your drug problem?"

"I don't have a drug problem," she said. "If I need drugs, no problem. Heather gets them for me. Money, drugs, whatever I want. Sam, you and I are not friends. I paid you and you acted as my lawyer for the money. Heather, on the other hand, is my queen. I would die for her." She nodded at Heather with a sappy smile.

I returned my gaze to Heather. "Why?"

"I will not ask you again," Heather said to Bob. "Take off your fucking shirt and get into the stocks."

Bob did as he was told, lifting the top portion of the device and putting his head and wrists in the proper position. Heather nodded to Beth, who walked around me and closed the top of the contraption, securing Bob's neck and wrists. After locking it with an old brass padlock, she returned to her spot behind me.

"Now, Mr. Roberts, you may select a whip, mace, or riding crop from the wall to correct your friend for his disrespect."

I had a friend from law school who was brought up by her grandmother in Louisiana. If she misbehaved, she was told to go into the backyard and select a switch from an old tree. If the switch was too thin, she would be told to get another and the whupping would be worse. I pondered that dilemma now as I walked over to the wall to select my implement of torture.

I found a bullwhip similar to the type used by Indiana Jones. I hoped it was less formidable than it looked.

Heather stood, arms akimbo, like some evil, hefty Wonder Woman, and said, "Now, Mr. Roberts, we will start with five lashes. If a single lash does not draw blood, we will begin again."

Beth laughed and actually jumped up and down. "Many men have achieved an orgasm by the sting of that whip," she said.

"Isn't that a line from a movie?" I asked.

"Something like that was said in *Waxwork*," Bob commented.

"The one with Paris Hilton?" I asked.

"That's *House of Wax*."

"Then I never saw that one," I said.

"Yes, you have … at my house. It had the kid from *Gremlins* in it."

"Oh yeah," I said, hefting the whip to get a feel for it, "I do remember that. An old house was used for a wax museum and the displays came alive."

Heather lifted her gun. "Hey, I have an idea. Why don't the two of you shut the fuck up before I am forced to clean your brains off the walls?"

"Can I ask one question before the whipping?" I asked.

"Why not?" Heather said.

"Why set up Mr. May? I thought you liked him."

"This has nothing to do with Mr. May," she said. "I never liked or disliked him. I needed Mr. May to gain access to the mirror. Access to the Realm of the Dark Lord. So, despite being a high priestess of this temple, I pretended to be a lowly page."

"Like the people who help knights get on their horses," Bob suggested.

"No, like the people who help shelve books in the library, you idiot," Heather said.

"Why?" I asked.

"What better way to convince an agoraphobic science fiction fanatic to go out with me? I couldn't exactly meet him in a bar;

he never left the fucking house. No, I pretended to be fascinated by his selection of reading materials. It wasn't hard to convince him to invite me to his house. A few spells and the best and only sex in his pathetic life and he was hopelessly in love."

"How can a mirror help you?" I asked.

"A mirror would be a huge help to Heather," Bob said. "Just look at her hair and makeup."

Heather pistol-whipped Bob across the face. He grunted, and blood began to trickle from his mouth and nose. Heather touched the blood with a finger and put it to her mouth.

"This 'bar,' " she explained, "is my temple. It used to be a church. I have defiled the holy site and turned it into the place you see today. To appease the spirit within the mirror, I feed it blood, bone, flesh, and seven herbs and spices. Yet the main ingredient is pain. You, my friends, will soon be dinner. Can we begin with the whip? I want to see blood."

"Who eats blood? Is the mirror a vampire?" Bob asked.

"If you have drunk anything during your stay here, you have drunk blood. A few drops in each glass. Blood is power. It allows me to look into the mirror to see the ancient one trapped within."

"Shit," Bob said. "I'm glad I didn't have a Bloody Mary."

"Enough questions. I may be a priestess, but there are forces far greater than I in this world. You two, however, are not even on the map. Begin with the whip or die now."

I reluctantly lifted the whip I had selected. I was bracing myself for the downward swing, imagining the leather biting into my friend's back.

"This is why I never listen to you!" Bob yelled.

The wind whistled as the whip lashed against Bob's bare back. A welt immediately formed where the leather had struck. Bob grunted as a trickle of blood leaked from where the leather had made contact.

"My ankle!" Bob yelled.

"You stupid twit," Heather said. "The whip was nowhere near your ankle."

I ran closer to Bob to inspect the wound. Heather raised the gun. I could hear a round enter the chamber as she pulled back on the slide.

"Continue!" Heather demanded.

I lifted the whip and brought it down hard. Yet, this time I was too close to Bob to make contact with my friend. This was fine, since I was not aiming for him but for Heather's arm. The arm that held the gun.

I had no experience with whips and missed, of course. My blow still had the desired effect. The whip slashed Heather's face. She dropped the gun as she brought her hands up to her injury. Bob and the stocks blocked me from grabbing the gun, but I did not need it. Instead, I fell to the ground and grabbed Bob's left ankle, which had a Walther PPK strapped to it with a Velcro band. I was indeed pleased that Bob never listened to me.

I fired three times at Heather from my position on the ground and turned to Beth and fired again. I was pleased Bob did not have the safety on since I had no idea where it was. I could not see the impact of my efforts with Heather, but I had a clear view of Beth.

Her neck snapped back as her skull gave way, creating a kaleidoscope of gore on the white wall behind her. I heard a bullet whiz by my head like an angry wasp as Heather got to her feet, holding her gun in front of her. One of her eyes was bruised shut from the strike of the whip. This bruise perhaps impacted her depth perception, causing her to miss with her first shot. I unloaded two more rounds. My depth perception was just fine. A portion of her skull and a good amount of gray matter struck the wall behind her prior to her corpse striking the ground.

"Would you mind getting me out of this torture device?" Bob yelled.

I searched Beth's body and found the key to the padlock, allowing me to open the stocks and release Bob. "This place definitely has an evil vibe to it," I said.

Bob rubbed his wrists. "They will kill us if we aren't careful," he said. "We just wasted their queen."

"There is a back door, remember?"

I handed Bob his gun and removed the gun from Heather's dead hand. I also grabbed Beth's gun with the pink grips. One could never be too careful. For added measure, I kept the whip. Bob put his shirt on, wincing in pain as he did so.

We were about to head down the steps when I stopped. There was something bothering me beyond the blood and corpses. It was a noise. One of my shots had made a strange noise when it hit. I looked at the padded mat against the wall behind the place Heather had been standing.

There was a large hole in the mat where the bullet had struck. I removed the mat to see that it was hiding what appeared to be the door of a large steel dumbwaiter similar to that in Mr. May's room, only this one was a lot bigger. There was only one button pointing downward.

"Any thoughts?" I asked Bob.

"Not a clue."

"Do you have your cell phone?"

"Yes."

I pushed the button and the steel door opened, revealing a space big enough for me to fit into. The smell of old food made my stomach turn.

"I'm taking it down."

"You are kidding me."

"I have to know."

"Curiosity killed the cat."

"Meow."

I crawled in and Bob pushed the button. The door closed and I was trapped in darkness. The smell of rot became overwhelming. I felt the elevator begin its descent.

Chapter 29

~~

A FEW MINUTES later, the door opened. Thrilled to escape from the metal claustrophobic box from hell, I did not look before pulling myself out and getting to my feet. I was in a dank, poorly lit basement that smelled of death.

It took a moment for my vision to adjust. A large bearded man in a white butcher's apron stood in front of a stainless-steel table, the type normally found in a morgue. On top of the table was a man whose head and limbs had been removed. The bearded butcher looked over at the dumbwaiter, shocked at my presence. Raising the bloody cleaver, he began walking toward me.

The gun with the pink grips was in my pocket. I whipped it out and fired four shots. Red flowers appeared on the man's apron and he fell backward to the ground. I could hear him coughing. He gurgled as his lungs filled with blood.

The room had a huge steel hopper with a large crank attached to the side of it against the wall. It looked like a giant version of an antique coffee grinder. I could see a human leg sticking out of the top of the hopper and felt dizzy with disgust. Upon closer inspection, I noted that a steel screen was used to filter the remains with a large steel bucket below. The holes in the filter were maybe a square-centimeter in size. It was clear that after the body was ground up like hamburger, the larger portion would end up sitting on top of the screen, where it would have to be removed. There was an opening in the machine to allow the removal of the larger parts. I noted what appeared to be a garden hoe and an old cast-iron pitchfork that must have been used for that purpose.

In addition to grinding up the bodies, the machine belched steam. I assumed the remains were heated to kill bacteria in an effort to delay spoilage, like pasteurizing milk. I had no expertise on the subject matter, so that was just my best guess.

On the floor near the machine was a black plastic trash can filled with what looked to be white sand. Stenciled on the outside of the can was "Sodium Nitrate." A large metal scoop was pushed part way into the mixture.

On a table next to the opening in the machine was a mound of bones, hair, and skin. The bucket below contained a slurry of human remains. The room also had a pile of clothing and a smaller pile of glasses, jewelry, and teeth, as well as a pile of old buckets stained with rust and blood.

This was a one-man assembly line of horror and death, organized in a manner that would make the Nazis proud. I looked up when I heard a noise and sensed movement. A rat had found its way onto the steel gurney and began to nibble at the stump where a head had once been attached.

The telephone rang in my pocket. It took three rings before I answered. I was completely mesmerized by terror.

"What the hell is going on?" Bob demanded.

"I am in the basement. It is a fucking human butcher shop."

"Shit."

"Is there any way out?"

I looked around and found a door, which opened easily. It led up a staircase.

"I think I can find my way out. I will meet you at the car."

"Be careful."

"You too."

I took some pictures of the chamber of horrors with my telephone and then ran out the door. After heading up a flight of stairs, I located a second door, this one made of solid steel. I was lucky; the door was not locked. It was clear the doors were designed to keep people from getting in, not getting out. That meant the victims were dead before the dumbwaiter brought them downstairs.

I expected to encounter armed assailants but found none. I ran to the car and got in. Bob was in the passenger seat already, breathing hard.

In a few minutes, we were back on the road. I showed Bob my blurry iPhone pictures of the human butcher shop. For a moment I thought he was going to vomit.

"Shit," he groaned, "I think I get the 'meat' part of 'Snuggle and Meat.' "

"I get the 'snuggle' part as well. They had a good time with Helga and Heather before they became 'meat.' "

"Should we call the cops?" Bob asked.

"Let's wait until we are back in town."

"All right."

"Sorry about whipping you."

"No need to apologize. You only created a bloody gash down my back, but no worries, my fucking socks will sop it up like bread sops up gravy at Thanksgiving. Besides, it could have been a lot worse, given the photographs."

"So, no hard feelings."

I turned on the radio. Neil Young was crying out in his nasal voice, "The King is dead but he's not forgotten."

Heather was dead. The war was over and we had won. It was Heather who had been killing people to feed the mirror. Heather and her minions of evil. With Heather gone, the mirror would harm no one else. After all, it had no arms or legs to catch its own food. It was over and we had survived. I could return to my normal life, knowing that once again the world was in balance. At least for now. On top of that, Blake was free.

We could relax and bask in our victory.

Chapter 30

~~~

WHEN WE GOT into town, we drove to the drugstore and I purchased two rolls of tape, gauze, antiseptic, and a bottle of bourbon. From there we returned to my house. I poured Bob a juice glass full of Maker's Mark and handed him a cold Coke from the refrigerator.

Bob took the whiskey and Coke and had a seat on the sofa. I was worried he would get blood on my furniture, but it seemed shallow to complain. I wetted down a few kitchen towels and had Bob remove his shirt. The welt looked painful, but there was no permanent harm done. Bob had finished the bourbon, leaving the Coke untouched.

"I know we have won but it feels unsatisfying," I said while dressing the wound.

"Why, because we still don't know what the mirror does?" Bob said.

"We also don't understand why Mr. May was set up."

Bob stretched out, face down, on the sofa. "There is a mystery to that house, one that goes back to a time before it was built, and we are no closer to an answer."

I sat in the easy chair across from the couch and let out a long sigh. "When I give a closing argument in a criminal case, I tell the jury that sometimes all their questions won't be answered.

That the question is not what happened, but can the state prove beyond a reasonable doubt each element of the offense."

"And I should care for what reason? We aren't in court."

"Okay ...."

"Sorry," he said, propping himself up on his elbows and wincing in pain. "I am feeling a bit snarky. I get that way when I drink whiskey after a whipping."

"I understand. It's just that this case is like dinner without chocolate cake for dessert. I feel good that we have dispatched Heather but not fully satisfied."

"Do you have any ...?"

"Satisfaction, no, 'I can't get no satisfaction.' " I made my lips jut out like Mick Jagger's.

"Cake, you idiot."

I got up and fetched a piece of Black Forest cake and a spray can of whipped cream from the refrigerator. Adding a generous dollop to the cake, I grabbed a fork and placed it on the coffee table in front of Bob. He was sound asleep.

I returned to the kitchen with the cake and ate it while standing at the counter. After I finished, I laid the dish in the sink, along with the fork. I sat down at a small oak writing desk in the living room, picked up the telephone, and dialed the Champaign County Sheriff's Department. I was told to call 911. When I finally was able to get a person on the line, I provided my name and number and informed the operator that I had been at Snuggle and Meat and heard gunshots but gave no further information about the incident.

When they found the bodies, they would of course call me back. The man who guarded the stairs would likely be able to identify Bob and me, and in addition, there were surveillance cameras—although our hosts might have turned them off, given their plan to murder us.

I expected the sheriff to appear at my door with handcuffs and an arrest warrant, but nothing happened. I poured myself two fingers of Maker's Mark, drank it down, and went out onto my back porch to let the cold mix with the warmth of the liquor.

My porch is small and built of treated two-by-fours. There is a large bench-style wicker swing, a stainless-steel gas grill, and a glass table and two chairs. I took a seat on the swing. I could observe my backyard from this vantage point and the apple orchard and pumpkin patch behind it. The orchard and my yard are separated by a waist-high wooden fence on my end and a slightly higher chain-link fence on the side.

It was near Halloween and the pumpkin patch was normally filled with cars. At the moment, of course, the field and parking area was empty. Other than the pumpkins, who waited patiently to be dissected and mutilated by children. The thin layer of frost on the orange gourds reminded me that it was unusually cold for this time of year.

The moon was hidden behind the clouds, giving them an eerie glow. The edges of the clouds were brighter than the middle, as if the light was trying to hold back an ominous dark cottony monster.

I thought of the saying, "Every cloud has a silver lining," and wondered if that was true. Maybe Bob and I had just ended this madness. Perhaps darkness had been held at bay. The evil priestess was dead and Blake was free.

A black crow alighted on the top of the chain-link fence and faced me, its eyes glowing a pale green. The illumination from the sky was behind it and did not appear to be the source of the reflection in its eyes, which seemed to glow from within. I shivered involuntarily.

Back inside the house, I locked the French doors behind me. Bob was still asleep. I went to my bedroom, got undressed, and slipped into bed. As I closed my eyes, the telephone rang.

"Hello," I said.

"This is Deputy Douglas Van Dyke of the Champaign County Sheriff's Department."

"How can I help you?"

"You called about hearing shots at Snuggle and Meat, the bar on Route 150."

"Yes."

"What were you doing there?"

"I was thirsty."

"Mr. Roberts, that establishment is only open one day a week—Saturday. It is not open tonight."

"Are you sure? Did you go out and investigate?"

"I am sure, and yes I did. The bar is most certainly closed. In addition, there are no indications of any criminal activity at that location."

This was odd. "Maybe I was mistaken," I said. "Is there another bar nearby?"

"No, Mr. Roberts. Have you been drinking this evening?"

"Officer, what did you see at the bar?"

"An old church converted into an empty bar. I will give you the benefit of the doubt this once and assume you were 'mistaken.' As a lawyer, you should appreciate that it is preferable to be mistaken than to be charged with obstructing justice."

Something was up with this guy. "Have we met?"

"Nice to know I make an impression. Yes, more than once."

The line went dead. I didn't remember Deputy Van Dyke, but I assumed I had annoyed him in some manner. His tone did not strike me as that of a man I had given flowers or a fluffy kitten to. From his attitude, you'd think I'd had sex with his wife or spit on his doughnut. I would certainly remember if I had done either of those things and I had not. I have a great deal of respect for all doughnuts and most women. Heather, Helga, and Mrs. May might be the exceptions.

I do not mean to imply I respect doughnuts more than people, yet given my run-ins with evil embodied in both men and women, I have found humans to be wanting in the same quality standards I would apply to a breakfast pastry. This is true despite a common internet rumor that one of our country's great doughnut stores allow their product to arrive at the store in a frozen state. All I can say is, it's best when the doughnuts are made right in front of you.

In the past, I have had a problem with officers of the law. I worried that perhaps the deputy had some connection to Heather's organization. I decided to think long and hard before getting involved further.

I was now too ramped up to sleep. I got out of bed and walked to the kitchen. I thought about drinking warm milk, but I rarely keep milk in the house, and when I do, it is unlikely to be fresh. I heated up a cup of sour cherry juice and added cherry brandy and a cinnamon stick. Then I returned to my perch on the back-porch swing. The crow was gone.

I returned to bed a half hour later. When sleep crawled down my body, I let it overtake me.

I was back at the Frost Home, but this time I was not in Mr. May's room but on the second floor, standing in the middle of the compass rose. In front of me was a man with long wavy hair wearing a black suit and long fur coat.

"Good evening," the man said with a slight Irish accent.

"Good evening," I replied.

"Do you not recognize me, good sir?"

"Should I?'

"I am Oscar Wilde. I am an author and playwright. I can only assume that since this is your dream, you at least know of me."

"I saw the movie *The Picture of Dorian Gray* recently."

He cocked his head. "Movie?"

"The motion picture."

"Yes, I know what a motion picture is—the art form was invented around the time I wrote my novel—but a motion picture could hardly be expected to represent my thoughts without sound, colour, or texture. Although, maybe I should say 'color,' you being an American."

"Color and colour are pronounced the same," I told him. "They are only spelled differently."

The word "colour" appeared in the air, written in lime-green Arial font. It evaporated like smoke before my eyes. As I tried to make sense of this, Mr. Wilde continued, "That is how you can tell you are in a dream, dear boy. I don't have to make sense. Have you read *The Picture of Dorian Gray*?"

"Yes, but years ago."

He made a mournful face. "At first the critics were not kind. Did you like it?"

"Yes," I said, "I liked the use of language and the play on words. It has aged well, I might add. Most Victorian books are slow reads and get bogged down in the language. If I might cut to the chase, why are you here? My problem has been resolved."

He wagged his forefinger at me. "You are overly optimistic, dear boy. As I say in the book, 'The basis of optimism is sheer terror.' "

"So there is more ahead?"

"What was the moral of *The Picture of Dorian Gray*?"

"I don't know. Perhaps that beauty can't be fully trusted. Mr. Gray remained young and beautiful but his soul did not reflect his true appearance."

Mr. Wilde made a little slashing gesture in the air. "No."

I tried again. "That the upper class as a whole is suspect."

He shook his head and again slashed the air. "No."

"I'm afraid I am ignorant of the message you intended to convey."

"Balls, if you are not careful, you will go to blazes. The moral is if you want to uncover someone's secrets, search their dratted mansion. What they are hiding, the answer to it all, is in the Frost Home. Shall I write it down for you?"

"So, it did not end with Heather. Will you come with me?"

"Alas, no," he said, making a little moue with his mouth. "I am not real. I am a dream. You must face your fears without me. Besides, I hear the striking of the clock. Do you not hear it?"

I awoke to the sound of my iPhone. I looked at the time before answering. It was five a.m.

"Hello," I said in a sleepy voice.

"Sam, it's Susan. I woke you. I will call back."

Chapter 31

~~~

"No, it's fine. I am awake," I said, truthfully, since hearing her voice drained the sleep from my mind.

"I guess I needed to talk with you."

"I haven't sent an RSV but I plan on attending your pending nuptials."

"It is RSVP, not RSV, the latter being a respiratory virus. You need not bother. We are calling off the wedding."

I tried not to sound happy. "I'm sorry."

She paused. "Are you really sorry or is that an attempt to be polite?"

"Both," I said. "I want you to be happy. If this marriage would have made you happy and you had to call it off, then I am sorry. I won't pretend that I wasn't a little jealous when I got the invite. I also won't pretend that I still don't love you.

"I see."

"Is that why you called off the wedding?"

She sighed. "No ... maybe. No, I do love you, but that is not why I called off the wedding. I still don't see how you and I could have a future. At the same time, I don't see a future with him either. Maybe I am destined to be an old maid."

"I'm not a fortune teller," I said, "although I knew a fortune teller once … but things didn't turn out as she predicted. Anyway, I am sure you will never be an 'old maid.' "

"You knew a fortune teller?"

"Aren't you getting a bit off topic?"

"You would think a fortune teller would know what was going to happen, unless she wasn't very good at it."

"No she did have the gift. You don't want to talk about yourself and the wedding, do you?"

"I don't know. You have been my best friend for so long, and it has been hard not being able to talk to you. Yet now that I have you on the telephone, I don't know what to say."

"Do you want me to talk to you as a best friend or a former lover?"

"I don't know."

I guessed it was best to assume she wanted friendly advice. "As a best friend I would point out that maybe you are just having cold feet. You should look into your own heart and decide if you love this man. I assume a part of you must love him or you wouldn't have agreed to the union. You have many interesting traits, but you have never been frivolous."

"And as a former lover?"

"I love you. How could I not at some level be happy you are calling off the wedding?"

Another sigh. "I have a lot to think about."

"I know."

"Maybe we could get together and talk."

"Let's give it some time. I want you to think about it without my influence. I will give you a call in a couple of weeks and if you still want to get together I will be there with bells on."

"You have bells?"

"Of course."

"I love you."

"I know," I said, giving my best impression of Han Solo.

She hung up—or ended the call. She might still have a phone on a cradle. There had been pain and sadness in her voice. I also felt pain, but despite that, I was unspeakably happy. Yet, was that fair? I couldn't change and she needed me to change. I have seen people who were presumably in love do horrid things to each other during divorce proceedings. It would be better to have Susan marry someone else than for the two of us to hate each other.

Of course, I could never hate Susan. Not even if she stuck a fork in my eye and danced the Macarena on my bleeding head.

Well, maybe if she did all of that.

Chapter 32

~~~

I WANDERED INTO the kitchen.

"Who was that?" Bob's voice rose from the sofa.

"Susan," I said.

"I thought you two no longer spoke."

"She is calling off the wedding," I said, putting the kettle on.

"Because she wants to get back with you?"

"No," I said, walking into the living room and sitting across from Bob, "at least I don't think so. I guess she decided she is not ready to get married."

He sat up on the couch and stretched. "You must be as happy as a dog with two tails."

"No, it is still up in the air. I don't know if I should be clam-like in my happiness or down in the mouth."

He frowned. "Since when have we talked in clichés?"

"You started it."

"Well, people who use clichés definitely aren't the brightest bulbs in the box."

The kettle whistled. "Agreed," I said as I stood up, "no more clichés. I have been thinking about this party at the Frost Home."

"Do share."

"Give me a moment." I made a cup of Earl Grey for me and

an instant coffee for Bob, then returned to the living room. As I put the coffee in front of Bob, I began, "Well, I had a dream …."

Bob snorted. "If you are going to quote from Martin Luther King's speech, I have already heard it."

"No, this one involves Oscar Wilde, and I will cut to the chase. It did not end with Heather. That house hides some very dark secrets."

"Well," Bob said, sipping his coffee and making a face, "I hope you've learned your lesson, because I am not going to that party unarmed. By the way, 'cut to the chase' … isn't that a cliché?"

"Your mother is a cliché."

"Real mature," he scoffed. "I am supposed to be the immature one."

"Sorry, this has got me a little upset. I am not myself."

He put the coffee cup down. "You know what I like to do when I am upset."

"Let me guess, go to Mary Ellen's for breakfast?"

Bob put a finger to his nose. I responded by pushing up my nose just a bit and making a pig grunt. Bob laughed at my juvenile gesture.

"You realize the pig grunt thing is Susan's," he said.

"Hell, she doesn't have a corner on pig references."

"Speaking of pigs, I'm not sure you heard me the first time: I don't intend to have to haul our bacon out of the fire without an arsenal this time. So don't tell me to leave my gun behind."

"Agreed. I heard you the first time. Do you have one of those mini Uzis I can borrow?"

"In fact, I just obtained a Micro Uzi SMG with a twenty-five-round clip. It would be perfect for you. I prefer a gun I can aim with greater precision. Yet, given your skills with a weapon, the point, pray, and shoot method is good for you."

We got dressed and headed out to the Mary Ellen's in downtown Champaign. Bob got the Horseshoe and a cup of coffee while I had the Number Seven, which included corn beef hash with basted eggs, dry toast and a cup of hot tea.

After we ordered, Bob said, "We know that whatever is behind this magic mirror or haunted house or whatever the hell it is has been around a lot longer than Blake, his mother, or Heather."

"How do we know that?" I asked.

"The history of the place goes back to a time before there was a house. Remember what the son of Black Hawk said."

Bob was gesturing a little too close to my face with his fork. Feeling vaguely threatened by the implement, I gently moved his hand aside. "So we should be looking for Native American mythical creatures?"

Bob laid the fork down but kept up the broad gestures. "Most of those myths deal with physical manifestations of creatures in nature or some kind of animal-human hybrid. Black Hawk's son said that the land itself was cursed."

"So," I said, "do we believe the mirror is a portal or a trap?"

"The mirror must have captured the evil presence that was a part of the land."

"Why do you think that?" I said. "Maybe the land is just as it was and the mirror is simply on the land."

We paused as the waitress brought my tea and his coffee.

Taking a sip of coffee, he replied, "I thought of that, but I don't think so."

"Why?"

"You said the land was barren, no trees or grass. Yet, the house has grass and trees, even if it is not a forest. In addition, there was blood all around the mirror."

I nodded. "The mirror is definitely the center of all this. Just being in the same room with it gives me the heebie-jeebies."

He laughed. "Old dolls, soft tofu, uni, masks, lenticulars, lentils, and episodes of *Clutch Cargo* all give you the heebies."

"Uni is made of the gonads of a sea urchin," I said, "and that is just plain creepy. In addition, everyone gets the heebies from a cartoon with people's real mouths. Besides, given what we have been through—"

Bob interrupted me. "Fine, you win. Besides, in this case, I think your instincts are dead on."

"So, the mirror must be evil if it feeds on blood. If we break the mirror, do you think that will free the evil spirit, for lack of a better name?"

Bob raised his eyebrows and started fiddling with his cutlery again. "Perhaps it will free the spirit and allow it to take over the world or allow it to settle in the land where it was prior to the mirror being made. Either way, worse than keeping it locked away in the mirror. Plus, the need for blood does not make it evil."

I frowned. "How do you get that?"

"Thomas Jefferson said, 'The tree of liberty must be refreshed from time to time with the blood of patriots and tyrants.' Blood is sometimes needed for change, and change can be good."

I threw up my hands. "I am at a loss. What are your thoughts? What do we do?"

"Arm ourselves to the teeth, show up at the party, and hope some course of action comes to mind. If we spill the blood of evil, I am cool with that."

"That's your solution to everything."

"What are your ideas?"

I shrugged. "Got nothing."

"I hope they have shrimp puffs."

"You don't have to do this."

"Dude, I would feel awful if you died alone."

"I won't be alone," I said. "I will be with an evil mirror and the rest of the party."

"Either way, I want to be there. I need someone to bitch at in the afterlife. Complain that you got me killed and all."

Good ol' Bob. "Thanks," I said.

"No problem."

We ate in relative silence, with only Bob's enthusiastic

chewing and slurping as an accompaniment. It was nice to see that his appetite was back. My mind was more on the mirror than my hash. After breakfast, I was going to stop by the insurance agent and ask about the cost of life insurance. I didn't have a wife or child to leave my estate to, yet the odds of my dying were pretty good. This was an opportunity to beat the actuaries at the insurance company, and that doesn't happen too often. Those dudes are better than Las Vegas bookies when they have all the information.

I was obviously not going to tell them I was walking into the haunted house from Hell this Halloween. Maybe I could give Susan a bit of a surprise after I was sliced and diced and fed to a hungry mirror. Nothing like a million bucks to erase those feelings of sadness.

Maybe I was being melodramatic. There was no reason to believe that this party on Halloween was more than a celebration of my legal victory against the man. Yet, I couldn't shake the feeling that it was much more than that, most likely a confrontation against the forces of evil. Maybe my past was making me paranoid. Yet, bitter experience told me to trust my intuition.

Chapter 33

～～

I SPENT THE next couple of weeks working and keeping my mind off the party on Halloween. I planned to go to sleep early on October 30 but called Susan before I got into bed.

"Sam, it is good to hear from you." She sounded tired.

"I was thinking we could get together. How about brunch on November first?"

"Why not tomorrow?" she said in a perkier voice. "We could do the Halloween thing."

"I can't. I have plans I can't get out of."

"A date?"

"No, a party, but it is business related. No way to get out of it."

"Cool. November first works great. When and where?"

"Golden River at eleven?"

"I will be there."

"I love you."

"I know," she said.

I got into bed and tried to sleep. Nightmarish images flitted by—none that made any sense. I was plagued by a sense of dread, as if some malevolent force was hiding just beyond my vision. At around three in the morning, I must have finally drifted into a deep sleep. I awoke at six as the sun was beginning to rise. I felt worse than if I hadn't slept at all.

It was the day of the party and perhaps the last day of my time on Earth. I got up and went to the kitchen to make a cup of tea. Since there was no point in trying to go back to sleep, I put on a white terry-cloth robe and slippers and headed into the living room.

I turned on the television. Scooby and the gang were running from a phantom through an old Southern mansion. The green ghost rattled its chains and a chill danced down my spine. I turned off the television.

I sat on the sofa drinking tea and allowing the morning to wash over me. I tried to think of something other than the party and that damn mirror, but with no success. I felt as if I had all the pieces but no ability to put them together. It was like a jigsaw puzzle with no picture on the lid. No, it was more complex than that. Perhaps a better analogy would be if I was handed a string of DNA and asked to sketch the animal it came from. I had the information; it was just in a form I couldn't comprehend.

I made breakfast. I was unlikely to die of old age so I decided on a three egg mushroom and cheese omelet, sausages, and a custard-filled donut with chocolate icing. Just as I was about to eat, my iPhone rang.

"Hello," I said.

"Dude, what's up?" Bob replied.

"I'm in shock," I said. "It's six something in the morning. I have never know you to be awake this early."

"Couldn't sleep."

"Me neither, but the party starts at eight this evening. We have a lot of time to kill. So to speak."

"Who said, 'There's never enough time to do all the nothing you want'?"

"You. You just said it."

"I meant originally, I think it was Bill Watterson."

"From *Calvin and Hobbs*?"

"One and the same, but let's not kill all this time."

I took a sip of tea. "What did you have in mind?"

"I bit of recognizance and a lot of preparation."

"You should have been a Boy Scout," I said, although I just couldn't picture it. "When do we start?"

"No time like the present."

"I just made breakfast," I protested. "Give me an hour."

"What did you make?"

"Eggs, sausages, and a donut."

"You made a donut? I am impressed."

"The Old Donut Shop made the donuts. A hen made the eggs, and a turkey made the sausage. I just put it all on a plate."

"The turkey's mother made the turkey," Bob said. "A poultry company made the sausage."

"Thanks for the clarification."

"I will be there in twenty minutes. Make some coffee as well."

"See you then."

Bob arrived in less than fifteen minutes. He managed to eat an omelet, two sausages, and three donuts. With his love of guns and donuts, he should have been a police officer.

We began to talk about our plans for the party. Although I could not imagine how we could prepare for the unknown, I had little doubt Bob had some ideas. It might not be a good plan but any plan was better than none.

After breakfast, we agreed to meet at Bob's house in twenty minutes. Bob was the one with the equipment. This gave me time to pull myself together. After Bob left, I put on a black suit with a black shirt and a maroon tie. I was not trying to look like Johnny Cash, I just wanted an outfit that would allow me to fit in at the party but also disappear in the dark.

On the way to Bob's, I stopped at the drugstore to pick up a four pack of Red Bull and a bottle of Pepto-Bismol. I bet James Bond never had to pick up a bottle of Pepto before heading to the headquarters of some arch nemesis. Although if he did, he would probably combine his Pepto with an energy drink in a cocktail shaker and have it served shaken, not stirred.

I arrived at Bob's twenty-two minutes after we had left my house. He had apparently used that time to turn on a movie I had never seen—*Constantine,* starring Keanu Reeves.

Bob had assembled a small arsenal on his coffee table. He laid the guns out on an old Mexican blanket in order of largest to smallest. There were five guns, four knives, what looked like a grenade, and two pairs of night-vision binoculars.

"What's with the flick? I figured we were set for an action movie."

Bob sat down and pointed to the spot next to him on the couch. "Sit. I want you to see a scene in this movie."

"Which scene? How will I know?"

"Just watch."

It didn't take long to get to the scene. Constantine performs an exorcism that traps a demon in a mirror and the mirror is shattered, presumably destroying the demon. I understood why Bob wanted me to see the scene.

"So you think we need to destroy the mirror?"

He shook his head. "No, I actually think it's a bad idea. A demon has got to be less dangerous trapped in a mirror than released. Seven years of bad luck and all."

"So, what is the point of making me watch?"

"It's just kind of cool. I will put on some James Bond or *Rambo* if you prefer."

"I prefer Bond, James Bond."

"Cool," Bob said.

Bob picked up the remote and switched to *Goldfinger,* which he had saved on his DVR. He then picked up the micro Uzi on the blanket. When I'd mentioned an Uzi earlier, I had of course been kidding.

"It is a nine-millimeter with a clip that holds twenty-five rounds. Not the most accurate of guns, but you asked for it." As he spoke, Bob demonstrated the folding butt and the manual safety as well as a grip safety that had to be depressed prior to firing. "This gun goes from semi-automatic to fully automatic as well."

I pointed at the weapon. "That is the smallest machine gun I have ever seen but it is still too big for my pocket."

"I have a long overcoat that would be perfect."

"So, possession of a firearm without a FOID Card is illegal, carrying a concealed weapon without authorization is illegal, and carrying a fully automatic weapon is illegal. If we get pulled over, we will be spending some quality time in the pokey."

Bob waved his hand in the air in an inconclusive gesture. "I think the odds are better that we will need it at the party than we will get pulled over on the way there. It *is* Halloween, after all. The police will think it is just part of our costumes."

"What do you intend to bring?"

"Walther PPK, just like James."

"What's with the grenade?"

He picked it up and held it out so I could see it better. "Smoke grenade. I bought it at a swap meet. I don't think we will need it tonight, but I thought you'd think it was cool."

Bob put the grenade back down, carefully, and picked up two small knives. The knives did not have grips and looked like hacksaw blades with a tip. "I have Velcro ankle bands these fit into. I also have a plastic folding knife that fits in my wallet."

"What, no laser weapons or exploding cigarette lighters?"

He made a sweep with his arms, Carol Merrill style, that took in the entire array. "Afraid not, but take any other weapons you think might help. Otherwise I will pack them up and put the rest in my van."

"The Uzi and the ankle knives should work for me."

"Cool."

In truth the weapons provided me little comfort in the face of a supernatural enemy. Yet, clearly Bob felt better with a gun in his hand. I had to admit, guns have saved my life many times. In my experience, even when ghosts, spirits, and demons are involved, there is usually someone somewhere in the background pulling the strings. A gun may stop the flesh and blood wizard behind the curtain. At the same time there was something in that house that I was fairly certain could not be stopped by a piece of lead.

"I've been thinking," I said, "given that it is Halloween, maybe we could dress up ... hide our true identities. If the soiree was big enough, we could blend in for a while before they know who we are."

"I might have something," Bob said. He left the room and returned with two masks that went over the nose and were held on with elastic: a rubber pig snout and a bird beak.

I made a face. "A little weak, for a disguise. Besides, do you really think they are not going to check to see what guests will be at the party?"

"Can't hurt."

"Fine, give me the pig."

In reality there was not much else to do to prepare for an unknown enemy. We spent most of the afternoon watching television and avoiding talking about what lay ahead. The party was at eight, but we agreed to leave an hour early to scope out the mansion.

At five, Bob showered and put on a pair of black pants, a black suit jacket, and a black T-shirt. The jacket was oversized to conceal his gun. We both fastened the Velcro bands holding the knives on our ankles. Bob gave me an oversized black coat with an inside pocket to hold the Uzi. He kept his gun in a shoulder holster.

We decided on dinner at the Groovy Sushi and Smoothie. There being a good chance this would be our last day on Earth, I felt we deserved sushi and smoothies. We took Bob's van, in part because there was so much audio equipment in the back that if we were pulled over, the cops would be unlikely to locate all our guns.

There at the restaurant, among the familiar neon lights and

the indoor koi pond, I thought I would feel more comfortable. I didn't. The waitress recognized us and immediately approached and bowed in a formal greeting. We were taken to a small table near the back of and ordered the sushi for two along with a Kobe beef appetizer. I asked for a smoothie and Bob opted for a decanter of a sweet plum wine.

Bob's wine came in a ceramic container shaped like a fat samurai, and the waitress brought two small clay cups that were glazed on the inside. My smoothie was in a large pink-colored glass. It was a sharp contrast to the dark maroon contents of the drink. The waitress left and returned a few minutes later with strips of beef on bamboo skewers next to a pile of bamboo shoots, pickled ginger, and an eggplant-shaped bowl filled with a dark liquid.

"Yui?" Bob said. I was surprised he knew her name, but Bob was good that way.

"Yes, do you need something else?" she replied.

"You are of Japanese descent, aren't you?"

"I was born in this country. My parents are Japanese, or were. They're dead."

"I am sorry for your loss, but could I ask you a question?"

"Of course."

"Do the Japanese have any myths, stories, or folklore about mirrors?"

This seemed like a strange conversation to have with a waitress, but Yui didn't hesitate to answer. "My grandparents were Shinto, and as a child we went to a Shinto shrine with an octagon mirror within it. I was also told a story of a sun deity being coaxed out of a cave using a mirror. Does that help?"

"Can you think of anything else?"

She tilted her head. "Why do you ask?"

"My friend here is writing a blog about scary stories involving mirrors."

"Oh, I did not know you wanted scary stories. I cannot think of anything else." The waitress left with a bow.

"I am impressed you remembered her name and a little embarrassed that we have been coming here for five years and I didn't," I said.

"She was wearing a name tag."

"Oh." I paused, then said, "You realize this may all be silly. The craziness may have ended with Heather's death. My dream is the only reason we have to believe the threat is not over."

"Your dreams have a good track record," Bob said.

We sat in silence when the waitress returned with the sushi. She placed it on the table, but rather than walk away, she hesitated. After an awkward pause, she looked over at Bob.

"My grandmother would cover the mirror in her bedroom when she slept."

"Why?" Bob asked.

"She said she had heard that covering the mirror would protect her from a malevolent spirit from some other place that would come at night and suck her energy until she was no more. It was of course a silly superstition."

"Is there a name for this malevolent creature?"

Brow furrowed, she gave it a moment's thought. "I don't remember. I was only a girl when she died. I do remember that when she passed on, I wondered if the creature in the mirror had caused it. Of course I am no longer a girl and don't believe in such nonsense."

"Thank you," Bob said.

After Yui walked away, Bob seemed lost in thought. After a few minutes he said, "Have you seen the movie *The Ring*?"

I nodded. "Sure. Cursed videotape, girl comes out of a television, vengeful spirit. I think I saw it with you."

"It was based on a Japanese flick, *Ringu*. A girl coming out of a mirror at night is not so different than coming out of a television set."

"So you think the mirror at the house contains a malevolent Japanese spirit?" I asked.

"No, but I think every culture has some myth about mirrors

as gateways or traps. Breaking a mirror is bad luck. The need to cover mirrors when someone dies. Malevolent creatures hiding within or beyond the surface of the glass."

I picked up my glass with its dark-red smoothie. "Don't forget vampires. They hate mirrors."

"That is because mirrors reflect not just a person's image but a part of the person's soul. Vampires lack souls. Thus, they don't appear in mirrors."

"You never saw *Blacula*. That African Prince had a lot of soul," I pointed out.

Bob had his glass to his mouth but put it down, swallowing hard to avoid a spit take. "You are now questioning me on my horror movie knowledge. I have watched *Blacula* and *Scream Blacula Scream* any number of times. There is even a pornographic spoof of *Blacula* called *Lust of Blackula*. I haven't seen that one. It never made it to Netflix."

Bob is a bit sensitive on the subject of his horror-film expertise. "Of course," I said, "I didn't intend to question your encyclopedic knowledge of horror movies."

We finished eating and paid our bill. I left a large tip since we had not only ordered food but inquired about Japanese mythology. Not to mention that the food and service were excellent.

I was in no hurry to leave the restaurant. It would have been simple not to go to the party. We could have gone home and forgotten the whole thing. The only reason to go to the party was for the purpose of looking for trouble. We drove to the Frost Home in relative silence.

We were early and Bob parked across the street. The house looked different. The round stained-glass window with a daisy-like design now looked ominous. The glow of the incandescent light within the house made the glass appear an eerie yellow. The center of the flower resembled the pupil of an eye with the straight lines from the petals forming the iris. It all called to mind a malevolent Cyclops.

"Shit I just thought of something?"

"What? Bob asked.

"We didn't leave a bowls of candy out for the Trick or Treaters in front of our houses. What if our houses get TP'd or egged?"

"My guess would be that is the least of our troubles."

The driveway and front porch were lined with luminary bags. The large stone piles in front of the house each had a lit jack-a-lantern balanced on top. The lights on the second and third floor of the house all appeared to be on, while the first floor was almost completely dark. The driveway was already occupied by two cars and a van. One car was a black Cadillac and the other, a silver Mercedes four-door sedan. The van belonged to a catering company, Miche's. This was a good sign, since they always served excellent food.

As we watched, a red Maserati pulled into the driveway. I recognized it as belonging to Charles Frisk, whose fast-food chain was known for providing organic alternatives to burgers and fries. Although the grilled tofu tortilla was good and the service excellent, his character was questionable. There were rumors he sexually assaulted an employee before his business acquired a national following. Apparently he was never charged with the offense. In addition there was a lawsuit claiming his "organic" tofu was anything but.

An older Rolls Royce Silver Shadow arrived. A lawyer I recognized got out, along with a young blonde woman who was not his wife. This was followed by a red Ferrari. I recognized the older man who emerged but could not recall why. Two more cars arrived—a silver Jaguar and a red Corvette. In addition, a black Chevy SUV and a black Lincoln SUV pulled up. Four men in leather trench coats went up to the front door and entered the house. There were various other luxury cars parked around the home and on the side street.

Yet, there was something missing. It took me a moment to realize there were no children in costume anywhere near the property. This further confirmed what I already knew: this house was creepy as hell.

I suspected this was a very exclusive party, and I was the guest of honor, just as a turkey is the "guest of honor" at a Thanksgiving feast. We were already ten minutes late for the party and I nudged Bob, indicating we should go in. He looked at the time on his cell phone and nodded as he opened the door. We each put on our rubber noses.

Chapter 34

~~~

W E GOT OUT of the van and walked up the lighted walkway. Before I could ring the bell, the arched oak door opened, sending a chill jittering along my spine. Ms. Frost's assistant answered. He was wearing a tuxedo with a black bow tie and cummerbund. Knowing Malcolm Conrad was mute, I took it upon myself to introduce Bob.

"This is my friend, Bob Sizemore."

Malcolm Conrad bowed slightly and pointed to the stairs. There was no reason to further hide our identity from Malcomb. First of all, he clearly recognized me and additionally, who could he tell? When we arrived at the second floor, the stairs opened up on the center of the room where the compass rose was drawn on the wooden planks. The door to Mr. May's room had been removed and replaced by an archway. I recalled that the door frame had been cracked when the police broke in, so it had probably been just as easy to remove the entire door.

Mr. May was an exceedingly private person. I couldn't imagine he would be pleased with the change. I suspected I would not want a party in his living space either, but that was where we were celebrating.

As we walked through the entrance, Mr. Avery came up to shake my hand. He wore a tuxedo and a half mask of a black crow's beak and face. Behind him were four men in matching black suits but no ties. Their white shirts had rounded collars and frog buttons like those worn by the actors in Kung Fu movies. One was Asian, one was Caucasian, and the remaining two were African American. All four were huge, muscular, and serious.

"Oh, I do apologize," said Mr. Avery. "I am afraid Mrs. May was so shocked by recent events that she cannot abide the thought of weapons in her home. These gentlemen are here to search everyone. They searched me as well, to give you an idea of their thoroughness." He raised a hand to silence me. "I know, I find it incredibly rude as well, but if you do have any weapons, they will be returned after the party."

"I would rather not be searched," I said.

In response, one of the men removed a handgun from his suit coat and pointed it at me. The other men patted us down, first me and then Bob.

"Why do they get guns?" Bob asked.

"Life is unfair," Mr. Avery said.

"So, are we guests or prisoners?" I asked.

"I am not into labels, Mr. Roberts. By the way, I like the pig snout. It adds something. Perhaps an apple in the mouth might complete the look. Think of this little gathering as a Halloween luau where a pig is always the guest of honor."

I removed the rubber snout and Bob removed his beak. Clearly there was no point in disguise. The Asian man walked up to me and removed the Uzi from my coat and the white guy found and removed the Waltham PPK from Bob's. Mr. Avery put on a show of being shocked. He waggled a scolding finger at me.

"It is considered rude in some circles to come to a party armed to the teeth."

"Yes," I said, "I went to charm school as a child but was asked to leave. You see, I suggested that my instructor would benefit by shoving her salad fork up her ass. Please don't tell anyone about my lapse of manners." I gave Mr. Avery a coquettish look that included batting my eyelashes.

"Yes, Mr. Roberts, it requires no stretch of the imagination to picture you acting boorishly. Do come in and enjoy the party. Mrs. May has spared no expense for this soiree in your honor. Prime rib, caviar, lobster, and all manner of hors d'oeuvres." Mr. Avery pointed to a large table in the area where Mr. May's bed had been the last time I was here.

"Is that a cutting station?" Bob asked, pointing to a large prime rib under a heat lamp where a man in a chef's hat was carving. "Shit, there is a whole poached salmon next to that," Bob added excitedly.

"Are you out of your mind?" I said. "They just took our guns and are going to hold us prisoner or eat us like a pig at a luau. Our murder does not seem out of the question. Besides, we ate less than an hour ago."

"Let's not be melodramatic, Mr. Roberts," Mr. Avery said. "No one is going to eat you. Frankly, you do not look the slightest bit appetizing."

Bob headed for the buffet and I followed. It appeared Mr. Avery had nothing more to say to us and walked in the opposite direction. On the positive side, no one had taken our ankle knives. On the negative side, what the hell good is a knife at a gunfight?

Bob started filling a plate with all manner of food. There were maybe eight members of the caterer's staff, a bartender, the four bodyguards, and perhaps twenty guests. If I had to guess, most of the people in the room were not packing heat.

I looked over at the mirror, which was still in the same location. Next to it sat Mr. May in a wheelchair. I had begun to walk in his direction when Dr. Hyde stopped me. He was wearing a brown suit and had his face half painted to look like Two-Face in the batman comics. It seemed an appropriate costume. I found it odd, given the holiday, how few people were in costume.

The guests as a whole were dressed as if at a formal dinner. A few wore tuxedos but most were in suits. The women all wore cocktail dresses. A few of the guests carried masquerade masks on sticks or wore simple masks that covered their upper faces.

"Mr. Roberts," Dr. Hyde said, "what a pleasure."

"I am sure. I was just walking over to speak with Mr. May."

Dr. Hyde cleared his throat. "I will go with you," he said. "I am afraid his treatment has not been as successful as we hoped."

We walked toward Mr. May, who was staring into nothingness, unaware of our approach. I had a feeling Dr. Hyde was not going to tell me any good news.

"What is the matter with him?" I asked.

He uttered something like a deranged giggle. "That reminds me of a joke."

"What the hell are you talking about?"

"An asparagus is walking down the street and gets hit by a car. The doctor is doing everything he can for him in surgery but things are not going well. He steps out of the operating room, and guess what he says to the asparagus's wife?"

"What are you talking about?"

"No, he says I have good news and bad news. The good news is he is going to live. The bad news is he is going to be a vegetable for the rest of his life." Dr. Hyde began to laugh outright now, a dry, humorless sound.

I am not violent by nature. I didn't even realize I had hit Dr. Hyde until I found myself standing over him, kicking him in the ribs. He looked up at me, blood trickling from his nose, without surprise or anger. He just laughed.

"Just as I thought," he said, "no sense of humor."

Before I could finish pummeling his face into oatmeal, two of the men in dark overcoats had pinned my arms behind my back. I could hear the familiar voice of Mrs. May behind me. I heard Bob's voice too, but I couldn't make out what he was saying other than a few choice curse words.

"You are correct, Mr. Avery," Mrs. May said. "They could not manage to be civilized for long enough to enjoy the party. What a shame. It is one thing to bring guns but quite another to strike the good doctor. Bring them to me."

Bob was in a similar position, his arms held behind his back by one of the large bodyguards. I could see from the pain in his eyes that they were not being any gentler with him than they were with me.

It was clear this woman was about to pronounce sentence upon us.

Chapter 35

~~

THERE WAS NOWHERE to run, so there was no reason for anyone to aim a gun at us. The large men were more than a sufficient guarantee of our compliance. Yet, despite our hosts' obvious advantage, they were still pointing three pistols in our direction. Mr. Avery, the good doctor, and a man I did not recognize were all armed. Mr. Avery had obviously lied when he claimed he'd also been searched for weapons.

Mrs. May walked up to us, tapping her cane. She wore an old-fashioned black dress with high-collared white blouse. Her long gray hair was wild and fell to her shoulders. She was old and blind and a small part of me felt sympathy for her.

"What do you intend to do with us?" Bob asked.

Mrs. May touched the tip of her cane to his forehead and dragged it down his body until it hit the ground with a thud. She then raised it, and with all her might struck Bob hard in the testacies, causing him to go limp. The man holding him released his grip so that he fell hard against the ground.

Bob tried to roll into a fetal position so he could catch his breath, but the man behind him lifted him to his feet, where he wobbled, looking like he wanted to throw up. I no longer felt the least bit of sympathy for this awful woman.

"In answer to your question, I believe you and Mr. Roberts

will be going for a ride to the police station." Bending down so that only Bob and I could hear, she added, "There will be an accident on the way. Neither of you will survive. So sad."

"Why do this to your own son? Why feed him to that … thing?" I said, pointing to the mirror.

Bending over again, she said in a whisper, "Why should I bother to tell you anything? You're already dead."

"Don't we deserve to know why we are going to die?" I asked.

"Why not just feed us to the mirror?" Bob added, his voice muffled by the pain. "Why waste the blood?"

"You did a good job for my son. Of course you were not supposed to do a good job and as a result my son is a fucking vegetable. That is okay; I don't blame you for that." She looked over at Mr. Avery, who she clearly did blame.

"You are too kind. May I ask why you wanted me to lose the case?" I asked.

"I needed my son out of the house so I could try with someone else. The mirror didn't like him and Heather was a greedy bitch. The problem is that my son owns the house … or, I should say, it is held in joint tenancy. I couldn't force him out when he didn't want to leave."

"So, if he were found guilty but mentally ill, you could do what you wanted, but not if he were found not guilty," I said.

"Yes, that was a problem."

"Now, however, the good doctor has made it so that he is in no position to oppose you," I said.

"Mr. Roberts, you are not half as stupid as Mr. Avery led me to believe," Mrs. May said.

"I didn't say he was stupid," Mr. Avery clarified. "In fact, I assumed he was smart enough to keep the money without making waves. Now he is neither smart nor stupid, he is simply dead."

"The mirror is a portal to another world, isn't it?" Bob asked.

"Did I miss a transition?" Mrs. May asked. "No, the mirror is not a portal to another world. It is a prison. A prison for a god."

"I get it. The prisoner gets hungry so you fed your son to him," I said.

Mr. Avery lifted his gun. "Why are you wasting time with this?" he asked.

Mrs. May turned to Mr. Avery. "It is my time to waste. May I continue?"

"Forgive my interruption," Mr. Avery said, making it clear that she was the boss.

Mrs. May continued, "You obviously think you understand, but you do not. Before the Indians, before mankind, there was the Creator. A goddess who helped to seed our world with life. She had a brother, however, who fed on the life she created. They were twins, yin and yang, opposite forces that formed a whole."

"That is certainly common in mythology," Bob said when she paused for breath. "Some Native American tribes believed that Gluskap was the Creator and had an evil twin, Malsum. In ancient Egypt there were the twins Geb, the earth god, and Nut, the sky god. You can find twin gods, one good and one evil, in Greek, Roman, Hindu, and Norse traditions."

"Not to mention that episode of *The Simpsons* where Bart has an evil twin," I added.

"It is like God and the Devil," Bob said.

Mrs. May listened to our interruptions with a vague look of disgust, though her ancient face came by that expression naturally. "Perhaps," she said, "most of mankind would think so, but there was neither good nor evil intent in this story. They were what they were; she was a creator and he was a destroyer. Is mankind evil for killing plants and eating animals? We kill to survive. They were twins, but neither was good nor evil. They simply had complementary natures.

"When life evolved, the sister was nowhere to be found. The native peoples prayed to the brother and sacrificed the living to him because they were afraid he would destroy them if he were not fed. They would slit the throats of their enemies and bathe the land in blood. Soon the land became so saturated with blood that no crops, trees, or grass would grow there."

I broke in, "Blood is so salty, it was like sowing the ground with salt."

"Yes," Mrs. May said, "like in the Bible. Judges 9:45 states, 'And Abimelech fought against the city all that day, and he took the city, and slew the people that was therein, and beat down the city, and sowed it with salt.' "

Bob nodded. "Without life nearby, the brother was trapped on the barren land."

"Yet you have trapped him further, capturing him within the mirror, haven't you?" I demanded.

Mrs. May tilted her head in my direction and stared at me with her blind eyes. "Not me. The mirror came with the house. Mr. Frost was a sailor. He learned about magic from different cultures throughout the world. He learned even more from his wife, who had the real power. When she came across the land, she could sense the magic here.

"Mr. Frost bought the barren land for a song and built this house here. His wife was able to pull the creature from the land and trap it in the mirror. She had far greater command of the craft than I."

"What use was the mirror?" I asked.

Bob answered, "They could now address the creature directly and try and control him. In exchange for blood, he would tell them things. He would advise them as to what land to buy and investments to make."

I looked at Bob and added, "Plus, the mirror was safer, wasn't it?"

She rapped her cane on the ground. "Very good, both of you. Yes, the creature could see into the future. In exchange for being allowed to live, it would provide financial advice. You are also right, Mr. Roberts. It was indeed safer. What if people accidently died on the land or life returned? The brother could escape. Yet, within the wood and glass of the mirror, the only life it could feed off was what was provided to it."

I tried to lift my arm to scratch my head, but one of the men behind me twisted it painfully behind my back. After a nod from Mr. Avery, he released it.

"The Frosts fed it just enough for it to remain alive and do as they asked," Bob said.

"Yes, until the mirror tricked Mr. Frost by convincing him that his son had died."

"So you took over where the Frosts left off," I said.

"I am a very powerful sorcerer, Mr. Roberts. My mother was even more powerful and that was why they thought her mad. She acquired the house and harnessed its magic. I inherited the house when she died; actually, I killed her, but that is another story. I became very rich and powerful. I also helped all the people in this room to become rich and powerful." Mrs. May spread her arms to encompass the room.

I now thought I understood. "Yet," I said, "it stopped working for you. The creature in the mirror stopped giving advice and stopped appearing when you spilled blood, so you moved your son in."

"Yes, it feeds on the person it gives advice to. It took my sight and my soul and left me with nothing it wanted, nothing it could feed off of. I hoped it would feed on my son, but apparently my son lacked something. The mirror did not like my son and my son had no interest in the mirror. Perhaps he did not possess the greed, desire, or magic I had."

There was still some detail I was missing. "You bring it food," I said, "blood. Why does it need anything else?"

"It needs blood, but something or someone else is needed as well. Maybe to help it digest or get through the glass. It is as though the blood is invisible to the man in the mirror without someone to feed it. It must feed from the zookeeper and the bucket. I didn't understand that at first. It took years before it stole my sight and my magic. It was slow and subtle."

I nodded. "So you brought in Heather, who was also a witch and on top of that was greedy and hungered for power."

"Yes," she said with an annoyed rap of her cane, "my son was immature and gullible. When Heather pretended to share his interests and gave him her body as well, it was easy to hook my son. The creature did so enjoy feeding on Heather."

"Then why the police, the blood on the floor?" I asked.

"Heather would wait until my son slept to get information from it. She was greedy and thought she was better than me. She had her followers at the church and tried to hide information from my followers. The agreement was that she would talk to the creature within the mirror and share his insights. She was holding back on me."

"Then why didn't you get rid of Heather?" Bob asked.

Mrs. May turned her blind eyes in his direction. "She did provide the blood and the bodies. We intended to get rid of her at some point, but we had no immediate plans. She was simply too greedy, too dangerous. Yet the mirror caused our plans to fall apart."

"How?" I asked.

"The creature within the mirror got to Ms. Kline, and she paid Ms. James to act on her behalf. Heather provided a couple of buckets of blood and remains to Ms. James, who waited for Blake to go to sleep and then poured the slurry on the floor of his room. She called the police and there you have it. I have keys to all the rooms in the house. It was easy for Ms. James to steal a key from a blind woman.

"The creature within the mirror needed to get the mirror out of the house. The plan was for Ms. James to take it to Snuggle and Meat, a location not protected by magic. It promised Heather that once she set it free, it would make her the richest and most powerful woman alive. Although, I suspect it would have just killed her."

"How?" Bob asked. "How would one free it?"

"You need not waste brain space on such things," Mrs. May said.

"I assume Ms. James is dead," I said.

"In tiny little pieces," she said with some satisfaction. "I, of course, didn't see the body. Yet if her screams are any indication, she suffered as she deserved. Would you have her suffer any less? She sought to free the devourer. She put the world at risk."

"Ms. James' plan helped you," I insisted. "It got your son out of his room. You wanted him to plea to something and were disappointed the case was dismissed."

Mr. Avery interjected, "Sam, you are so arrogant, you think your great lawyering put an end to our evil plot. The police always accuse the boyfriend first. We decided it would be good if Mr. May was charged. It would give us complete access to his part of the house. We didn't need Heather to get to the mirror with Blake out of the way."

"Yet it was Heather and her cult who supplied the blood," I said. "You needed her."

From Mr. Avery's smug expression, I could see how clueless he thought I was. "We paid for that bar so Heather and her followers could supply our needs. Sort of a secret partnership. Unfortunately it had to end; she was too greedy. If you hadn't killed her, we would have."

"So, it was not my great legal skills that brought you down?" I asked.

"Even without you, the case would have been dismissed. Heather was not dead. At least not at the time. The case never mattered, anyway. Dismissed or convicted, who cares? *You* lost from day one. Once Blake was brought to the mental health facility and began treatment by our hand-picked psychiatrist, he would no longer be a problem. He will never be a problem again."

Bob, who was now steadier on his feet, asked, "How do you know about the man in the mirror or any of these strange folktales you have gone on about?"

Mrs. May replied, "Mrs. Frost had a diary and many books

on the subject. I grew up reading them. My mother was also an expert and taught me well."

"So, are you going to chop us up like Ms. James, make us suffer?" I asked.

"Of course not," Mrs. May said in an almost soothing voice. "You will die in a humane manner. A car accident, I think."

"Gee, thanks," Bob said. "Any chance you would at least let me finish my plate? Why waste the lobster tail and prime rib?"

Mrs. May stared in his direction and said, "The question is if we should give you morphine or heroine first?" She was thinking aloud. "It would help with the pain."

"Why shouldn't they suffer?" Mr. Avery butted in. "They *did* kill Heather and Beth. They were also armed to the teeth when they arrived. They would have gladly murdered us all."

"Gladly," Bob agreed.

Mrs. May pounded her cane on the ground. "We can afford to be generous. They need not suffer."

Dr. Hyde walked up and removed a pencil box from inside his suit jacket. He opened it to reveal a syringe and a small bottle filled with a golden liquid.

"I am nothing if not resourceful," Dr. Hyde said with a laugh.

"Can I ask what that crap is?" Bob said.

"Don't worry, it will be just fine. Hell, if not for the whole being dead thing, you would thank me," Dr. Hyde replied.

The men had loosened their grip on my arms, but now it tightened. Bob, who was quicker than I, head-butted the man behind him. I could hear a satisfying crunch as the man fell to the ground with a broken nose. Another man hit Bob with the back of his gun and he crumpled to the floor.

The man holding me picked me up and slammed me to the ground with the skill of a professional wrestler. He once again twisted my arms behind me as I lay facing the oak floor. His knee was placed in the small of my back. I was completely immobilized.

I pictured Dr. Hyde pushing the needle into the medication

and using the syringe to draw the liquid from the bottle. I could see nothing but the oak floor. I braced myself for the prick of the needle.

Chapter 36

~~

I HEARD A scream, and for a moment the weight on my back was gone. I fell forward on my hands and knees. The room was silent as Mr. May stood before the mirror, holding a wooden chair as if to strike it.

"It is evil," Blake yelled. His voice was slurred as if he were intoxicated.

The four men in black overcoats all had pistols pointed in Mr. May's direction. The party guests were looking back and forth between Mr. May and his mother as if watching a tennis match. The eerie silence spun out. We seemed to be suspended in time.

Mr. Avery spoke first. "Put down the fucking guns. You may accidentally strike the mirror, you idiots," he yelled.

"What the hell is going on?" Mrs. May demanded.

"Your son is threatening to break the mirror," Mr. Avery shouted.

"Then stop him, but don't break the fucking mirror," Mrs. May yelled back.

I was not surprised that she had greater concern for the mirror than her own son. It did give me an idea. From my hands and knees, as if at a track meet, I sprinted toward the mirror. I half expected a bullet in the back but none came.

They could not risk the mirror. I grabbed the chair from Mr. May and he sat down on the floor. I held the chair before the mirror.

"Let Bob up before I give us all seven years of bad luck or worse," I said, pressing the chair legs to the glass.

"You're bluffing," Mrs. May said.

"To paraphrase Bob Dylan, the guy with nothing has nothing to lose. I am a dead man already."

"You want to risk the world by freeing that thing?" Mr. Avery said.

"What do I care? A world with witches like you in charge is not worth saving."

Two of the men started to move toward me. I began my swing with the chair toward the looking glass. A nod from Mr. Avery stopped them. Bob got up and joined me, unmolested by anyone in the room. We were at a standstill, no one wanting to make the first move. The tension continued to build. After a few minutes that felt like hours, Mr. May walked over to the buffet.

Blake took the long butcher knife and fork from the meat station and cut an inch-thick slice of prime rib. He picked it up with a fork, walked back to the mirror, and showed it to Bob. Bob took the meat and began to chew on it.

"You are eating now?" I asked.

"I'm hungry." Bob slurped the juice dribbling down his chin. "It's fucking prime rib. We are not talking about a fast food burger."

Blake stared into the mirror for a moment. Then he took the butcher knife and drew it across his own throat. The blood sprayed across the mirror. I ran to Blake, trying to pull the knife away from him and stop the flow of blood. He dropped the knife and with both hands pushed me hard toward the mirror.

Chapter 37

~~~

I FELL BACKWARDS, not into the mirror but through it. It was as though I was falling into water. The world around me passed in shades of black and gray. Not the kinky type of shades of gray but the disconcerting type. I was falling for what seemed like a long period of time, but when I landed, I had traveled no distance. I was in the same room, but none of the people were here. At the same time I could see them through the mirror.

There was no furniture on this side of the mirror either. The room was empty, other than for a large stone arch. A moment later, a man stepped out from behind the arch, at least something resembling a man. He was bald, his body was hairless, and his head was easily twice as large as any man's I have ever seen. His eyes were also oversized and reflected the world around him like a mirror.

His skin was gray and lifeless. His body was so skinny that it reminded me of the starving children in those commercials. The emaciated man's body looked so out of proportion to his head that he reminded me of a scarecrow topped with a pumpkin.

He stared at me and smiled, revealing large teeth. His greenish black tongue licked his lips. He grunted and then spoke in a voice that was shockingly human. If I closed my eyes, I could picture a grandfatherly figure or a friend.

"Why have you come?" he asked.

"I fell through the mirror. Are you going to eat me?"

He sniffed the air and waited before speaking. "No, there would be no reason for that."

"Why, is my blood less tasty than most?"

"I am not a vampire," he said. "I don't drink blood." The creature sounded annoyed.

"Haven't they been feeding you blood since time began?"

"Blood opens the gate; it allows me to interact with your world. But I feed on greed, power, and dark magic. I don't feed on blood but on the person who spills that blood. It has always been thus."

"I thought you were trapped in this place because you fed on life, and the spilled blood killed the grass and trees all around you."

He shook his giant head. "I was trapped here by my sister, Taiwo. She cast a spell around the land to keep me trapped. Another spell was cast by Ms. Frost to create this prison within the mirror. The trees and grass may have died from spilled blood, but not because I demanded it. This land has always been a magical place. Spilled blood helped open the portal within the stone arch. It opened the portal to the world we are trapped in. Not worth killing for, if you ask me. My sister knew of this place and trapped me here."

I looked around at what looked like a deserted chamber. "Are there others trapped here?"

"No, a few skeletons, but no company."

"I thought your sister, Taiwo, trapped you to keep you from destroying the world."

"I feed on evil," he said with a shrug. "I feed on greed and black magic. The only people I destroy deserve their fates."

"Why should I believe you?"

He grimaced, an expression that made his horrible visage

even more fearful. "I don't care what you believe. We will be trapped here forever." His tone expressed profound weariness.

"You know that because you know the future."

"I can see the future and past," he explained patiently. "Time goes by as images within the arch. I can tell you to wait and not purchase the iPhone 9. The iPhone 10 is much better. I can tell you that Amazon and Google will develop a drone that far surpasses anything you can now imagine. Yet I can't see my future or yours."

"Does that mean we don't have a future?" I was trying to fight the panic.

"I don't think so," he said with an otherworldly sigh. "I have been here forever and time has gone on, but I have never seen myself within the images of time moving forward or backward."

I pointed at the mirror. "Why can't we climb out?"

"The mirror needs blood to open the gate and will only open on the side with blood on it. I have already tried, thousands of times."

"Why not cut yourself and spill blood on this side of the mirror?

"I don't have blood, not human blood anyway."

"I do."

The creature looked at me like a starving man looks at a hamburger. We walked up to the mirror together. He made no move to attack me.

"Do you have a name?"

"Kehinde, and you?"

"Sam," I said.

I pulled the knife out of the Velcro strap on my ankle and pulled it across my hand. The blood began to ooze. I rubbed my hands together; then I began finger-painting the mirror.

"You believe me. You understand that I am not evil," Kehinde said in a voice full of awe and hope.

"Yes," I said.

"Why?"

"If you were evil," I explained, "you would not have needed me to spill my own blood to open the door to our world. You would have done it yourself."

When I was done painting the back of the mirror, the image of the room on the other side became clearer. I could easily distinguish the portion of the mirror painted in blood from that I had not touched. It was the difference between high definition television and regular television.

I dove, headfirst, into the mirror.

Chapter 38

~~~

Bob was being held down by two men. Blake, covered in blood, lay on his side in front of the mirror. He was not moving.

Two of the guards in leather trench coats had guns pointed at me. Mr. Avery had a gun as well. Even Mrs. May was armed. This seemed rather reckless, given her blindness.

A moment later Kehinde appeared from within the mirror. I dove to the ground as bullets whizzed past my head. I could hear the mirror shatter from the impact of the bullets. I could not see if Kehinde had been hit.

Instantly the people in the room began to scream. I could feel their agony. Kehinde was feeding off them. His body appeared to expand like a basketball being inflated.

Kehinde no longer looked like a monster, just a large man. His body expanded until it was in proportion to his head. His mouth no longer seemed dangerous but satisfied. He was not smiling so much as grinning.

Most of the people in the room lay on the ground unmoving. I did not know or care if they were dead or alive. The bartender and the caterers ran out of the house, apparently unharmed. Mrs. May oddly also appeared unharmed. Perhaps, after previously draining her of her vision and magic, Kehinde could find nothing more of interest. That had been Mrs. May's theory, anyway.

Kehinde walked up to Mrs. May, who dropped her cane and put her hands on his strong upper body. Kehinde lifted her into the air by her head, a hand on each ear. He pushed hard, and with an unsettling crack, blood began to pour from her mouth and sightless eyes. He dropped the lifeless body, which landed with a muffled thud.

It happened so quickly, the ensuing silence was shocking. I looked over at Bob, who was also unharmed. He stood up and walked over to me. The two men holding him down had run out the door.

He pointed at Kehinde. "So, this is the man in the mirror. I assume he is saving us for a snack when he gets hungry later on."

The man shook his head. "I feed on ambition, desire, dark magic, and evil. I do not feed on obnoxious. Only the dark ones are dead; the others are allowed to escape. I am all about justice." This last sentence had a smug flavor.

"Are you still trapped on this land?" I asked. "Caged by your sister's magic?"

"I don't know. It may not matter, of course." He pointed to a hole in his chest where a bullet had struck him. No blood oozed from the wound.

"We need to get you to a hospital," I said.

"I will die or I will live," he said without concern. "Your 'hospital' won't change that. Either way, I am grateful. You have ended my torture, starvation, and imprisonment."

"Is there anything we can do?"

"I know of your world. I can see the darkness within it. I know of desires and magic. Even within the cage, all of this came through. Yet, I know that this world is not all darkness and desire. I could hear Blake watching what you call television. Show me this."

We led Kehinde to the large television against the far wall.

Bob instructed him in the ways of the remote control. We of course warned him that if he wanted to avoid darkness and evil, he would have to skip most of reality television.

I informed Kehinde that we would have to call the police if the caterers had not already done so. He seemed undisturbed.

After a moment, the room was silent, other than the television. Mr. Fluffinator had come in. He stood before the prime rib at the carving table. Then he sat and stared, waiting patiently to be served. The server had left or was dead. I walked up to the beef, took the entire roast and placed it on a plate, which I placed before the dog. I walked toward the room's exit and Bob followed. As we were leaving, we heard Kehinde laughing hysterically. I looked over to see he was watching a cartoon. A bald man with a shotgun was chasing a bucktoothed rabbit holding a carrot.

I still didn't know for sure if I was putting the world at risk by freeing Kehinde. Yet I had a feeling that anyone who laughed with such delight at a cartoon rabbit couldn't be too evil. Then again, you never know.

We walked down the stairs to discover Malcolm Conrad still standing by the door. He looked dizzy and confused. I grabbed him by the shoulders, afraid he might fall.

"She is dead, isn't she?" Malcolm rasped.

"I thought he was mute," Bob said.

"It was the old witch—she did this to me. Yet, now that I can speak, I am free. I can move of my own will. Is she dead?"

"Does the phrase 'Ding Dong' mean anything to you?" Bob asked.

"Yes, she is dead," I said, to clear up the confusion.

"Good," Malcolm said with a satisfied nod of his head. "I am her slave no more."

Mr. Fluffinator rushed down the stairs with the roast in his mouth. He dropped the meat at Malcomb's feet, then ran around, wagging his tail in delirious happiness. I gathered he didn't like Mrs. May much, either.

Bob and I left the house, and Malcolm and Mr. Fluffinator followed. We asked him if he needed a ride, but he refused. Apparently he had some experience as a car thief since as we got into the van, he passed us driving the Maserati. Mr. Fluffinator's head could be seen hanging out the passenger-side window, his tongue lolling in doggy ecstasy.

We were a few miles away when we heard the sirens. Against all odds, we had survived. All and all, this had been a damn good day.

"I was thinking …" Bob said.

"You were thinking that we might have just unleashed some unspeakable evil into the world?" I said, finishing his sentence.

"No, that is not what I was going to say."

"Do tell."

"What is going to happen to all those rich guys' fancy cars, assuming they are dead? Maybe we should follow Malcolm's example and take one."

"It is still theft. I assume their families will inherit them," I said. "Their families might be nice."

"Damn, I would love a Ferrari."

"I am never going to get to sleep after that," I said. "What do you say we head downtown and get a drink?"

"Cool."

"You know, I am kind of curious what is in the attic."

"Do you want to check it out?"

"No, I have had enough mystery for one night. And besides, the police should be there by now."

After the dream with Oscar Wilde, I realized I probably should have checked the attic. Perhaps there was a portrait of interest there. Maybe it contained the diary and history book Mrs. May spoke of. That would shed some light on this land and this house. Yet, the truth was I simply didn't care. I knew as much as I needed to know of the house and its secrets.

We had a few drinks at a bar called the English Gentry. It was known for exotic beers, steak sandwiches, and fried vegetables. We had some of each.

"Bob," I said, "something has been bothering me, but I've been afraid to say anything. I know I am not your mother."

"Dude, you know you can say anything to me."

"I guess I was concerned about the Ecstasy and the lack of appetite."

"Lack of appetite? Did you see how much I ate tonight? More than anyone, other than Mr. Fluffinator."

"Nothing else going on?"

"I don't know," he said. "It's hard to deal with all the shit we have seen. I guess when I was dating that woman from Snuggle and Meat, it made me feel good. The drugs didn't hurt, either."

"Should I schedule an intervention?"

"No. Truth is it wasn't just her boyfriend or husband or whoever she was seeing who scared me off. I just couldn't keep up. I would wake up in the morning feeling like hell."

"If you do need help, don't be afraid to ask."

"I know."

"So, everything is cool?"

"Yeah, but I don't want you giving me a dirty look every time I drink a beer or smoke a joint. I will let you know when I need an intervention."

By the time I got home, it was after midnight. I showered and got into a clean gray T-shirt and boxers. I was about to slip under my fluffy feather blanket when I noticed that I had a voicemail.

It was Susan, my ex-girlfriend, calling about brunch tomorrow at the Golden River. It was too late to return her call, so of course I did anyway.

"Hello," Susan said, not sounding particularly tired.

"Sorry to call so late, but I wanted to confirm that I will be there at eleven for brunch."

"I am glad."

We spent the next hour talking about nothing. I felt no urge to discuss my evening. Like Kehinde, I'd had more than my fair share of evil and wanted nothing more than to hear what

Susan had for dinner that night and what she had bought at Target.

Apparently, Susan had adopted a kitten after we broke up. She named him Fluffer, and I avoided making a reference to the job title in the porn industry. I assumed that with the magic of chemistry, those jobs no longer existed. It also reminded me of the Mays' dog. I guessed he would be happy with Malcolm.

She told me she would bring pictures of her cat to brunch the next morning. I pretended to be excited to see them. Don't get me wrong: I love a good kitten picture. I watch kitten videos on Facebook and Pawmygosh all the time. Yet the truth was, Susan was the only one I wanted to see.

Chapter 39

~

I ARRIVED AT the Golden River fifteen minutes early and parked. Not wanting to seem over-eager, I decided to walk around. I walked onto the bridge above the small river by the restaurant, my mind filled with thoughts of Susan. I struggled for clarity. What was best for her and what was best for me might not be the same. Could I risk getting back together with her? Could I risk it not working out? How many people have paid the ultimate price simply for the crime of knowing me? How many people have died at my hands? Was it arrogance on my part to believe that I deserved to be with someone like Susan? That I deserved any measure of happiness?

"Why are you standing out here?"

I turned around to see Susan. She was wearing a tight black dress with a lime-green belt, and her long red hair was in a ponytail tied in a lime-green ribbon to match the belt. As always, she looked fantastic. At the same time, cheese cake drizzled in chocolate fudge and topped with raspberries is fantastic too, but that does not make it good for me.

"I didn't want to arrive too early. Then the time got away from me."

Susan pointed to the entrance. "If you don't mind, I am freezing."

I walked over to her. I wanted to put my arm over her shoulder to warm her but that would be awkward after so much time apart. Instead I walked over to the entrance and she followed. I opened the door for her. She asked the hostess to seat us near the fireplace.

I sat with my back to the fireplace facing the door of the restaurant. I know etiquette demands that the lady face the door, but I will always be afraid of not seeing someone enter the room armed with a gun or spell. Since I am not a mobster, this might seem paranoid to strangers but those who know me, including Susan, understand that there will always be those who are out to get me.

"You look fantastic," I said.

"You are just being kind. I own a mirror and have more wrinkles than when I last saw you."

"I would never trust a mirror."

"The evil queen in *Snow White* trusted her mirror."

"Look where it got her. Beauty is too subjective to entrust to a mirror," I said with a little too much emotion. I didn't want to scare Susan. "Who's to say that one person is the fairest in the land? After all, the queen was considered beautiful, despite her dark soul. Do you really need to be the fairest in the land?"

She tilted her head and smiled. "You have spent a lot of time thinking about this, haven't you?"

The waitress brought us a basket of bread and we each ordered an iced tea. We opted for the buffet. I was not hungry but needed the distraction.

Susan selected a slice of bread and buttered it. "Have you been reading a lot of fairytales since I last saw you?" she asked.

"Just studying mirrors. They can be dangerous."

She took a bite of bread. "How so? Because they encourage vanity?"

"Antique mirrors used mercury in the backing. That can be poisonous."

"I missed you."

"I missed you too."

"I can tell."

"How?"

She jutted her chin in the direction of the buffet. "Because we are less than a hundred feet from a table with a platter of smoked salmon, capers, and bagels and you have not gotten up yet."

"I am not Bob," I said. "I can delay temptation even if it is impossible to completely resist."

She sighed. "I need you in my life ... even if our relationship is not what it was."

I smiled. "I missed that transition from food talk." Her right hand was resting on the table, and I covered it in mine. I felt her warmth and could see the fire reflected in her eyes. "A part of me will always love you, and I have missed you a great deal. Yet at the same time you have almost died because of me. I don't know if love is enough."

She nodded. "Maybe it is enough for now that we simply enjoy each other's company."

We sat in silence, gazing into each other's eyes and lost in our own thoughts. I was afraid to look away. I was afraid that this was simply a dream and Susan would be gone if I averted my eyes for even a moment. I wanted to hold her in my arms so I was sure she would not disappear. She was so achingly familiar—the expression on her face, her hair, her scent. They were all a part of me, yet at the same time she was a stranger. She had another life without me.

After a few minutes, Susan said, "What are you thinking?"

"Lox and that breakfast casserole might be nice," I lied.

"I was thinking the same thing," Susan said.

Susan took my hand, and together we walked to the buffet table. I filled my plate with smoked salmon, breakfast casserole, and roast beef. Susan looked over at me and grunted like a pig as she pointed to my overflowing plate. We laughed together and for a moment, it was as if no time had passed. I was happy and content. Perhaps life is not about achieving some goal but instead about embracing moments of joy.

AUTHOR AND ATTORNEY **Scott A. Lerner** resides in Champaign, Illinois. He obtained his undergraduate degree in psychology from the University of Wisconsin in Madison and went on to obtain his Juris Doctor degree from the University of Illinois in Urbana Champaign. He is currently a sole practitioner in Champaign, Illinois. The majority of his law practice focuses on the fields of criminal law and family law.

Mr. Lerner lives with his wife, their two children, and their cat Fern. Lerner collects unusual antiques and enjoys gardening, traveling, reading fiction and going to the movies.

You can find Scott online at:

scottlerner.camelpress.com.

NOW READ THE OTHER SAMUEL ROBERTS THRILLERS!

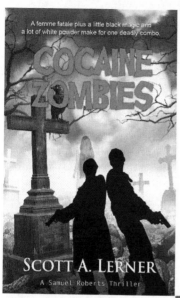

Soon after small-town lawyer Samuel Roberts takes on the case of a man accused of selling cocaine, he is plagued by terrible nightmares. Only, when he dreams of death, people die. His investigation will involve an exotic beauty named Chloe and a synthetic cocaine combined with Voodoo herbs so addictive that its inventors have the ability to enslave mankind. Unless Sam can stop them.

Three nuns—in Chicago, Paris, and Jerusalem—have been killed in a religious ritual. Someone is following a recipe provided on an ancient text to unleash the forces of hell on earth. The final sacrifice must occur on the Winter Solstice. Once again it falls on Sam and Bob to stop the cultists before it is too late.

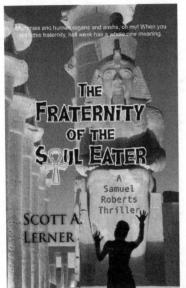

THE
FRATERNITY
OF THE
SOUL EATER

A
Samuel
Roberts
Thriller

SCOTT A.
LERNER

Sam seems to have a calling when it comes to stopping evil entities from destroying mankind. While investigating the case of a fraternity pledge who claims to have witnessed a human sacrifice, he and Bob uncover a nefarious plot: a group of men are combining magic and genetic engineering to bring the bloodthirsty gods of ancient Egypt back to life.

After attorney Samuel Roberts has his fortune read by a sexy witch, he finds himself having to defend her before a coven court against charges of using dark magic. If found guilty, she will be burned at the stake on Halloween. As they comb the area for clues, quiz the locals, and take a crash course in witchcraft, Sam and Bob can't shake the question: is Bridget a good witch or a bad witch?

THE
WICCAN WITCH
OF THE
MIDWEST

SCOTT A. LERNER

A Samuel Roberts Thriller

Keep Reading for an Excerpt from

COCAÏNE ZOMBÏES

I'VE BEEN A lawyer for about ten years. In that time I have always worked for someone else; first for a small law firm and then for the public defender. For the first time in my career, I had opened my own office. The office itself is nothing special, a ten-by-ten-foot room on the top floor of a six-story white masonry block building. It has about the same dimensions as the jail cells I try to keep my clients out of. The building was originally designed to house apartments, but the architect did not put in enough closets. So the owner was trying to attract anyone who would bite. The result is that some floors contained offices, and others, apartments.

After I moved in, I gave the walls a fresh coat of white paint. Actually, eggshell was written on the can, but it looked white to me. I bought two file cabinets, three chairs, and a wooden bench at a used office supply store. I arranged the office so that the one comfortable chair sat behind the large desk and the two armchairs faced it. The desk is the only nice piece of office furniture I own. It is mission-style and made of smoked oak, built around the turn of the century. My father, who gave it to me, claimed it was made by Stickley, but I doubt it. I have a laptop computer and a printer on my desk and pay enough money to get all the research tools I need online.

I also have a secretary named Susan who comes in a couple hours on the weekends to help with typing and filing.

Looking around, I realized I had everything I needed to practice law—other than clients, of course.

As if in answer to my thoughts, the phone rang. "Law Office," I responded in a too cheerful voice.

"Is Samuel Roberts there?"

"This is he," I said, grateful it wasn't a call for Domino's Pizza. They had a phone number similar to mine and despite just opening the office I had already received a number of calls for pepperoni and extra cheese.

"I was told you do criminal work."

"Sure, what can I do for you?" I asked.

"It's not for me but for my friend. Can we make an appointment?"

"Sure," I said, pretending to be looking at something other than a completely empty calendar. "How about Friday at nine a.m.?"

"Could we get in today, by any chance?"

"All right, how about four?"

"Thanks."

The caller sounded like she had money but it might have been wishful thinking. In the world of criminal law, most potential clients don't have money. It is always a mistake to allow clients to pay over time in a criminal case. If you lose, your clients will have to pay fines and costs, and your bill isn't a priority. If your clients go to jail, they're out of work and have no way of paying. Also, clients who go to jail tend not to care about their lawyers being paid. If you win, clients don't need you anymore and so won't feel the need to pay you.

I played Halo on the computer until four p.m., when there was a knock on the door. "Come in," I said.

In came an African-American man with a shaved head. He was six feet two and couldn't have weighed less than three hundred pounds. He had a four-inch scar above his right eye.

With him was the woman I must have spoken with over the phone. She was probably five feet six and had long, straight black hair and bright green eyes. She looked tiny compared with her friend, but there was no doubt who was in charge. She was wearing a green dress in a snakeskin pattern. It was so tight I was concerned that it would rip when she sat down. Her perfume filled the room, replacing the smell of my fresh paint with a scent both sweet and hot, like a mix of honey with Tabasco sauce.

The woman wore a gold necklace with a strange pendant strategically placed so as to draw the maximum attention to her large breasts. The pendant was a gold chicken's foot squeezing a very large, pink, heart-shaped diamond. If the diamond was real, money was not an issue. Her gold men's tank-style Patek Philippe watch probably dated back to the 1940s. This woman could more than afford my rates. Her friend, however, was wearing torn blue jeans and a white muscle shirt. She might be able to pay, but my guess was he couldn't. I sure hoped she liked this guy.

The woman spoke first. I couldn't place her accent. "My name is Chloe," she said, extending a hand, which I shook. "My friend is Thomas. Thomas is charged with selling cocaine. He didn't do it. He needs a lawyer to get him off. Can you do that?"

"I can give him good representation. If you want a fortune-teller, I'm afraid I can't help you." I immediately regretted the sarcasm, but she ignored it.

"He is being charged with a Class X felony. With his record, he could be in the Department of Corrections for the rest of his life."

A class X felony subjects a defendant to a term in the penitentiary from six to thirty years. In addition, if convicted, the defendant would serve eighty-five percent of the imprisonment rather than fifty percent for most crimes. There is a possibility of an even lengthier sentence, depending on other factors such as the defendant's record.

"Why don't you sit down and tell me what is going on," I said, looking directly at Thomas. Chloe began to speak. "Chloe," I interrupted, "what Thomas and I speak about is privileged. The attorney client privilege assures our conversations can't be used in court against him. If you are present, it would be considered a waiver of that privilege and you could be subpoenaed to testify about our conversation. Would you mind waiting outside?"

What I said was legally correct, but I doubted that the State would know to subpoena her. I was really just trying to get rid of her and I think she knew it. She left without another word.

Thomas seemed more at ease the minute she left. I entered his address and phone number in my computer. From his slight accent, I guessed he must have spent time in the Caribbean. He had a tattoo depicting two snakes intertwining around a cross on his left upper arm that reminded me of the symbol doctors use—the caduceus. Although the symbol used in the medical profession has only one snake, not two.

"I have sold crack in the past," he said, "but just to get money or drugs for my own use. I spent some time in the Illinois Department of Corrections and don't want to go back." I nodded. "While in the joint, I found Jesus and accepted him as my Savior."

Of course, I thought, *everyone finds Jesus when they have all day to look.* From my experience, more people find religion at the Stateville Correctional Facility in Joliet than Jerusalem, Mecca, and Mississippi combined.

He continued, "I have a ten-year-old daughter, and I don't want to miss being a part of her life. That's why I wouldn't risk selling drugs and going to prison. Since I got out I have been completely clean."

"Are you still on parole?" I asked.

"Yeah," he responded.

51055067R00158

Made in the USA
San Bernardino, CA
12 July 2017